A Swee

WORKING After All

Happily Ever After All Series: Book 4

CECE LOUISE

ISBN 978-1-7330636-7-8

Cover design by DLR Cover Designs.

Proofreading by Tess Marie of RomanceProofreader.com.

Published by
Jabberwocky Tales

Printed in the United States of America

Also by Cece Louise

THE HAPPILY EVER AFTER ALL SERIES

Christmas After All

Perfect After All

Faking After All

Falling After All (coming soon)

THE FOREST TALES SERIES

Desperate Forest

Mazarine

In a Dark, Dark Wood

Saving Vengeance: A Prequel

The Jabberwocky Princess: A Companion Novel

THE SHATTERED TALES SERIES

To Escape a Wonderland

For our soon-to-be-here baby girl.

Thanks for being my companion while writing this story. Looking forward to lots of snuggles and less nausea.

We can't wait to meet you and discover who you'll become!

Prologue

AUDREY

It was the perfect night for magic.

There was something in the late-spring evening air that promised it. The warmth of the daytime cooling to a comfortable level. The scent of lilacs floating on the gentle breeze. The occasional hum of a passing car as I walked down the quiet lamplit neighborhood street.

That serenity was broken the closer I got to my destination. Shouts, laughter, and thumping music filled the air. Less magical, but all the more exciting. The party was in full swing by the time I strolled up to the Jorgens' front lawn. A couple were making out on the porch swing. A group exited a car parked on the side of the road. A few late-comers, like me, made their way up the walk. But it was clear the real party was happening in the backyard.

I crossed the grass and turned the corner. Oh yeah, it

was packed. People clustered on the patio, around a bonfire in the yard, and at the edges of the massive in-ground pool.

My footsteps faltered. It was even more crowded than I expected. I flung my long red braid over my shoulder, suddenly annoyed by my hair. It always felt too heavy. I yearned to cut my hair short, but my mother insisted I keep it long so it could "be styled." Even though the only style I ever wore was a braid or ponytail to keep it out of my face.

I bit my lip, glancing around. I wished I had been successful in convincing Penny, my best friend, to come with me. Walking into a party like this alone made me feel even more awkward than usual.

But Penny had insisted she had no time for a party tonight. She had plans to meet up with Camden Clarke to go over his final paper, and she was not going to miss that. The best I had gotten out of her was a promise to stop by after if they got done early. But by the tone of Penny's voice, it didn't seem like she had much interest in getting done early. She had started tutoring Camden this past year, and even though she wouldn't admit it, I had a feeling she was invested in more than his passing grade at this point.

I wasn't sure how I felt about that. Camden seemed nice, I guess. I mean, everybody liked him. He was a fun-loving guy and the star of the basketball team.

But he was also super popular, and Penny and I weren't. I was worried any feelings Penny had developed for him were one-sided.

Case in point when I spied Camden on the far edge of the pool, drink in hand and arm around a cheerleader.

I glanced at the time on my phone. Penny had left to meet him a half hour ago. Either Camden's academic skills had improved so much under Penny's tutelage that he'd written a paper so perfect it needed no improvements—highly unlikely, considering his grades were so bad at the start he'd needed Penny's help to avoid getting kicked off the basketball team—or the jerk was standing her up.

No longer intimidated by the large crowd, I marched forward, blood boiling, ready to confront Camden. But my way was blocked when a lanky figure stepped into my path.

"Hey, Odd Aud— Er, Audrey Miller! You made it." Ty Jorgen grinned and shoved a red cup in my hand.

"Hey, Ty. Yeah, thanks for inviting me." I gave him a smile, but made sure it wasn't too enthusiastic. Penny had not been happy when I'd told her our invitation to this party had come from Ty. He was two years older than us—in college now—and he had a reputation for trying to score with high school girls.

Yeah, he was a creep. But it didn't matter because I had no intention of being one of his conquests.

Something he had probably already realized by the way his glassy eyes shifted, searching around me. "Ya bring any friends?"

"Uh, Penny's probably going to stop by later."

"The Crow?" He frowned, and I did too over his use of Penny's nickname—so imaginative, given her black hair and last name being Crowe. Never mind that she had gone through an Edgar Allan Poe phase in middle school. I was pretty sure our classmates weren't astute enough to get that connection.

At least the nickname they had given me was a little more original—not that that made me like it any more.

"Greeeaaat." The way he drew out the word made it obvious he did not think that was great. But his eyes lit up, catching sight of something—or more likely, someone—over my shoulder. "Catch you later."

With that, he was off, heading over to a group of three more-popular girls in my grade—no doubt invited by him as well.

I sniffed the drink he'd given me, which smelled heavily of alcohol and slightly of fruit punch. Nope—there was no way I was drinking anything tonight, especially being here on my own. I discreetly lowered it and tipped the contents into the grass. I held on to the empty red cup though, to avoid having more drinks shoved into my hand.

I raised my gaze to find Camden again, but he wasn't where I'd last seen him. I scanned the crowd. There were a lot of people here I didn't recognize. And a few of the ones I did were older than me—Ty's age or even above. I guess that made sense since the Jorgens siblings were a few years apart and had likely both invited friends tonight. But before I could start putting names to faces, a loud whoop sounded nearby, followed by a splash.

Camden emerged from the water, now shirtless in the pool, and the crowd around us started cheering. A few more guys stripped off their shirts and followed suit, jumping in after him. But since they were merely followers of Camden's antics, they didn't earn quite as much enthusiasm.

Eyes on my target once more, I glared at Camden from the other end of the pool. He certainly didn't seem like he was in a hurry to meet Penny. I was going to talk to him before he had a chance to disappear again.

I was about to make my way toward the deep end of the pool, but unfortunately, the crowd that had gathered at the edge was so big—and loud—there seemed little chance I'd be able to get Camden's attention from over there.

With a sigh, I set my empty cup and cell phone on a patio table and kicked my sandals off. Then I hopped into the shallow end of the pool.

I ignored the catcalls, whoops, and crass comments as I trudged through the waist-deep water, waving a hand, trying to get Camden's attention. He was oblivious to me, too busy sinking baskets in the hoop at the far end of the pool, each shot followed by an exaggerated muscle flex. I rolled my eyes. What did Penny see in this guy? He was such a moron.

"Camden!" I waved both arms above my head. "Hey, Cam—" My words were cut short as I unexpectedly hit the slope of the deep end and slid down. My head dipped under, water filling my mouth. I came up sputtering.

I had just started treading water, about to swim Camden's way, when I heard a splash behind me. An arm looped around my waist and tugged me back.

"Hey!" I protested and flailed, splashing, about to swing at whoever thought they had a green light to get handsy. Until I saw who was dragging me back toward the shallow end.

Jackson Crowe. Penny's brother and my lifelong crush. Four years older, he was the reason why guys like Camden held no interest for me. They all seemed so immature compared to him—always had.

"Jackson!" My outrage turned to pure delight. "What are you doing here?"

"What are *you* doing here?" he shot back, frustration in his deep voice. "Don't you know how stupid it is to go swimming when you're drunk?"

I couldn't help but laugh. "I'm not drunk." Was that why he thought I'd jumped into the pool?

"Right. I'm sure Ty gave you Kool-Aid." He released me and gave me a little push toward the pool steps.

"I didn't drink what Ty gave me. I'm not an idiot." Wait—had Jackson been watching me? Had he actually *noticed* me? My heart picked up its pace. I knew coming here tonight was a good idea.

I climbed out of the pool, Jackson following close behind, and the evening air hit me like a slap in the face. Out of the heated pool and now dripping wet, it felt a lot colder.

Whistles and hoots sounded from the crowd, and I glanced down to find my clothes plastered to my body. My yellow T-shirt had turned see-through, revealing my striped pink-and-green bra underneath. Apparently, yellow wasn't much better than white when you got it wet.

"Animals," Jackson muttered under his breath, then he stooped and picked something up off the ground and shoved it into my hands. "Here."

It was a soft gray sweatshirt—his sweatshirt. I quickly slipped it over my head. It was warm and dry and smelled way better than the chlorine from the pool. And it was Jackson's, so I might never take it off.

"If you're not drunk, why did you jump in the pool?" Jackson grabbed my arm and led me away from the crowd, who didn't seem to have much of an interest in me anymore now that I was wearing his sweatshirt. As we passed the patio, I scooped up my phone and sandals.

"I was trying to talk to Camden Clarke," I said. "He was supposed to meet Penny tonight—"

"Penny's not here, is she?" Jackson's head swiveled to look back, scanning the crowd.

"No, relax. I wanted her to come with me but she had other plans."

He did seem to relax, but then he scrubbed a hand down his face. "Did you come with anyone?"

"No, but Penny was maybe going to meet me later—"

"You came to a college party alone? Real smart, Audrey. Real smart."

"Hey!" I may have appreciated his sweatshirt, but I did not appreciate his condescending tone. "There are plenty of people my age here. And besides, I'm not a kid." I tried to stand taller. "I turned eighteen last week, you know."

Jackson just sighed and looked at the sky. I glanced around to see where he had led us. To the porch swing in the front yard. I recalled the couple I had seen kissing on it earlier. Was this the party make-out spot? I quickly sat down and looked up expectantly. Unfortunately, Jackson made no move to join me, so after a beat, I began putting on my sandals.

"What brought you here tonight?" I asked casually. *Please don't say another girl.* "Penny didn't even tell me you were back from college." I was a bit annoyed, but I could also guess why she hadn't. She had long ago stopped approving of my one-sided crush on her brother.

"Yeah, I graduated last weekend and moved back last

night. My buddy invited me here." Jackson finally sank down on the seat next to me and the swing swayed under his weight. "But it's not really my thing. I was actually about to leave when I saw you." He frowned. "And I saw Ty give you a drink."

"Yeah, Ty invited me."

"Ty's a creep, Audrey." Jackson's jaw ticked. "Please tell me you're not getting involved with him."

"I'm not. Gee, calm down—I just came to check out the party." I laughed, but at the look on his face, another thought dawned on me. An absolutely wonderful one. "Wait—are you jealous?"

"No." He scoffed. "I just don't want to see you get hurt." His answer was vehement. Maybe too vehement—like he was in denial? I was delighted.

"C'mon." He slapped his legs. "Let's get out of here. I'll take you home."

Before he could stand, I leaned forward, grabbed the front of his T-shirt, and brushed my lips against his.

His response was immediate and intense—but not in a good way.

"What the—" He bit back a swear as he pushed away from me, taking the swing with him so quickly that I slid off it and landed in a heap on the porch. "What are you *doing*?"

"Kissing you." I stood up, tucking a few strands of my wet hair behind my ears that had come loose from my long braid. My heart thudded in my chest. "I thought that was obvious."

Jackson groaned with frustration as he released the swing and stepped a good few feet away from me. He scrubbed a hand down his face, then faced me, meeting my eyes. "Audrey, listen to me." He gestured as if explaining something to a child. "I don't know what you read into with that, but I do *not* want to kiss you."

Then for good measure, as if that wasn't clear enough, he added. "I will *never* want to kiss you. Why don't you understand that?"

"I-I thought—" I felt like the biggest idiot in the world, my words failing me. I gulped, trying anyway. "I thought because I'm older now that maybe—" I twisted my hands together, then dropped them at my sides. "I thought we were having a moment—"

"We were *not* having a moment!" His voice rose. "I was babysitting you."

That did it.

"*Babysitting* me? Get over yourself, Jackson Crowe. I don't need you to babysit me! I'm not a kid anymore, and just because I'm Penny's friend doesn't give you the right to treat me like your little sister. Go babysit her."

"I don't need to," he shot back. "*She* doesn't act like a psycho."

Of all the things he could have said to me right then, that was the absolute worst. It was like he had physically bruised my heart, and tears pricked in my eyes, my throat tightening. Psycho. Crazy. Odd Audrey. It was bad enough that was how all my classmates saw me. Was that really what Jackson thought too?

I'd like to say there was a reasonable explanation for what I did next. In hindsight, maybe it was leftover adrenaline from jumping in the pool. Maybe it was all those Regency romance books Penny liked to read passages out loud from where girls seemed to get away with stuff like that. Or maybe it was years of pent-up aggression from being called "Odd Audrey" by my peers.

Most likely it was a combination of all three. Whatever it was, I'm not proud to say I slapped him.

Like *really* slapped him. I took two giant steps toward Jackson, pulled back, then let my arm fly. My palm connected hard and fast across his cheek.

He stumbled, then stared at me like I was crazy, his eyes confirming what his words had said only moments ago. What kind of girl slaps a guy after he turns her down? The crazy kind, that's who.

So I fled.

The sound of my sandals slapping the pavement was muffled only by me bursting into tears when I reached the sidewalk.

Chapter 1

AUDREY

Six Years Later

Sometimes you need to hit rock bottom to know which way is up.

At least that's what I told myself that late-spring evening as I drove into Halften, my old hometown.

Was I being dramatic? Possibly. But after making the last leg of my journey on a dangerously low fuel tank, a depleted bank account, and the recent memory of having just been fired from my job and dumped by my fiancé, it was the only pep talk I could come up with.

In truth, I was tired, hot, hungry, and cranky. And unfortunately, I wasn't the only one. No sooner had I passed the faded Halften welcome sign than did my poor car shudder and protest, like it was saying *I got you this far. You're on your own now.*

"No, no, no," I cried out. "You can do it, baby, we're almost there!"

Shudder, grunt, grunt was my car's reply. I managed to pull over to the side of the road next to a farm field before it died completely.

"Great. Just great." I leaned my head back against my seat and squeezed my eyes shut, willing myself to teleport away from my useless car.

I peeked an eye open and sighed. No luck. Not that I really expected it to work when it hadn't the other forty times I'd tried it in my life. It was amazing the number of situations I found myself in that had me wishing I could teleport away. Modern science really needed to get on that one.

I exited my car and crossed to the passenger side, which left me standing at the edge of a vacant, slightly muddy field. I glanced down at my heeled shoes, hoping they wouldn't collect too much mud while I waited. I didn't exactly want to be tracking in dirt when I arrived at my cousin Tucker's rehearsal dinner—now, late to boot.

I powered on my phone and waited for it to load up. I'd shut it down to conserve the dying battery once I had hit Rocimac, the closest big city to Halften, and no longer needed the GPS.

As I waited for my ancient phone to do its thing, I contemplated who I could call. My parents would have already arrived at the rehearsal dinner, I was certain. Plus, I didn't want to hear a lecture from my mother about responsibility. I'd already had my fair share over my twenty-four years.

Tucker was obviously out, even though he would have

been my first choice. More like a big brother than an older cousin, he'd be so happy to see me he wouldn't even have minded coming to pick me up. But since it was his rehearsal dinner that was about to start, I knew I couldn't pull him away.

My friend Caleb Ellis would be my best bet. Even though he was the bride's brother, his other sister, Kelsey, was notorious for running late. It was possible they had carpooled and she had delayed their arrival. If they were still driving, maybe they could swing by and pick me up on the way.

Just as I was about to hit Caleb's number in my contacts, a black truck drove by, slowed, and then stopped a few yards past me. I shaded my eyes against the setting sun and stared as it reversed, trying to see if I knew the driver. Halften was a small town, so there was a good chance I did.

The car pulled up behind mine and the door opened.

And my heart stopped.

Oh yeah, I knew him.

Of all the rotten, stinking luck.

Instantly, I wished for those teleportation powers again. Maybe the forty-first time would be the charm?

"Audrey?" He slammed his door shut, dark brows drawn down above his sunglasses.

"Hey, Jackson." I gave a half-hearted wave to Tucker's best friend and my long-ago former crush. "Yeah, it's me."

"What are you doing here?" He strode toward me. "What happened?"

"I was on my way to the rehearsal and my car died."

His frown deepened as he turned toward my car. "Did

it overheat? Dead battery?"

"Um, no . . . I think it ran out of gas." I shrugged sheepishly. "I'm no mechanic but the gauge says empty, so . . ."

Jackson pulled off his sunglasses and turned his critical gaze to me. "Where were you coming from?"

"Uh, Chicago."

"You made a trip like that without checking if you had enough gas?"

"Well, traffic was worse than I expected. I was afraid I wasn't going to make it on time if I stopped, and I thought I had enough." I lifted my hands. "I mean, it got me this far."

He muttered something unintelligible and then, "You're lucky you didn't break down in the city."

"Right." I nodded, trying to look solemn. "Imagine if some grumpy, judgmental man had stopped to give me a hand. What a nightmare."

The look Jackson shot me said he wasn't amused.

And just like that, our dynamic was restored. I was still his little sister's flaky, annoying friend that he had to watch over.

Granted, that wasn't always our dynamic, but the last time we exchanged this many words? Yeah, that was about how it went down—except way worse.

Since that incident was the last thing I wanted to think about, I waved my phone. "Thanks for stopping, but I've got it under control. I was just about to call Caleb. He's a mechanic, you know. Or he was." It had been a little while since I'd seen my friend, and I almost forgot he had stopped working as a mechanic to open his own gym.

"Caleb's probably already at the rehearsal." Jackson

didn't seem impressed by my solution. "Like *we* should be. And you don't need a mechanic to fill your car up with gas. You got an empty can?"

"Uh . . ." I did a quick mental inventory of the junk I had stashed in my backseat and trunk. "I think I have an empty gallon of orange juice." I never relied on coffee to keep me awake during a long drive. Give me sugar, vitamin C, and upbeat tunes.

"It's fine, I have one. Why don't you lock up and we can head to the rehearsal? We'll get you gas after."

"If you're sure. . ." I guess that made sense since we were headed to the same place, but still, my pride prickled at having to accept his help. If he in any way referred to this as "babysitting" me, I wouldn't be responsible for my actions.

"Yeah, let's go." Jackson pulled up the cuff of his dress shirt and checked his watch. "We're already late."

"Okay, thanks." I grabbed my purse from inside my car and hit the locks. Not that I was worried anyone would steal my stuff. For one thing, it was Halften. For another, I didn't really own much worth stealing.

As I headed toward Jackson's truck, I tried to put a positive spin on the situation. "At least *you're* off the hook for being late now. You can say it was because you had to stop for me."

Jackson grunted, like he didn't appreciate me accusing him of not being punctual. "I was managing some last-minute things at the Inn for the wedding."

Oh, right, Tucker's wedding reception was being held in the barn event venue connected to the restaurant that Jackson and Tucker ran together.

"That was nice of you," I replied cheerily as I slid into

the passenger seat.

Jackson started the truck and the cool air from his vents hit me.

I exhaled happily. "Ahhh, air-conditioning." Granted we weren't quite into the main heat of summer yet, but sitting in Chicago traffic without air-conditioning in my car had been less than fun.

Immediately, that memory sparked another. My gaze shot down to my armpits, and sure enough, I had forgotten to take out the Kleenex I'd stuffed in there to stop my sweat during that leg of my journey.

Shoot.

I swiveled awkwardly in my seat, facing away from Jackson, and tried to discreetly peel the mangled tissues from under my arms. Since there was really no way to discreetly do that, I failed miserably.

Hastily, I stuffed the two wads into my purse, making a note to toss them into the trash the moment we reached the rehearsal.

Then I leaned back in my seat and squeezed my eyes shut.

Number forty-two?

Nothing.

I opened my eyes with a small sigh.

It was bad enough having to be rescued at the side of the road by my former crush who once epically rejected me. Doing it with sweaty tissues sticking out of my armpits made it ten times worse.

CHAPTER 2

JACKSON

Even though I hadn't seen her in years, Audrey was the same as I remembered. At least, almost.

Clearly, she was still irresponsible and scatterbrained. How anyone runs out of gas is beyond me. I mean, there is literally a gauge and a warning light. What more do you need? A flashing message across the windshield that says *Stop driving now or you'll regret it*? Then a minute later, the image of a shaking finger and a sign that says *I really mean it!*

But that was Audrey for you. Never one to heed any warning, she seemed to barrel through life with an unhealthy amount of energy and optimism. And when life knocked her off her feet, I swear, she just dusted herself off and did it all over again.

I tried to keep my eyes fixed on the road as she

fidgeted next to me, but when I glanced over, I found her extracting what looked like mangled tissues from beneath her arms.

I resisted the urge to laugh and averted my gaze.

Yup, same old Audrey. She was always doing, well, weird things. That was why her classmates had given her the nickname Odd Audrey—which, I know, was super mean. I never called her that. Until maybe our last major run-in when I implied it.

Best not to dwell on that at the moment.

As we climbed the rural hills that led to Tucker's mom's house, where the rehearsal dinner was being held, I racked my brain trying to make small talk. Not that I wanted to, it just seemed like I should.

But now that Audrey was done digging in her armpits, she seemed to be content enough fiddling with my radio controls, switching stations—even though she hadn't asked permission. Then she pulled out a compact mirror from her purse and began fussing with her hair.

I did my best to focus on the twists and turns of the road. This was the Audrey I was not so familiar with, and the reason I'd had to do a double take when I saw her standing on the side of the road.

Simply speaking, Audrey Miller—my little sister's best friend and the thorn in my side most of my life—was all grown up.

Her red hair was darker than I remembered and not long and frizzy anymore, escaping messy braids and ponytails. Now it hung in lively but shiny waves around her face, just grazing her bare shoulders. And the kid I once knew was definitely all woman now, filling out her royal blue cocktail dress in all the right ways. But the only reason I noticed was because I didn't initially recognize her.

Now that I did, I certainly wasn't a single guy noticing a pretty woman. I was the idiot who was recalling our last real interaction together—and praying she had somehow forgotten about it.

It was right after I graduated college when we'd both been at the Jorgens' summer kick-off party together. When I'd thought she was drunk and had hauled her out of the pool. Then she'd tried to kiss me. I'd been so shocked, she'd succeeded for a split second.

It turned out she was stone-cold sober and just enjoyed making questionable decisions.

I'd told her off for once and for all. Looking back, it was definitely harsh, but the good thing was, after that, she had *finally* gotten the hint. She had no longer followed me and Tucker around, or stared at me when she was at our house hanging out with Penny. I honestly hadn't seen her much at all that summer—it was nice. That fall, she and Penny had gone off to college in Chicago and I'd seen her even less. All our interactions after that were short and uneventful. And she certainly never tried to kiss me again.

Which, I told myself, was a good thing, as I focused on the road and tried to ignore her swiping a fresh coat of gloss on her lips.

"So you in town for a while?" I finally thought of something to ask, recalling her packed-to-the-gills car.

"Just for the summer," she replied as she closed her purse, then went back to fiddling with the controls on my dash. It seemed like she was trying to aim the vents toward her armpits. "With Penny going on book tour and our lease being up, it seemed like a good time since I had to come back for Tucker's wedding."

"Right." I said it like I knew this, but really, I didn't. I mean, of course I knew about my sister's book tour. It was a pretty big deal.

But even though Audrey and Penny were roommates, whenever I talked to Penny, I never really asked about Audrey.

As Audrey's left hand fiddled with the controls, something shiny caught my eye. She was wearing a ring, and that's when I remembered Tucker telling me that Audrey had gotten engaged.

At the time, I think I had mumbled an unenthusiastic "That's great," when really, I was wondering who the poor sucker was. I know that might sound mean, but the thing about Audrey is . . . she's a lot. It wasn't that I disliked her, per se, it was that we just didn't mesh well.

In an effort to keep things friendly now, I said, "Congrats on the engagement, by the way."

"Oh, thanks." Audrey jerked her left hand back almost as if one of the buttons had shocked her, then began twirling the ring on her finger. "Mercer really wanted to be here for Tucker's wedding, but he's studying for his bar exam in July and interning at a big law firm, so his schedule is really intense."

"Bummer," I said, assuming Mercer was her fiancé, although I didn't recognize the name. I did recall that Tucker had mentioned the guy was going to be some big-shot lawyer. It baffled me now as much as it did then. Audrey with a serious, stuffy lawyer? I just couldn't see it. But then again, maybe it was one of those opposites attract things that people talk about.

I killed the engine and before I could say anything else, Audrey threw open her door and practically jumped out of my truck.

"Well, thanks so much for the ride." She waved and shut the door behind her, then began heading the rest of the way up the driveway.

Despite myself, I let out a light chuckle. Audrey running away from me wasn't something I was used to. But maybe she felt as awkward about our history as I did and just wanted to end our encounter as quickly as possible.

That was fine by me. And even though she was back in town for the summer, I assumed I'd barely see her at all.

"Hey, Jackson," the bartender Randy said as he handed me my drink. "Who's your date?"

"My date?" My brows furrowed. "I didn't bring a date."

"The redhead I saw hopping out of your truck when you got here. She's hot."

"Oh, that's not my date. That's Tucker's cousin Audrey. She had car trouble so I gave her a lift." I guess it made sense that Randy wouldn't know her since he only moved to Halften recently.

He snickered. "I'd give her a lift to the nearest motel."

"She's engaged," I said quickly. "And watch your mouth." Randy was one of our newest bartenders at the Inn, and to be honest, I had mixed feelings about him. He was a hard worker and super reliable—which was why

Tucker hired him to bartend for the rehearsal dinner tonight. But what Tucker was less aware of was that he also had a habit of making off-color jokes. This wasn't the first time I'd given him a warning.

Which seemed to be about as effective as the other times. In fact, it didn't seem to register at all, by the way he swore loudly. "Engaged? Isn't that just our luck? Man, this town really needs some fresh meat."

Before I could retort that Audrey was a person, not "meat," he crossed to the other end of the outdoor bar to serve his next customer.

As I walked away, I made a mental note to sit down and have a talk with Randy about his professionalism—or lack of it.

But even after deciding that, I was still irritated. Probably because his crass comment was directed toward Audrey. I mean, she was Penny's friend and Tucker's cousin—practically his sister. As annoying as Audrey was growing up, I always tried to look out for her. That must've been why I had the urge to go back and punch Randy in the jaw.

Instead, I headed toward the main crowd and commanded myself to mingle. The last thing I needed to do was cause a scene at Tucker's rehearsal dinner.

Before long, Tucker found me.

"Hey, man," he said, "great news. I think I found my replacement for the summer."

"Really? That *is* great news." The first person we had hired flaked on us a few days ago. "You found someone who's got the experience, but is good with it being a temporary role?" I had to admit, when Tucker told me his plan to take a three-month-long honeymoon over the summer, my stress had risen to dangerous levels—even though I'd tried hard not to let Tucker see it.

But really, who could we possibly get to fill his shoes who would be experienced enough to handle the event venue portion of his job—booking shows and managing musicians? I mean, hello, he was a country superstar—it was kind of his thing. And on top of that, who would only want the role for three months?

I wasn't about to hire an intern back from college for an important job like this—those shows brought in a big portion of our business. But I was also way too swamped with managing the restaurant to properly handle it myself, which was how it was looking as long as the spot stayed vacant.

"Yup." Tucker grinned. "She's perfect. I don't know why I didn't think of it before. Experienced with event management. Great with people. Excellent taste in music. The best part is, she only wants a job for the summer. And you already know her."

"So don't keep me in suspense. Who is it? Just please don't say your mom." I took a swig of my drink.

"Audrey."

I coughed, swallowed, and my beer burned as it went down my throat. "Audrey?"

"Yeah, I was just talking to her. It turns out she's planning on staying in Halften for the whole summer and is looking for work."

Really? *That* was his great solution? Tucker's mom would actually be better. At least she didn't drive me insane.

"I don't know, man." I chose my words carefully. "Her and me working together . . . probably isn't the best idea."

"What are you talking about? You guys have known each other forever. She's your sister's best friend." He chuckled. "Is this about her crush? Don't worry, she's moved on. Didn't I tell you she's engaged?"

Her being engaged didn't erase our years of awkward history. And more importantly, I didn't feel confident that she really had what it took to do the job. How reliable could she be when she couldn't even remember to put gas in her car? Overall, the thought of working with her sounded like a huge headache.

Not wanting to insult Audrey, I chose a different route to convince Tucker this was a bad idea. "I thought you said she was experienced? Since when has Audrey worked in the music industry?"

"She hasn't officially, but I have no worries there. One of the things that bonded us growing up was our shared love for music. She's even more up on the indie scene than me. And she's worked in the people industry. She's been in hospitality since she graduated, and I've seen her in action—she's great. She can definitely handle it."

Tucker frowned, his expression turning puzzled. "Honestly, I thought you'd be excited too. Someone you already know. Not having to deal with all that awkward small talk. I mean, I know she had that crush on you, but that was ages ago." He laughed. "It's not like she's going to call her wedding off because of you."

I forced out a laugh too. The thing was, I'd sound like a conceited jerk if I said our past was why I was hesitant. Sure, Tucker knew all about her crush on me, but I'd never told him about the incident at the Jorgens' party. I'd wanted to wipe that completely from my mind. And admitting to my best friend that I'd locked lips—albeit unwillingly—with his younger cousin just wasn't something I wanted between us in our friendship.

"Look," Tucker went on. "Why not just give her a chance? It's not like we have anyone else lined up."

He had a point. Summer was our busiest time of year for shows. We did need someone—and we needed them now. "Did you offer her the position already?"

"Not yet. I wanted to talk to you first. But I won't if you aren't on board with it."

I glanced across the lawn to where Audrey was chatting with Melissa and Kelsey Ellis.

I took a long pull from my beer, then said the words I really hoped I wouldn't regret. "Let's see what she thinks."

CHAPTER 3

AUDREY

I felt so much better now that I'd had a glass of lemonade, lots of fresh air, and what was probably more than my fair share of hors d'oeuvres. I felt a little guilty as I swiped another crab rangoon off a serving tray, but my limited funds had meant surviving my little road trip on trail mix and orange juice instead of stopping for lunch. I needed to refuel. And everything here was delicious.

As hesitant as I was to move back to my hometown for the summer, I had to admit, it was great seeing familiar faces and catching up with some old friends. That was the mixed blessing of growing up in a small town. On the plus side, everyone knew you. On the downside, well, everyone knew you—and their memories were long.

I had no doubt that if I'd grown up somewhere with a

larger population, I may not have carried for so long the unfortunate nickname I'd been branded with at a young age.

The seeds of it were sown on my very first day of school. The day had started out promising—I was excited to finally be around kids my age, especially as a rambunctious only child. We lived on the rural outskirts of Halften, so we had forest and farm fields surrounding us. No neighborhood with other children for me to play with in my preschool years.

Never one to be deterred by my circumstances, my imagination had filled in the gaps. My imaginary friend Perluna was born, and since my mother's main mantra at the time was for me to go play and leave her alone, I had done just that. I spent most of my time outside, roaming the nearby woods, and so I wasn't lonely, I brought Perluna along—in my mind at least. Which basically consisted of me carrying on one-sided conversations or narrating our adventures.

Before long, Perluna was a staple in my life, and my loyalty to my fictional friend grew to the point that when the time came for me to start school, there was no way I could leave my beloved companion behind.

You would think that kindergarteners would be imaginative enough to be a little more understanding of their peer with an invisible friend. However, it didn't help that I took it a step too far—insisting Perluna be acknowledged during four square at recess, talking to her openly and loudly during class, and even pitching a fit when my teacher didn't reserve an empty chair for her at snack time.

While my parents were called in for a special meeting

to discuss my "vivid imagination" and "unhealthy attachment," my classmates' solutions ranged from ignoring me to ridiculing me. Friendships were formed and I stayed on the outside. No one wanted to be friends with the "weird" girl.

By the time I had adjusted to school and left Perluna behind, the damage had been done. Maybe I would have slowly recovered if not for my pageant stint that ended in second grade.

Yes, I had done child pageants, although the credit for that goes to my mom. When she wasn't ignoring me, one of the ways she dealt with having me was by trying to become the ultimate pageant mother. She poured all her energy into trying to get me to shine brighter than the other girls.

One of my first memories was of her putting me in a poofy pink dress that, sadly, was not meant for playing a princess slaying pretend dragons. No, it was for me to wear while practicing my pageant wave.

Call me a buzzkill, but at three years old, I had no idea why mechanically crooking my hand back and forth was better than stabbing imaginary green monsters with an empty paper towel tube.

Unfortunately for me and my mom, we soon found out that I hated the spotlight. And frilly dresses. And makeup. Yes, makeup. I swear, I'd worn more makeup as a six-year-old than I'd ever done as an adult.

When we'd first started working the pageant circuit, I'd been excited. My mom showed an interest in me like she never had before and she called it our special "mother and daughter bonding time." However, the weekends of waiting, parading, and judgment soon wore on me.

I was never a first-place winner, but that only seemed to push my mother harder. My curls got tighter, the dresses got frillier, and the list of talents for me to try got longer.

Of all the unsuccessful talents my mom tried to coax out of me, none was a worse fit than tap dancing. Which was made apparent at the Halften Lil' Honeybees competition. After six weeks of intense tap-dancing lessons, my mother had deemed I was ready to share my tapping with the world.

The time came for me to start my routine. The bubbly music started playing in the background, and when everyone's eyes fixed on me, I froze. In all my sequined, teased-haired, fake-eyelashed glory. I swear I can still feel the heat of those stage lights beating down on me and the critical gazes of the judges while my heart pounded madly in my chest. I couldn't remember a single step from my tap-dancing routine.

But plucky eight-year-old that I was, I decided all was not lost. Instead of remaining frozen onstage, I channeled my inner Babette Finch—my idol at the time.

Much to my mother's chagrin, Babette was not a dancer, a singer, or a gymnast. No, she was the weather woman on our local channel. I'm not entirely sure why I was so enthralled with Babette. Maybe it was her big smile that always seemed friendly or her knack for making atmospheric conditions sound so interesting.

Whatever the reason, instead of breaking out into my tap-dance routine, I broke out into a full-detailed weather report set to the tune of "Little Bitty Pretty One."

Any points I may have scored with the judges for originality and accuracy—because, don't worry, I had watched Babette's report only that morning—was entirely lost on my mother, who was fuming mad at me afterward. She didn't buy my stage fright excuse, and the way she reamed me out after in front of all the other stage moms was the nail in my social coffin.

That was the end of pageants, much to my relief, but the other mothers quickly began to buzz about "that odd Audrey Miller." Of course, the gossip was overheard by their daughters, who were only too happy to entertain their parents with stories of my strange behavior at school, and so "weird Audrey" morphed into "odd Audrey."

And years later, I still worried that returning to Halften meant living in that shadow.

I shook the melting ice cubes in my empty glass, pushed the thought from my mind, and instead contemplated whether it was worth dealing with the creepy bartender to get another lemonade when Melissa Ellis—Tucker's fiancée—said, "But enough about us. Congratulations on the engagement, Audrey. Is your fiancé here?"

My smile slipped from my face, just for a second, and I quickly pasted it back on again, hoping Melissa and her sister, Kelsey, hadn't noticed. Here it was, the topic of conversation I had been hoping to avoid tonight. And tomorrow at the wedding.

I took a deep breath, hoping I could say something generic enough to satisfy them and then change the subject. "No, unfortunately, Mercer couldn't make it. He's studying for the bar exam *and* interning at a big law firm this summer, so his schedule is really intense right now." It was the same rehearsed response I had given

Jackson in the car. My predecided cover story. Everyone seemed to buy this excuse without question, even though I knew it was a lame one.

Not that the bar exam and Mercer's internship weren't intense—they were. But for Mercer, they were both pretty much just technicalities.

His dad had worked for a big-shot Chicago law firm his whole life and Mercer basically had a spot lined up for him there since he could walk.

But since I wasn't about to tell them the real reason Mercer was MIA, that was my story.

"Hey, Melissa, sorry to interrupt." Tucker appeared and slipped an arm around his fiancée's waist. I was so happy for the interruption, I resisted the urge to join them for a group hug—because that would be weird. But his timing was perfect. "Could we borrow Audrey for a minute?"

Yes, please, borrow away! Unless he was planning on questioning me about my love life too, in which case, I would be excusing myself to hunt down more finger food.

"Of course." Melissa gave Tucker a quick kiss. "I know you're dying to catch up with her." Melissa stepped back and continued talking to Kelsey.

"Thanks." Tucker took Melissa's spot, and to my surprise, Jackson was with him—although he was standing a little farther back, with his hands shoved in his pockets.

After dashing out of his truck, I hadn't expected to interact with him for the rest of the night. I tried to ignore the way my heart picked up, just slightly, seeing him standing there with an unsure smile on his face. Darn him, why did he still look so good after all these years? Especially in his dress shirt and tie? Now that I wasn't taken up by being embarrassed about running out of gas and rogue tissues under my armpits, I had the mental clarity to notice how handsome he still was.

Familiar things, like the deep blue of his eyes and the sheen of his jet-black hair. And other, newer things that came over the years since I'd last seen him. His beard, while neat and trim, was fuller now, the perfect complement to his strong jawline. And his crisp button-up shirt was well tailored, accentuating the muscles of his arms and broadness of his chest.

Nope, I was shutting that down.

Get a grip, I commanded myself. *Absolutely no ogling the best man or there will be no dessert for you tonight.* There, that was telling myself. Melissa Ellis owned her own bakery, so I knew there were some delicious treats on the line tonight if I didn't get my act together.

"What's up?" I directed my smile at Tucker.

"Jackson and I were just talking and we want to offer you a job. My job, actually, as Head Event and Music Coordinator at the Inn."

"What?" My eyes widened, which I was sure made me look like a deranged cartoon, but I couldn't help it. That was the last thing I was expecting. I glanced at Jackson and only now did I notice that his smile seemed more forced than anything.

"Are you serious?" I asked, wondering if they were both going to laugh and say they were kidding.

But no, Tucker looked dead serious as he went on. "We want to know if you're interested in taking over at the Inn for me while I'm gone."

I laughed as I tended to do when I found something unbelievable or strange—his suggestion was both. "But I don't know anything about running a restaurant."

"I don't run the restaurant. That's all Jackson." Tucker gestured to his still-silent best friend. "I handle the live music and other events. It's really not that different than what you did event coordinating at the hotel. You'd be perfect, and the best part is, we'd just need you for the summer. That's what you're looking for, right?"

"Well, yeah, that actually sounds perfect." I brushed a hand through my wavy hair. Despite what I'd led others to believe, I was only planning on staying in Halften for the summer because I didn't really have anywhere else to go. My goal was to get a job and save enough to move somewhere new in the fall.

I'd thought that using most of my salary to pay down my student loans was a wise move. But between that and the money I had already sunk into my now-canceled wedding, I had very little savings to fall back on. If I wanted a fresh start, I needed a good job this summer. Was this it?

"So you're interested? I'm telling you this will be great. I won't have to worry about taking an extended honeymoon because I know you'll be handling things at the Inn. It will be such a relief. And you won't be stuck doing something boring, like working at the local bank." With that, Tucker went into some details about the position, including my main responsibilities, hours, and salary.

I bit my lip. Okay, I had to admit. Tucker was making this sound pretty darn good. I mean, the pay was way better than what I'd made before, and since I was staying at my parents' house, I could save it all and use it as a down payment once I figured out where I was going next.

And the work? Despite how things had ended at my last job, I knew I could handle it. I loved music as much as Tucker did—I just hadn't been gifted musically like he had. But I would love finding new talent and coordinating the shows.

But there was still one big problem.

"Are you sure about this?" I asked, finally turning my attention to Jackson. It was time to mention the elephant in the room—at least for me, and probably for Jackson. I got the feeling Tucker was oblivious to certain, uh, hiccups in our history.

"As long as you can handle the job, I'm fine with it." Jackson's reply was all business, but I wasn't quite sure I believed him. His body language said otherwise. Had Tucker twisted his arm to agree to this? Or were they really so desperate for help that he would take what he could get?

Before I could question Jackson further, his phone rang and he pulled it out of his pocket. "Sorry, I've got to take this. It's the restaurant."

"See what I mean?" Tucker said as Jackson walked away. "All he does is work. He really can't take on my job too. We need you. So what do you say?"

"Are you *sure* Jackson is okay with this?" I crossed my arms.

"Yeah. Why wouldn't he be? It's a great solution. And you guys already know each other, so it will make things a lot easier."

Oh sweet, naive Tucker.

"You're forgetting one thing." I dropped my voice,

even though Jackson was well out of earshot and on the phone. "He hates me."

"What?" Tucker laughed. "What are you talking about? He doesn't hate you."

Okay, maybe *hate* wasn't the right word, but he definitely didn't like me. "Have you forgotten about all the years he spent avoiding me like the plague?"

"That's what you're worried about?" Tucker waved a hand. "That was kid stuff. It's not like we're teens anymore. You're both professionals. And besides, you're engaged. What's the issue?"

Right, my engagement. My engagement that had ended last week when Mercer had dumped me—a mere twenty-four hours after I'd gotten fired from my job. But I was not telling Tucker about my broken engagement—not yet.

Why? Because it was the night before he was marrying the love of his life—the girl he'd pined over for years and finally won. There was no way I was putting a damper on his big day.

I knew Tucker, and the minute he found out about Mercer dumping me, he'd be all sympathy. His role as my stand-in big brother—even though he was only my cousin—would kick in, and he'd oscillate between being sad for me and worried about me.

Nope, definitely not telling him about my failed engagement until after his wedding.

And yeah, I'll admit it. There was a selfish part of me that didn't want to admit to the rest of my family—heck, the rest of Halfen—that "Odd Audrey" was just as odd as ever. Couldn't hold a job. Couldn't keep a fiancé.

It was bad enough that I was forced to come home with

my tail between my legs, but I didn't want everyone to know what a colossal failure I was.

And Tucker had a point. The reason Jackson was so uncomfortable around me was because of my massive crush I'd had on him all through middle school. And high school.

He'd made it clear in no uncertain terms that he did *not* feel the same, and I'd finally, *finally*—though it had taken most of college—gotten over him.

But I could only imagine how he might have groaned when Tucker suggested I come work for him.

No way, man, I could hear him say in his matter-of-fact voice. *I can't deal with her making googly eyes at me all day long. I've got a restaurant to run. Find someone else, just not your crazy cousin.*

But the more I thought about it, the more I realized I *did* want this job. It would be a dream come true. And even though it wasn't permanent, it would look great on my resume. And the pay Tucker mentioned was fantastic. It was just the thing I needed to get myself out of the hole I'd fallen into.

"No issue." I cleared my throat. "I mean, as long as Jackson's okay with it." My eyes turned to where Jackson stood under a tree, talking on the phone, his back to us. I smoothed my hands down the front of my skirt. "Obviously, I'm a happily engaged woman, so I won't be anything but professional. But you have to make sure he's on board. I don't want to work somewhere that I'm not wanted."

"Trust me," Tucker said, "he's fine with it. He'll love having you there."

"So when do I start?" I asked, my excitement growing

as I mentally went over my new plan in my head. This was exactly what I needed to get my life back on track.

I could do this. I could work with my old crush. After Mercer, I was so not looking for a relationship. And even if I were, it wouldn't be with a guy who thought I was a total joke.

Nope, Jackson and I would never work romantically. I had accepted that long ago and moved on.

But could we work together? I guess I was about to find out.

CHAPTER 4

AUDREY

Early afternoon on Monday, my soles crunched against gravel as I made my way toward the huge restored barn behind the Stonewall Inn where Jackson had asked me to meet him.

The gravel lot was empty, which was no surprise since the restaurant and event space were closed on Sundays and Mondays. That was why Jackson had asked me to meet him here today for my first day of training, so he would have time to go over everything with me.

I felt a little bad that he was using one of his days off to train me, but I was relieved to have a pressure-free environment to learn the ropes.

I gazed up at the formerly dilapidated structure I remembered from my childhood, now restored. It still had a rustic charm, but the once-rotting beams were fresh, and rather than looking sad like I remembered it, it stood tall and proud—like a stalwart fortress, every bit as mighty as the thick backwoods surrounding it.

That could be you, I encouraged myself. *All you need is a fresh coat of paint.*

Okay, as far as internal pep talks go, it wasn't my most inspiring, but I was trying to be positive as I approached my future. It wasn't the future I had planned, but it was the one available, and I was determined to not mess it up.

I swung open one of the huge barn doors and stepped inside the grand space, now much emptier than it had been two days ago when it hosted Tucker and Melissa's wedding reception.

The whole wedding had been beautiful, everything that Tucker and Melissa deserved. And not only that, I had succeeded in keeping it together.

Absentmindedly, I twisted the fake engagement ring on my left hand, the one I had purchased at a steep discount before heading home. Despite being a little loose, it had worked perfectly to keep my family from discovering that Mercer and I had broken up, just like I'd hoped. Except for a few cheery "You're next!" comments, all focus had been on Tucker and Melissa, exactly like I wanted.

Well, except when I'd experienced a slip of the tongue and confessed the truth to Caleb Ellis's new girlfriend, Victoria. But I wasn't too worried about that. She seemed trustworthy, and since she wasn't from Halften, I had been able to tell her the truth without her judging me.

I knew telling my mom wouldn't be so easy. She *loved* Mercer, and sometimes I wondered that if given the choice between me or him, she'd pick him.

Nope, that wasn't a conversation I was looking forward to having. But I had time to figure that out. Right now I needed to focus on my new job. I had already done the math, and if I saved most of what I earned, I'd have enough at the end of the summer to start fresh somewhere with a few months' rent and the ability to job search at my leisure.

I just had to make sure I did my best here these next three months.

"Audrey." Jackson's voice sounded behind me and I turned as he stepped inside the barn. "You're here early."

Was it just me, or did he seem surprised by this?

"Yup, I'm excited to start working." I smiled broadly. It was true. And even though punctuality wasn't always my strong point, I had set three alarms, left early, and made sure I had a full tank of gas before heading out. Like I said, I was not about to mess this opportunity up.

"Great, well, let's get started." Jackson started walking down the center of the barn floor. "Obviously, you already know the layout because you were here for Tucker's wedding, but let me go over some of the different setups we use depending on the event we're hosting." He handed me a black binder. "You'll find the floor plans in here. We pretty much rotate between four different setups depending on the occasion."

"Awesome, thanks." I flipped to the tab labeled *Floor Plans* and easily found the one Jackson was describing, same as I recalled it being over the weekend for Tucker and Melissa's wedding reception.

"With a show," Jackson went on, "we do one of two setups."

I flipped the page and found show setup plans and

nodded along as he detailed how the crew might arrange the chairs and tables to best accommodate the expected crowd.

"Obviously, the bar and the stage don't ever change." He gestured to the built-in wooden bar off to one side of the room, and then the stage all the way in the back of the building.

I nodded, made a few notes in the binder he had given me, while Jackson went on. "Our setup crew is great and they know the drill, but you'll need to oversee things. Lighting is where it can get tricky, but we'll go over that later." He waved a hand. "C'mon, let me show you the bar setup."

I followed him behind the bar and he opened a built-in fridge. "It's pretty basic compared to the bar we've got in the restaurant. Two beers on tap, the rest is generally bottles and cans in here. As far as mixed drinks go, we've got the basics . . ." As he outlined that, I nodded along. The setup was similar to the hotel I had worked at, with a lot less options. I wouldn't have trouble keeping any of it straight.

When he finished, I asked about restocking procedures and when orders came in, and as Jackson answered, my brain popped a completely unprofessional question.

Do you think he looks better in a tux like at the wedding or jeans and a T-shirt like today?

What? Where did that come from? I was so not answering that.

Shut up, brain!

". . . so we usually only need one bartender here to handle the events. But we are short-staffed at the moment, so you and I are going to need to coordinate scheduling so we don't double-book anyone. I still need someone in the bar at the restaurant when we have shows."

"Right," I said. "Got it."

It's a simple question . . . my mind persisted.

One I'm not answering, I shot back.

"Do you know how to change a keg?" Jackson looked up from where the lines to the tap beers connected.

"I think so. I did it at the hotel a few times."

"Great. Let me just show you this one. It's a little different than most. The connection is kind of finicky." He knelt down to unhook the empty keg from the lines.

Oh, I'm definitely voting jeans! my brain declared.

"No, you're *not,*" I muttered under my breath.

"Uh . . . what?" Jackson looked up at me, confused. "You mean you want to change it?"

Shoot.

"Um, yeah, why don't you let me do it?" I said quickly, kneeling beside him. "I'm a hands-on learner, so I might not remember if I don't."

"Okay, go for it." He leaned back, giving me ample room to access the connections, but whether it was my awkwardness or his closeness, I found myself fumbling around.

"Hang on," Jackson said, leaning closer. "You've got to pull the ring to remove the coupler—" Jackson's hand closed over mine, and I jerked suddenly, causing beer to spray out.

I yelped and dove to the side, hands flying to my face, while Jackson yelped, and, luckily, quickly stopped the shooting stream.

"Sorry," I said weakly, shaking my dripping, sticky

hand. "I guess it's been a while . . ."

"No problem," Jackson said stiffly, yanking a clean towel off the counter and wiping his foam-covered face. "Let's head to the office next." I sensed his unspoken *That seems safer . . .*

"Sure."

So much for my great first day.

As we left the barn behind, my brain of course had to have the last word, taking in Jackson's beer-soaked shirt clinging to his chest.

Definitely jeans and T-shirt . . .

I shook my head.

Clearly, working in close proximity to Jackson wasn't going to be quite as easy as I thought.

Okay, so I still found him attractive.

But finding him attractive and wanting a relationship with him were two entirely different things. And I was *not* looking for a relationship—not with Jackson, not with anyone.

Which worked out, because I was the last person in the world Jackson would want a relationship with either.

So, you know, fate.

"Here's the office." Inside the restaurant, Jackson opened a door down the hall off the entrance.

I stepped in behind him and surveyed the space. It was simple but decently sized. A large window took up most of one wall and there were two matching desks, side by side, with a computer on each. A filing cabinet in one corner and a small bookshelf in the other. The only thing lacking was some décor and personalization.

"This is Tucker's desk, so now it'll be yours." Jackson tapped the edge of the left desk, then sat down in the office chair in front of the other. "I set up profiles for you on all the accounts, and all the info you need should be in your binder."

"Great." I followed his lead and sat down in the chair behind Tucker's—now my—desk. It was low for me, so I reached for the lever and adjusted it as the computer fired up.

"Let's get started with the scheduling software. That's the one you'll use the most for the shows and the staff."

"Sounds good." I flipped open the binder to the tab labeled *Office,* then grabbed a pen from the silver cup on the desk for notes.

I was in full work mode.

Never mind the fact that Jackson sitting so close beside me made the office feel much smaller than it actually was.

Satisfied, I leaned back in the office chair and looked over the schedule and what I had accomplished today.

After Jackson had shown me everything I needed on the computer, he had left me to it and made himself pretty scarce.

I couldn't exactly blame him.

I had promised myself I'd do everything in my power to make working with Jackson not weird, but already, I seemed to be failing on that front. What was it about him that made my brain move at the speed of lightning and my limbs feel like they were stuck in Jell-O? Honestly, I thought I was long over that. But here I was feeling like the same nine-year-old who had first been awed by him.

Let me explain.

My social leprosy continued through elementary school, and it wasn't until Penny's family moved to Halften in third grade that I made my first friend. Although I even almost messed that up.

On Penny's first day, she chose the empty desk beside me, and even though it was simple logistics—it was one of the few empty desks in the room—I couldn't help but be amazed at the prospect of a new seatmate.

"You're sitting here?" I gaped at the dark-haired, bespectacled girl when she slid into the seat beside me.

"The teacher told me to," she replied calmly as she pulled out two perfectly sharpened pencils and a new pink eraser, then lined them up in a row on her desk. She glanced at me. "Shouldn't I?"

"No, I mean, yes. You should if Mrs. Galveston told you to. It's just—" I tugged the ends of my messy ponytail, wondering if I should enjoy the conversation while it lasted, or warn the new girl what she was in for if she associated with me.

As she blinked back at me with calm, yet curious eyes, my conscience won out. I took a deep breath and lowered my voice. "The other kids don't like me. And if you sit with me, they might not like you either."

She didn't react how I expected. Meaning she didn't grab her pencils and book bag and jump up searching for another seat. Nor did her eyes fill with pity. Instead, she cocked her head slightly and blinked again. "Why don't they like you?"

I laughed. "I don't really know. They never have. I mean, it started in kindergarten. They thought I was weird because I had an imaginary friend. I guess I was way too attached to her, but I haven't talked to Perluna in years and they still think I'm weird, so—" I shut my mouth abruptly.

Great. Just great. Finally I had a chance to meet someone who didn't think of me as Odd Audrey and I was giving her a play-by-play of why she should. I swallowed and finished with a shrug. "Anyway, they just don't."

"That's stupid," she replied. "Lots of little kids have imaginary friends."

I couldn't help but smile at the way she referred to "little kids." Like obviously as third graders, we were so much more mature than that.

"They do?"

She nodded. "You're not weird. You're just like Anne of Green Gables. She had an imaginary friend in a glass door. You even look like her."

"Who?"

"Anne of Green Gables. Haven't you read it?"

I shook my head.

"Here." She reached into her book bag, which I could see was loaded up with books—none of which I recognized as required reads for class. She pulled out a yellow hardcover book and placed it in my hands. "Why don't you borrow mine? It's one of my favorites."

"Okay." I glanced at the cover, and even though the girl with braids and an old-fashioned dress didn't really seem like my reading style—I preferred scary books, like Goosebumps—I slid it into my backpack with a smile. "Thanks," I said. "No one's ever lent me a book before. The closest thing was when Teddy Marshall stole my backpack on the bus and chucked one of my books out the window. Which, I guess, was pretty much the opposite of lending me a book."

"That's terrible." She gaped at me, horrified.

I shrugged. "It landed in the woods, so I comforted myself by telling myself that a squirrel found it and took it back to his family and taught them all how to read." Uh-oh, should I have admitted that? Was I being weird again? Everyone knew squirrels couldn't read. "Anyway, thanks."

But she just laughed. "You're welcome. I'm Penny, by the way."

"Audrey," I said with a smile, happy to have one person here know me by just my given name.

Class began and I smiled to myself the whole time. When I got home after school, I spent the entire afternoon—and late into the evening—reading *Anne of Green Gables* cover to cover.

I was right. It wasn't anything like my usual read—and there were lots of words I didn't understand. But still, I liked it. I liked how spunky misfit Anne was, and I was especially intrigued by her and Diana's close friendship. And even though Diana wasn't described as wearing glasses, I pictured the raven-haired girl looking exactly like the dark-haired new girl with glasses who had lent me the book.

"I loved it," I said when I set in on Penny's desk the next day. "Thanks."

"You read it already?" she asked, clear admiration in her eyes.

"Yup." I beamed. I certainly wasn't one to read a book in one sitting, but this one had been different.

"Wow," Penny said as she slid the book back in her

bag. "It took me two days to read it. What was your favorite part?"

We spent recess together that day, chatting about books and many other things, and for the first time in ages, I had someone to eat lunch with.

After dismissal, we waited outside and continued talking together. I hadn't talked this much at school since I'd given up Perluna. Having a conversation with a real person was so much better.

That is until Gwyneth Syracuse, one of my top tormentors, approached us and snickered.

"Hey, Odd Audrey, who's your weird friend? And why is she dressed like a boy?"

I glared at Gwyneth, only now realizing that Penny had on baggy faded blue jeans with a blue-and-red flannel shirt that did seem pretty boyish. She had such a refined air about her I hadn't even noticed before.

I glanced at Penny to see her face turning bright red as she scuffed the toe of her gray, slightly worn sneakers behind her.

"This is Penny," I shot back quickly. "She's from Oklahoma and that's what all the cool kids there wear. Don't you know anything?"

"Yeah, okay." Gwyneth snorted, clearly seeing through my bluff. "Then Oklahoma must be full of losers."

I took a step forward, ready to shove Gwyneth or at least tell her that Penny was ten times cooler than her and all the other girls in our class who wore bright pastels and sparkles, but before I could, another voice interrupted.

"Hey, Penny, sorry I'm late. Let's go."

Gwyneth took a huge step back as an older boy headed

down the sidewalk toward us. He had dark hair like Penny and looked to be about thirteen, standing a good two heads taller than most of my classmates.

I blinked as he approached. "Who's that?" I asked Penny.

"My brother, Jackson," she replied, turning as she hoisted her backpack onto her shoulders. "He's here to walk me home. See you tomorrow."

"Hey, how was school?" Penny's brother asked her once she joined him. "Everything okay?"

"Yup," Penny said, no longer red from Gwyneth's snarky remarks. "I made a friend." She turned to me with a wave. "Bye, Audrey. See you tomorrow."

"See ya."

As Penny walked off with Jackson, I couldn't help but stare after them. I could see where she got her calm demeanor from. Although with Penny, it seemed a little bit like she was in her own world. With her brother, it seemed much cooler. Like nobody was going to mess with him—he seemed so mature. Even stupid Gwyneth Syracuse had appeared in awe of him.

But the moment they were out of earshot, Gwyneth turned back to me. "So you starting a loser club or something?"

"Shut up, Gwyneth."

"What?" She held up a hand, blinking her big blue eyes. "I mean, if she's hanging out with you, she must want to be a loser too. She sure dresses like one." The kids around her snickered.

Before I could fire back, my dad's car pulled up, and rather than continue to battle, I glared at Gwyneth, then got in.

"Hey, kiddo," my dad greeted me cheerfully. "How was school?"

"Pretty good," I said, "I think I made a new friend."

"That's great."

But I was pretty silent on the way home. Yes, it felt like Penny and I were fast on our way to becoming great friends, but I couldn't get Gwyneth's last words out of my head.

She must want to be a loser too . . .

I swallowed thickly. Was she right? If Penny became my friend, would she be treated like a loser too? It seemed unfair. She had told me today that her family had moved here because her dad lost his job. It was bad enough she'd had to leave her old life and all her friends behind. It didn't seem fair for her to become a social outcast like me. She was so great. I bet if the other kids gave her a chance, everyone would like her. She would have tons of friends in no time.

I thought about the book Penny had lent me. Especially the part where Anne and Diana became bosom friends, but due to a misunderstanding couldn't associate anymore.

My mind made up, the first thing I did when I got home was head up to my room and write a long note on my best stationary. Then I called out to my mom that I was going for a bike ride and I'd be back before dinner.

It was a long ride to Penny's house, since she lived in one of the neighborhoods closest to school, not out by the farm fields like me. But I found her house easily based on what she'd told me about it.

Bravely, I marched up to the front door and knocked.

Her brother answered, holding a peanut butter

sandwich, somehow looking just as cool doing that as he had outside of school. "Yeah?"

"Is, uh, Penny home?" I swiped some stray hair out of my eye. "I'm her friend from school."

Jackson smiled, but shook his head. "Sorry, Penny's not here. She had a dentist appointment."

"Oh." Well, maybe it was better this way. I handed him the note. "Can you give this to her?"

"Sure."

"Thanks." I gave a half-hearted wave.

I walked slowly back to my bike, trying not to think too hard about how much fun Penny and I would have had if we could have stayed friends. We might have hung out at her neighborhood park together. Or she might have liked to explore the woods by my house with me. But none of that would be happening now. Not once she read my note about why we shouldn't be friends.

I was just pedaling out of the driveway, about to turn onto the sidewalk, when a voice called out behind me.

"Hey!"

I stopped my bike and turned to see Jackson jogging toward me, waving a hand, no sandwich in sight. "Wait."

"Audrey, right?" he asked when he caught up to me.

"Yeah." I nodded.

He held out my note. "I'm not giving this to Penny."

"You read it?" My cheeks flamed. I wasn't sure if I was angry or embarrassed.

"Yeah, and it's stupid. Penny doesn't care about being popular. She just wants a friend."

"You don't understand," I said. "It's not just that she won't be popular if she hangs out with me, she'll get picked on." I scuffed my toe against the cement. "She's new here. And she's really cool, so I bet everyone will like her as long as she isn't friends with me—"

"That's the dumbest thing I ever heard." Jackson crossed his arms. "And anyway, it sounds like all the other kids in your class are jerks. Why would Penny want to be friends with jerks?"

I stared at him, open-mouthed. For once, I didn't have an answer. Would I be that smart in a few years once I was a teenager like him?

He sighed. "Look, Penny wasn't popular at her old school either. In fact, she hardly had any friends. Usually all she talks about is books. But today, all she did was talk about you the entire way home. I haven't seen her that happy in a while. So I'm not going to give her your note." He pressed it into my hand. "But I will tell her you stopped by."

"Okay," I said slowly as I stuffed my note into my pocket. It seemed a little silly and dramatic now.

"Okay," Jackson said with a definitive nod, then started walking back toward the house. "See ya around."

"Bye," I said back.

I rode home with a much lighter heart than when I had ridden there. And after that, Penny and I were pretty much inseparable. As far as I knew, Jackson never told her about my dumb note that almost ended our friendship before it began.

Jackson walked Penny home from school the rest of the year after that. And even though Penny and I still got picked on during school, it was a lot easier to deal with when I was with Penny than it had been by myself. And while Gwyneth and her friends were still rotten to us during the day, they never said anything to us during pickup anymore. I guess they didn't want to get caught being jerks by Penny's teenage brother.

And whether it was the way he had encouraged me to be Penny's friend, or the way he made all the boys in my class seem silly and juvenile by comparison, from that day forward, Jackson Crowe was the coolest guy ever in my eyes.

What had started as admiration soon morphed into a crush the minute I hit puberty. A crush that grew every passing year until the summer before graduation.

While Jackson had never been unkind to me before that, he had made it clear that he only saw me as Penny's friend. Even when Tucker and his mom moved to Halften and Jackson and he became best friends, it didn't change anything. The more I saw him, the more he seemed to ignore me.

While that used to frustrate me, now given the circumstances, it was for the best.

I was here to work and I would do that better if I wasn't getting distracted by Jackson.

Pulling myself out of my memories, I returned my focus to the scheduling software in front of me.

Tucker had booked shows through the end of June, and he'd left detailed notes on the process. Jackson had said the best place for me to start was to contact bands and get the rest of the summer schedule in place. He'd handed me a printed schedule of their shows from last summer and recommended I start there. Between all my phone calls and emails, I had filled five more summer slots today.

Even so, I noticed that there were quite a few un-booked evenings. There was definitely an opportunity for growth here and I made a note to spend tomorrow scouring for some local talent to fill more spots. I was determined to prove to Jackson—and myself—that I was not only qualified to do this job, but I had the talent, time, and energy to really shine at it.

After saving my work, I glanced at the clock. It was late, the sun dipping low in the sky. I'd gotten in some solid work and the time had flown. That was a good sign.

When I left the office, I didn't see Jackson anywhere in the restaurant, so I headed out to the barn. Sure enough, I found him stacking boxes into a corner.

"Hey," I called out, walking over to him. "I got a hang of the scheduling software and some more shows booked. Is there anything else you want to show me tonight?"

"Nah, you're good." He glanced at me, then hoisted another load on top of the ones he had already stacked. "Thanks. I'll be heading out too once I finish moving these."

"Want a hand?" I glanced at the boxes scattered by the door. He had been here just as long as I had—on his off day too—and honestly, he looked tired.

"It's fine. I'm just getting 'em out of the way for now. I'll have one of the guys help me move them to the loft tomorrow." He pointed above us where, sure enough, there was a hayloft with a ladder leaning against it on one end. "We use it for extra storage."

"I can help," I said, setting my purse down on the ground. "We can put them up there now."

Jackson straightened, then swiped the back of his hand across his sweaty brow. "You don't need to worry about that. The ladder's kind of unsteady—"

"If Tucker were here, would he help you put them in

the loft?"

"Sure, but—"

"Okay, then. I'm Tucker's stand-in for the time being, so anything he would do, I should do." Without waiting for him to argue more, I grabbed a box and headed up the ladder. I tucked it under one arm and began climbing. The wooden ladder creaked beneath me. Luckily, the box I had grabbed was on the smaller side, because Jackson was right—it was a bit shaky. I was thankful to have one hand free to grab on to the side to steady myself as I climbed.

"Geez, Audrey." Jackson raced over and stabilized the quaking ladder. "Be careful."

"I'm always careful," I called back, then shoved the box into the loft and peeked over the top. It seemed like a great space, even in the dim light, but one side was filled with boxes. On the other end there was a large closed window.

I started to climb back down, but Jackson called up, "Climb up in the loft. I'll hand the boxes to you."

"Aye aye, Boss Man." I pulled myself over the loft edge and turned to face Jackson, where he was already climbing partway up the ladder with another box in hand. When he got close enough, I reached down and grabbed the box from him, then stacked it on top of the other one.

We worked that way for a while. I was a little annoyed because Jackson was doing the bulk of the physical labor, hauling the boxes up and down the ladder, but our assembly line approach worked well.

And the one time I suggested us switching places, he just grunted and said, "No way. It's too much of a liability having you on the ladder. If I fall, the only person I can sue is myself."

Before long, Jackson handed me a box and said, "That's the last one."

"Great." I stood and set the box on top of the others.

"Since you're already up there." Jackson climbed over the edge. "I may as well show you how everything's organized up here."

"Sounds good."

The system was pretty self-explanatory, one end starting with equipment, then décor, anything food prep or serving related, then some nonperishables. We stacked everything in its correct spot, and I had just set down a box of paper napkins when a loud crash behind us made me jump.

"What was that?" I whirled around.

Jackson cursed, then raced to the gap in the railing where we had climbed up. Then he cursed again.

I joined him and peered down.

The ladder had fallen over and was now lying on the ground to one side.

"Uh-oh," I said.

"Did you close the door after you came in?" Jackson asked.

"Was I supposed to?"

He groaned. "Those huge barn doors let in some pretty big drafts. The wind musta knocked the ladder down." He shoved a hand in his pants pocket but came up empty. "Shoot. I don't have my phone."

I looked down where my purse sat on the floor. "I left mine down there too when we started loading the boxes."

"Great," he muttered, then crossed to the other end of

the loft and freed the bolt across the closed window. He swung open the hinged door, letting in a burst of light and fresh air.

"Hey!" he called out. "Can anyone hear me?"

Silence.

I joined him at the window. "It's only been us here today, right?"

Jackson nodded, but still, I called out as well. "Hello! Can anyone hear us? We're stuck up here!"

Jackson joined in, but a minute later, all we had were hoarse voices.

"We're too far off the road for anyone to hear," he said, then headed back toward the edge of the loft. He looked down. "Maybe I can jump."

"Are you crazy?" I raced to his side and looked down, grabbing his arm on instinct. "It's way too high. If you do that, you *are* going to have to sue yourself. Besides, how are you going to run the restaurant with a broken leg?"

He threw his hands in the air. "So what do we do?"

"Wait." I plopped down on the floor and leaned my back against the stack of boxes. "The restaurant is open tomorrow. Someone will be by in the morning, right?"

"Well, yeah, but . . ." He faced me, not looking convinced by my solution.

"There you go. We're not going to die. Or starve." I pointed to one of the boxes we had just put up here. "We've got a year's worth of pickles."

Jackson crossed his arms and clenched his jaw, then looked back out over the railing as if trying to devise some other plan. As long as he didn't try to make a parachute out of tablecloths, I'd let him be.

I crossed over to the window and sat in front of it,

admiring the view. It was actually quite stunning. The sun was starting to set, casting a golden glow over the farm fields in the distance. But I would have enjoyed it more if I wasn't trapped up here.

Was this how Rapunzel felt in her tower? I brushed a hand through the ends of my hair, which grazed my shoulder. Too bad I didn't have her mighty locks to throw down so Jackson could climb out and get help.

I glanced back where he still stood brooding, then quickly looked away.

If my high school self had known I would one day be trapped in a tower of sorts with Jackson, I would have done backflips.

Now, I was honestly just tired and hungry.

So much for my stellar first day.

Chapter 5

JACKSON

I stood by the loft edge for a few more minutes, calculating the risk versus reward of jumping. Like Audrey had said, at this height, the odds were not in my favor.

Then I moved a little way down and contemplated climbing over the railing and shimmying down one of the large beams on either end holding the loft up. But they were so wide and awkward I wasn't confident I would actually be able to manage that.

Despite my desperate desire to get out of this situation, I had too much riding on the work I did here every day to risk getting injured. What was I going to do? Call Tucker up a day into his honeymoon and tell him he needed to get back here and run things while I nursed a broken leg?

No, I wasn't going to do that to him—or myself. I was

way too picky about how things were run to trust anyone but myself. So that settled it.

We were stuck.

I turned to face Audrey, who had already opened several boxes and seemed to be trying to make the best of the situation.

She sat cross-legged on what looked like a spread-out black tablecloth with a bottle of water next to her and held up two jars.

"What do you think?" she asked. "Pickles or olives?"

"Why choose?" Reluctantly, I crossed the room and sat across from her. "I say we feast and have both."

"I like the way you think." With a grunt, she popped the lid of the olives, speared a few with a plastic fork, and popped one in her mouth.

Following her lead, I twisted the top off the pickles and crunched into one. I swallowed. "How many tablecloths did you see in that box? Think we could tie them together and make a rope?"

"The old bedsheets out the window trick? I'd say it's your funeral." She grabbed the fabric between two fingers. "This stuff is pretty stiff and thick. Not sure it would tie together well. And I only saw four. I don't think that would be enough for a rope. Plus, I'll be honest, I don't trust my ninja skills to actually get me to the ground in one piece. How 'bout you?"

She had a point. I worked out, but I wasn't exactly a practiced escape artist. "What if I lowered you to the ground?"

"Don't take this the wrong way, Boss Man, but as much as I want this job, I don't recall anything in the job description requiring me to put my life in your hands."

"Would you stop calling me that?"

"Why? It's funny."

"Technically, I'm not even your boss. You're filling in for Tucker, and he and I are partners."

She shook her head. "Partner Man just doesn't have the same ring to it. Besides, you're training me and paying my salary. Plus, it doesn't take a genius to know that Tucker's the one who really wanted to hire me and you just went along with it."

I thought about denying it, but realized it was pointless. I cleared my throat. "Was it that obvious?"

"The hills have eyes," she said dryly. "And ears. And the hills are me."

"Yeah, I got that." Considering her reference was to a horror movie slash video game, I wondered if that meant she was annoyed with me. "I didn't mean to come off like that."

"Hey, I get it. Tucker put you in a hard spot. But I promise you, I'm not here for nepotism. I may not know the music industry, but I'm ready to learn, and believe it or not, I know a lot about the people industry."

I shoved another pickle into my big mouth and chewed for a minute. "What did you do before this again?"

"Hotel management. I was an event coordinator."

That's right—Tucker had mentioned that. It was relevant experience. Maybe I shouldn't have been so negative about Tucker wanting to hire her. I mean, it wasn't as if we had a bunch of qualified candidates lining around the block interested in the demanding, yet short-term, position. Was it her experience that I thought was lacking, or was it just the fact that I didn't want to work with her?

I released a heavy breath. "Look, I'm sorry if I came off as a jerk, and you're right, I should at least give you a chance. Especially when you're kind of saving my butt filling in for Tucker like this. So how about a deal?"

"I'm listening." She looked up from where she was skewering olives onto each prong of the fork.

"I'll give you a fair chance just like any other employee if you stop calling me Boss Man."

She grinned and stuck out her hand. "It's a deal."

Wiping mine free of pickle juice, I accepted her handshake, ready to make good on my promise to be more professional. Only when her hand slipped into mine, I wasn't expecting the strange tingle that ran up my arm. I pumped once and let go quickly.

If Audrey noticed my reaction, she didn't show it, her attention back on her food. "So what am I supposed to call you then?" She laughed lightly. "Mr. Crowe?"

"No." That seemed as weird to me as it no doubt did to her. "Not unless you're talking to my dad. Just call me Jackson. Everyone else does."

"All right, well, Jackson, I am really sorry that I didn't close the door when I came in here. Believe me, getting stranded with the Boss Ma—er, the Jackson—wasn't exactly how I planned to make a good impression today."

"It's not your fault. You didn't know about the door." I paused. "I gotta say, you've been pretty calm about it."

She shrugged. "I've learned the hard way that no matter how hard we try, sometimes we can't control our circumstances. Sometimes we just have to make the best of what we have. Olive?"

"Thanks." I took the jar and handed her the pickles.

"That's very mature of you."

"What can I say? I've grown wise in my old age."

She said it as a joke, but part of me envied her. I was pretty sure I had grown cynical.

"Hey"—a thought occurred to me—"where are you staying while you're in town?"

"My parents'."

"Really? That's great."

"Is it?" She wrinkled her nose. "Most people wouldn't consider living with their parents at the age of twenty-four *great*."

"No, I mean, they might get worried when you don't come home and come looking for you."

"Maybe . . ." She said the word slowly, doubtfully. "But I told them I might be working late on account of it being my first day. Plus, I think they're kind of out of the habit of waiting up for me, considering I've been pretty much moved out since college. And they go to bed super early. I don't even think they wait until it's dark in the summer."

"So you're saying the odds aren't great?"

"Sorry." She shook her head. "What about you? Anyone at home who might notice your absence?"

"Not unless you count old Darcy," I said, thinking about the old mutt who was technically Penny's, but who had more or less become mine since she'd left for college and I'd returned. When I'd moved out, I brought him with me. "But I took him out and fed him before I left this afternoon, so I don't think he'll miss me too much. He has a surprisingly strong bladder in his old age."

"Mr. Darcy! I forgot you took him after Penny left. I haven't seen him in forever. How's he doing?"

I chuckled. "Same ol' Darcy, except fatter, slower, and older."

"You should call him by his full title, you know. It's *Mr.* Darcy. Actually, Mr. Fitzwilliam Darcy to be exact."

I shook my head, recalling how Penny had given the dog that ridiculous name when she got him. "I forgot how Penny named him after some snob in a book."

"Excuse me? Mr. Darcy is not some snob in a book. He's only one of the greatest literary characters ever written." She placed a hand on her heart. "And the swooniest when portrayed on the silver screen."

"Sorry." I held up both hands in a show of truce. "I forgot how weird you two were about that guy."

Audrey seemed to forgive my offense. "Can Mr. Darcy still shake hands?"

"Eh, his social skills have regressed some since you last saw him. He's more into sniffing butts now."

She grimaced. "Poor Mr. Darcy . . . I guess that's what happens when you're reduced to living with a commoner. No offense."

"None taken."

"Can I come see him some time?" Without waiting for me to answer she went on. "Does he still like that canned liver? Remember when Penny threw him a first birthday party and served them to him on those fancy plates?"

"Yeah." I laughed, recalling the memory. "And my mom freaked out when she saw him slobbering all over her best china."

Audrey laughed too. "And your dad walked in and thought it was some kind of cracker spread and started eating it?"

When both our laughter died away, I said, "Come by

and see him any time. Bring all the liver you want, but you're not putting a bow tie on him again. That's where I draw the line."

"You're no fun."

I laughed again. I had to admit, despite my initial horror of us being stuck up here, it wasn't really so bad. How long had it been since I laughed like this? And with Audrey, no less? Maybe Penny was right and she was fun. I had just never seen it because I'd been too busy trying to avoid her. But we weren't kids anymore. And things were different now.

Reminded of that, I glanced at the ring on her left hand. I wondered what her fiancé would think about our predicament. Mercer, the city-slicker, soon-to-be big-shot lawyer. Was he fancy, like non-dog Mr. Darcy? Probably. That was probably why Audrey had fallen for him.

Since it wasn't my business, I didn't ask. Instead, I focused on the matter at hand. "Since our odds of being rescued aren't looking very good, we should probably figure out, uh"—I glanced around the open loft—"sleeping arrangements."

Audrey grinned, not seeming to share my discomfort about the situation. "Is it crazy that I kind of want to build a box fort?" She pointed to all the boxes stacked behind us.

I laughed. "Go right ahead." In fact, that wasn't a bad idea at all. We could each have our own private sleeping quarters. "I'll even help." I pointed to the far end. "You want that corner? It will probably be the warmest spot. It gets stuffy up here, so we should keep the window open, but it might get cold overnight."

"That sounds great, thanks. I thought you were going

to laugh at me." She grabbed a box and got to work.

I followed, hoisting one of my own. "I'm actually impressed by your survival skills." And my own. Separate sleeping arrangements meant I would be less likely to get a black eye when Mercer found out about this whole thing—or Tucker, for that matter.

By the time we finished, Audrey had an enclosed spot in the corner and I had one on the other end. I had just finished my wall, when Audrey dropped two of the folded black tablecloths into my space.

"I guess these are our blankets," she said.

"Thanks."

She nodded and grabbed the one we had been sitting on, then spread it out in front of the open window. Then she took the final tablecloth and wrapped it around her shoulders and sat down, leaning her back against a box.

"What are you doing?" I asked.

"Watching the sunset." She patted the ground next to her. "Come join me."

I hesitated for a moment. But then, why not? It was too early to go to sleep and we had nothing else to do.

Grabbing my own tablecloth, I headed over to her and sank down onto the floor beside her. A light breeze blew in from the open window.

Across the horizon, colors danced. Deep blue bled into red, which bled into a fiery orange.

"I can't remember the last time I watched the sunset," Audrey said softly beside me.

"Me neither." Although the truth was, I didn't think I had ever just sat and watched the sunset before. But it was kind of nice.

We sat in silence as the colors dipped, and I shifted,

leaning my head against the back of the box. That was nice too. The silence. The peace.

I closed my eyes, resting them for a minute. I worked such long hours at the restaurant, I rarely got a full night's sleep.

Sometimes we just have to make the best of what we have, Audrey had said.

I had to admit, despite our predicament, she had done just that.

Chapter 6

AUDREY

The sound of birds trilling awoke me the next morning. Man, they were loud.

I was all for appreciating nature, but why couldn't nature appreciate that I was not a morning person?

With an angry groan, I rolled over and yanked my comforter over my head.

But my comforter wasn't very comfortable. And the pillow I had rolled into wasn't very soft.

I blinked, then my eyes flew open.

And I came face-to-face with a sleeping, softly snoring Jackson.

Holy smokes! I did a double take. *I just woke up in Jackson's arms! Wait –* why *did I wake up in Jackson's arms?*

This had to be a dream. Then everything came rushing back. My first day at the Inn. Getting trapped in the hayloft. Building our box forts that we clearly hadn't slept in.

The last thing I remembered was Jackson and me watching the sunset by the barn window, side by side, but not talking or touching. And definitely not touching like this.

I tried to roll away discreetly, but it wasn't easy considering Jackson had one arm wrapped around me, securing me snugly to his chest.

At one point in my life, this would have been a moment to cherish. But now it felt like it was a moment to end. Quickly.

Spoilsport! that obnoxious other part of my brain chided me.

Ignoring it, I slowly tried easing Jackson's arm up and off of me, but I had only raised it an inch or so when Jackson startled and his eyes flew open, connecting with mine.

"Wha— Whoa!" His confusion gave way to realization and he jerked away from me.

With a thud, he rolled into the box behind us, the one we had sat against last night. It was a good thing he hadn't rolled in the other direction because that would have sent him flying out the barn window—which really would have been a shame, considering he could have just jumped last night and broken all his bones then, saving us from this current humiliation.

Because while this, at one point in my life, would have been my dream come true, clearly for him it was a living nightmare.

"What did we—" he sputtered. "I mean, we didn't—"

"Relax." I wadded up the tablecloth I—no, we—had

used as a blanket and chucked it at him. "Nothing happened. We must have fallen asleep." Stupid hypnotic sunset.

"Right." Jackson ran a hand down his sleepy face, and his shoulders slumped, seeming to relax. I could only assume his memory had returned and he knew that, of course, nothing romantic had happened between us.

I couldn't be sure what his last memory of last night was, but I now recalled turning my head when the final ray of sun had disappeared over the horizon and seeing Jackson slumped next to me, head back, snoring quietly.

My own eyelids heavy, I had smiled to myself, then shut them and leaned against the box, planning to just rest there for a moment before I woke Jackson up and we both moved to our prepared spots.

Apparently, that moment had turned into the whole night. And somewhere along the way, we had moved closer, probably for warmth.

"Audrey"—Jackson held up his hands—"I swear, I did not mean to fall asleep on you like that."

"It's okay." I stood up, grabbing the tablecloth we had slept on, bunching it up. "I know you didn't. Don't worry about it, I'm not mad—well, except for the fact that I lost a perfectly good chance to sleep in a box fort."

Call me crazy, but that was something on my bucket list. Had been ever since Penny and I had built a totally amazing one in my basement when we were eleven, and my mom had refused to let us sleep in it, saying it was a suffocation and fire hazard.

"I must have been really tired . . ." Jackson muttered to himself, running a hand through his already rumpled hair.

I couldn't help it, I grinned. He looked so adorable flustered and sleepy. And I swear, the spot on my waist where his arm had held me earlier still tingled—

Hold up—no. No way was I going down that road. I had promised myself that I wasn't going to let old feelings come back, and this changed absolutely nothing.

If anything, it reiterated the true nature of our relationship. I was oil to his water. The garlic to his vampire. The mud to his antique white sofa. Okay, he probably didn't have one of those, but if he did, I'd have my grubby fingerprints all over it.

We didn't mix and that was that.

But seriously, if he didn't stop acting so appalled, I might slap him again. Rejecting my advances long ago was one thing, but acting like sleeping next to me was going to give him the plague was another.

He went on. "I really hope this doesn't cause a problem between you and your fiancé."

Oh, right. My so-called fiancé. Was that what he was so worried about?

"It won't." I waved a hand. "Mercer will believe me when I tell him what really happened." Ha, if only that were true.

"Okay, good." Jackson finally seemed to relax. "I'd hate for a silly misunderstanding to cause a problem."

"It won't," I said again and forced a smile on my face, even though part of me wanted to fess up right there.

It won't cause a problem because it turns out my former fiancé cares more about his career than my honor anyway.

But I kept my mouth shut. Call it pride, but after Jackson's reaction to finding me in his arms this morning, I wasn't sure I wanted to own up to the fact that the man who had once claimed he would love and protect me forever didn't want me either.

My stomach growled loudly, an awkward but welcome distraction. I rubbed my abdomen. "Guess our feast didn't cut it last night after all."

Jackson frowned. "Let's see if we can find anything else to—"

The sound of a car door slamming cut him off. We both rushed to the window and started yelling when we caught sight of a man sauntering across the gravel parking lot, whistling to himself.

"Hey! Randy! Up here!" Jackson waved his arms.

"What the—" Randy raised his hand, squinting as he strode closer. "Whatcha doing up there?"

"We were unloading boxes when the ladder fell. Can you grab it for us?"

"Sure thing." Randy waved a hand and headed for the barn.

I blew out a long breath.

We were finally rescued.

CHAPTER 7

JACKSON

I yawned again, for what felt like the hundredth time that day.

As I took my place behind the bar to relieve Randy of his shift, he snickered. "The new hire keep you up last night?"

"What?" I turned to him, my brain slow to catch up. I'd been foggy all day, which made no sense considering when I did the math of the number of hours I slept last night, it was more than I usually got.

"You and the new girl stuck in that loft all night. Musta thought of something to keep you busy."

"Nothing happened." I didn't mention the fact that Audrey had woken up in my arms this morning. And not just because it hadn't meant anything. I knew Randy wasn't looking for tips on cuddling.

"Aw, c'mon, don't worry. I won't tell Tucker you got

busy with his cousin. So how was she?"

"Listen, Randy." I turned on him, more fire in me than I'd felt all day, ready to knock his head against the wall. "Shut your mouth about Audrey. Not only is she Tucker's cousin, but she is your superior. Treat her with respect, or you will not have a job here anymore, do you understand?"

Randy's jaw ticked and his eyes narrowed, and for a second, I wondered if we were about to have a real problem.

But like the flip of a switch, he laughed and held up his hands. "Loud and clear, boss. Relax—I'm not moving in on your girl. I was just hoping maybe you were gettin' some for a change. You really need to loosen up." With that, he sauntered out the bar's side entrance, leaving me to stack clean glasses with more force than necessary.

I hoped Randy would heed my warning. I hadn't forgotten the comments he'd made about Audrey the night of the rehearsal dinner. Or the way he'd grinned when I'd officially introduced her as Tucker's temporary replacement this morning.

But maybe I was overreacting—Randy seemed to value his job here, picking up extra shifts whenever we needed the coverage and even asking to take on extra responsibilities. And as far as I knew, he hadn't bothered any of the female staff here. But still, the thought of him around Audrey made me uneasy.

Is it him *around Audrey or is it any guy?*

I dismissed the question almost as quickly as it popped into my head. Of course it was him. Besides occasionally taking on the role of stand-in big brother due to Audrey's friendship with Penny and mine with

Tucker, I did not have any overly protective urges toward her. The one time I had, at the Jorgens' party, she had completely misinterpreted it.

So why'd you have your arm around her this morning?

I clanked another glass onto the counter as if pounding down the thought.

I had no idea. I certainly hadn't done it intentionally, but the fact that it had happened at all was . . . problematic.

And not just because she was engaged. Sheesh, if she was about to complain about anyone here having unprofessional behavior, it would probably be me.

But there was nothing I could do about it now. I'd already apologized, and luckily, she had pretty much laughed it off. She'd probably already forgotten about it. Which meant I should too.

Still, my foggy mind and sour disposition lasted throughout the afternoon, and the only thing that helped was that the bar wasn't busy.

However, when a new voice greeted me, I wished that it was.

"Hello, stranger. It's been a while."

I looked up from the drink I was mixing to find my ex-girlfriend leaning over the bar, a seductive smile spread across her face, and her smoky eyes gazing up at me like I was the only man in the world.

Same old Gwyneth.

Only difference was I wasn't falling for it anymore.

"Gwyneth," I greeted her but didn't return her smile.

She waited, then flipped her long caramel-colored hair, which I was pretty sure was extensions, over her shoulder. The last time I'd seen her, she'd worn it in a bob cut up to her chin. Or maybe Gwyneth had some Pinocchio-like power, but instead of her nose growing every time she lied, it was her hair. In which case, I was surprised it wasn't down to her knees.

"That's really all you have to say to me?" she said, her lips pursing into a pout. "What's it been since I last saw you – three months?"

Seemed longer, but I didn't say that. "Can I get you anything?"

Her smile turned amused, like she enjoyed the fact that I was being cold toward her. She pulled up a stool and sat down. "Vodka tonic with lemon." She looked around the bar. "The place looks good. And so do you."

I didn't comment, just mixed her drink silently and set it in front of her.

"I see you're still upset with me." She stirred her drink with her skinny straw. "I was hoping maybe the time apart would do us good."

"I'm not upset, I just don't have anything to say." I'd said it all when we'd broken up last fall. "And there is no us."

"But there could be." She flashed a teasing smile, one that used to make me putty in her hands.

"No, there couldn't be." I planted both palms on the counter and looked her square in the eye. "So if you came here hoping to reconcile, you're wasting your time."

A thoughtful sip. "We'll see. Lucky for you I'm back in town for a few weeks."

That didn't seem lucky at all, but since her family still lived in Halften, she tended to pop up every now and then, especially around holidays.

After we had broken up, I'd heard Gwyneth had

gotten a job at some fancy salon in Chicago. The distance had been good, finalizing things and giving us both the space we needed. Her, to do whatever it was she had been doing—I didn't know because we hadn't kept in touch. And me, to throw myself into my work, which was exactly what I'd needed.

It had actually been quite a while since I'd thought about Gwyneth, but having her show up out of nowhere was unexpected to say the least.

I turned my back to her to enter her drink into the computer—hopefully, she wasn't planning on starting a tab—when the bar door connecting to the kitchen swung open and Audrey walked in.

"Hey, Jackson." She looked up from the clipboard she was holding. "I'm going over inventory in the barn and I can't seem to find any bottled seltzer. Do you know where it is?"

"Yeah, there's a bunch in our cooler." I motioned to the bar shelf in front of us, the wall of which connected with the walk-in cooler behind it. "I think they forgot to split the order when they delivered it. Go ahead and take what you need."

"Thanks." Audrey checked off her list, then turned to go.

"Audrey Miller?" Gwyneth said suddenly from her spot at the bar. "Is that you?"

Audrey turned and faced her, but before she could say anything, Gwyneth smiled broadly and went on. "You look good." Any chance of that being a compliment died with her next words. "I almost didn't recognize you."

"Hey, Gwyneth." Audrey's eyes darted between me and Gwyneth briefly, and I didn't miss the question in them. No doubt she had heard about Gwyneth's and my messy breakup. I wondered just how much she had heard. "Yeah, it's me."

It was no surprise that Gwyneth and Audrey knew each other—Gwyneth had been in the same grade as her and Penny at school, and Halften was a small town. But given the tight smiles and brief words now exchanged, it didn't seem like there was much love lost between them. No huge surprise. Penny had never liked Gwyneth, so I could only assume Audrey felt the same.

Audrey said goodbye, and the moment she passed back through the swinging door, Gwyneth turned her attention to me. "How long has Audrey Miller worked here?"

"She just started. She's filling in for Tucker while he's on his honeymoon."

"I see . . . How convenient."

"It worked out well." I set her check in front of her. "We needed help and she was looking for work."

"And I'm sure she just jumped at the chance." She tapped a long, manicured nail atop her bill, looking thoughtful.

When I didn't comment further, she went on. "I mean, c'mon, it was no secret in high school how obsessed she was with you. Did she hear you were single again and come running back to Halften?"

I resisted the urge to scoff. Jealousy was not a good look on Gwyneth. And her accusation was crazy.

"She's actually engaged," I said flatly. I had no intention of rising to Gwyneth's bait, but at the same time, the fact that she thought Audrey had come back to town solely for me was, well, ridiculous.

"Oh, really?" Her pouty lips turned to a sneer. "Odd Audrey's engaged. How sweet. Who's the lucky guy?"

I shrugged. "Haven't met him. He doesn't live around here."

"So she's back for the summer without her fiancé?" She scoffed. "Wonder how long that relationship will last."

"Not everyone has as much trouble remaining faithful as you, Gwyneth."

"I already told you, that was a misunderstanding."

Right. Funny how anything that painted her in a poor light was conveniently "a misunderstanding." Too bad for her, I knew the truth.

CHAPTER 8

AUDREY

It's said that eavesdroppers never hear any good about themselves, and I could now confirm that it was true.

Not that I made a habit of eavesdropping, mind you. But when you caught your name on the lips of less-than-polite company, it was hard not to listen.

No sooner had I left the bar and entered the walk-in cooler, which was a room directly behind the bar, than did I hear Gwyneth caustically say my name through the walls.

So instead of grabbing a few cases of the seltzer water I'd come for, I stood rooted to the spot. Oddly enough, it even had a small glass window where I could just catch a glimpse of Gwyneth's snotty face through the liquor shelf. It was an interesting feature because it was obscured enough from the bar that I couldn't be seen. Not sure if it was built by design or a part of the old building that had been kept during renovations.

Either way, I easily heard Gwyneth's snide remarks about me.

"Like I said, Audrey's engaged," Jackson said for the second time. I knew he meant well—and thought it was true—but hearing him say it made my insides squirm.

Especially when Gwyneth voiced her thoughts on it. "For how long?"

"I would assume until her wedding." Jackson's dry reply brought a smile to my lips. His humor had always been one of my favorite things about him.

"You know what I mean." Gwyneth's snippy reply made it clear she was not a fan. "How long before that goes south and she's all over you again?"

My skin prickled more from her accusation than the freezing cooler. Her words were too close for comfort, except for the part about me being "all over" Jackson.

But the truth was, my engagement *had* gone south. Once I fessed up to it, would Jackson think Gwyneth was right? That it was because of him? Or that I had some ulterior motive for wanting to work here?

No, Jackson knew it was Tucker's idea for me to work here. And I'd accepted the position *despite* my former feelings for Jackson, not because of them.

So far, he and I had avoided the topic of my former crush, and I wanted to keep it that way. His rejection and my humiliation weren't things I wanted to relive. How would that conversation go exactly? "Hey, boss, remember that time I tried to kiss you and you jumped out of your skin? Good times."

Nope, I was perfectly happy to leave the past in the

past, but trust Gwyneth Syracuse to show up and stir everything up. She'd always been a total gossip and drama queen in school—not to mention a catty snob.

I'll admit, when Penny had told me last year that Jackson had started dating our former nemesis, I was shocked. Not because I was jealous, but because I truly could not understand what either of them had in common. Penny was as flabbergasted as me, and she'd had a few choice words to say about her "idiot brother" falling for that "fake, two-faced Jezebel"—Penny rarely insulted people, but when she did, she tended to do so in biblical or literary terms.

Wanting to prove that I wasn't at all irked at the thought of the girl who had once purposely tripped me in the cafeteria—resulting in me wearing traces of green Jell-O for the rest of the day—winning over my once former crush, I had attempted to take the high ground. I said maybe Gwyneth had changed since we knew her.

Penny had snorted and said a leopard didn't change its spots. And a few months later, she seemed to be proven right when she told me Gwyneth and Jackson had a messy breakup. And even though he hadn't disclosed to her any of the details, Penny was almost certain it had been Gwyneth's fault.

That, and what I was hearing now, made me fairly certain Gwyneth was the same old mean queen bee I knew in school. But reading between the lines of her insults toward me, one thing became clear—she seemed like she wanted Jackson back.

I had to give him credit, he did not seem to be taking her bait. But given her reputation for being able to get any guy she wanted in high school, I wondered if she'd eventually succeed in wearing him down.

But it was none of my business. Which was why I finally grabbed two wrapped packs of bottled seltzer, stacked them on top of each other, and was just about to head back to the barn, when the cooler door opened and Jackson stepped inside, muttering under his breath.

He almost bumped into me. "Audrey—" He grabbed my arm to steady us both. "Sorry, I didn't realize you were in here."

"Just grabbing the seltzer," I said brightly, lifting my load. But maybe my tone was a little too bright, because Jackson's gaze fell over my shoulder to where Gwyneth sat.

He frowned. "Did you hear all that?"

"Um, yeah . . . some of it. I mean it was kind of hard not to." Okay, maybe that was an exaggeration. I could have walked away, but I had frozen and listened intently. What can I say? Maybe a bigger person could walk away when they heard their name being slandered, but I was not that person.

"I'm sorry." If Jackson was annoyed by my eavesdropping, he didn't show it. In fact, he looked genuinely embarrassed. "Gwyneth is . . ." His voice trailed off, as if searching for the right word. I thought about supplying one, but since the only one that came to my mind was quite rude, I bit my tongue.

"Not the person I thought she was," he finally finished.

"It's fine." I lifted a shoulder, which was now getting sore given the length of time I'd been holding the seltzer cases. "I know how she is. We went to school together."

"Right. Well, for what it's worth, I told her to leave."

I glanced over my shoulder and saw Gwyneth stand up from her barstool, a sour look on her face. She tossed her long balayage waves behind her shoulder and sauntered toward the door with an exaggerated swing in her hips. It was almost like she knew she had an audience for her exit. Or maybe that was just how she lived her life, always assuming eyes were glued to her—every day was just another episode of the Gwyneth Show and the world was filled with her admiring fans.

"That's good." I lifted the cases of seltzer. "Well, I should probably get back to the barn."

"Right, sorry." Jackson seemed to realize that he was blocking my way and stepped aside. Not that there was that much room in the little walk-in cooler, so I still brushed against him as I passed.

It wasn't until I stepped out that I realized my face was heated, despite the freezing temperatures of the cooler.

Jackson followed after and headed back to the bar. The moment he disappeared behind the swinging door, a tinkling laugh caught my attention.

"Someone looks hot and bothered for coming out of the cooler."

I looked up to meet the appraising stare of one of the waitresses, Brittany, I had met this morning.

"Oh, I—uh, Jackson was just helping me find the seltzer—"

"Relax, I'm totally kidding!" Brittany broke out into a full laugh, then waved her hand, her hoop bracelets clinking together. "Even if you were trying to get cozy with the boss in the cooler it wouldn't work. Trust me. I've been trying to break down his walls since day one. The man's a fortress." She rolled her eyes. "He has a strict no-dating-his-employees policy."

"That makes sense," I said.

"Does it? I've worked in the restaurant industry a long time, and let me tell you, most managers are a lot more lenient with that. Trust me to work for the one boss with morals." She sighed heavily as if this were quite the sacrifice, then brightened. "But on the plus side, he's not a creep. I've known my fair share of those too." She laughed. "Dated quite a few of them. So if you want the rundown on who's worth your time around here, I'm your girl. Monty's cool, but he has a girlfriend, although I'd only give that a few weeks. Randy, on the other hand, creep. I didn't think so at first. We hooked up a few times, but—"

"Actually, I'm engaged." While I appreciated that Brittany was being friendly, I didn't want to gossip about my new coworkers on my first real day on the job. "So I'm not looking to be set up or anything."

"Oooh, you go girl!" She grabbed my hand and examined my ring. "Very nice. So what's his story?"

I gave my quick Mercer rundown, my insides squirming as I did. My cover story that Mercer and I were still together was meant to be for the benefit of my family, but I still hadn't figured out the best way or time to come clean about it.

"A lawyer? Some girls have all the luck." She sighed. "Well, next time he's in town, tell him to bring a friend." Brittany winked, then sashayed back to the kitchen.

Chapter 9

JACKSON

It was well past closing by the time I saw Audrey again that night. Which was good, since I was still embarrassed that she had overheard me and Gwyneth talking about her—and the worst part, that Gwyneth had implied Audrey was only working here because of me. How stupid. I only hoped Audrey didn't think *I* thought that.

I stood at the sink in the back room, rinsing the remaining dishes before starting the final load in the dishwasher. I could hear music and the chatter of the cooks cleaning up in the kitchen, but I had let the waitstaff go for the night.

"Hey, Jackson," Audrey greeted me when she walked in. "I finished taking inventory in the barn."

"Really?" I scraped a plate, then washed the scraps

down the sink and hit the garbage disposal for a few seconds. "That was quick. I wasn't expecting you to get it done in one night."

Once I flipped the disposal off, Audrey shrugged, handed me her clipboard, and said, "It was helpful to get an idea where everything is. We're in good shape for Friday's show."

"Awesome, thanks." I momentarily perused the checklist and her notes, then gave it back to her. "Would you mind sticking this on my desk? I'll look over it tomorrow morning."

"Sure thing." She pulled the clipboard toward her with one hand and gave a little wave with her left. "Have a good night."

"You too." I turned back to the sink, ran the faucet, and flipped the garbage disposal switch again. Maybe it was the hope that the hum might disguise the embarrassment in my words, but I found myself turning and calling after her, "Hey, Audrey—wait. I'm sorry again about Gwyneth. She had no idea what she was talking about."

"Oh gosh, don't worry about it—" Audrey flung her hand in the air, in what I'm sure was meant to be a carefree manner, but she and I both watched silently as the ring flew off her finger, soared through the air, then landed in the large industrial sink.

The whirring of the garbage disposal instantly turned to a clattering roar.

I dove toward the wall and flipped the switch. The noise died away as I turned to her. "Audrey—"

"It's okay." She wrapped her arms around herself as she slowly walked toward the sink, her eyes strangely calm. "It's not a big deal."

"Not a big deal?" I stared at her. "That's your engagement ring." I began rolling up the sleeves of my lightweight Henley. "The ring itself is probably demolished. Gold wouldn't stand a chance against that, but the diamond might be okay." I bunched my sleeve past my elbow and reached into the drain.

"Stop!" Audrey flew to my side and grabbed my free arm trying to pull me away. "It's not worth losing your hand over."

I faced her with a laugh. "I'm not going to lose my hand. I do this all the time."

"Well, you shouldn't!" She kept tugging at me, reaching up to grab my shoulder of the arm I was fishing around inside the dirty disposal with. "And trust me, this will be the time that you do. Bad things happen when I'm around, and I don't want to be the reason you walk around with three and a half fingers for the rest of your life!"

I almost laughed again at her dramatics, but when my gaze found hers, meeting her wide green eyes, the laughter died on my lips.

The last time she had been this close to me, she had kissed me. It was so long ago, but the memory that I really hadn't thought of in ages came rushing back.

And with it rushed a new and strange emotion. I didn't want to push her away this time. More the opposite. I kind of wanted her to stay here, or even move closer.

My heart raced and the fear in her eyes over me potentially losing my fingers was nothing compared to my sudden fear over losing my senses.

What was *wrong* with me?

This was Audrey.

I shouldn't want her in my arms. I shouldn't want her anywhere near me. Yet, I did.

And it was all wrong.

Not only for me, but for her.

She was engaged.

I quickly put my hand on her shoulder and gently pushed her away. I was firm, but this time, my words came out kind. "Don't worry. I'll be fine."

As I prepared to search for the ring once more, Audrey squeezed her eyes shut. "It's fake!"

I paused, my brows furrowing. "What is?"

"The ring." She pointed a finger at the sink.

My jaw dropped. "Your fiancé gave you a fake ring?" I couldn't help but feel insulted for her. First, the guy had made plans to spend his entire summer away from her. Then, he hadn't bothered coming as her date to her cousin's wedding, and now this?

"No, the one he gave me wasn't fake." She wrung her hands together. "But that one is. The whole thing is at this point." Her shoulders slumped and she sank onto the floor against the wall. "We broke up. I'm not engaged anymore."

Oh.

I extracted my hand from the grimy drain and gave it a good soapy rinse, trying to keep the surprise out of my voice. "When did this happen?"

"Before I came back here." Audrey looked up at me, the fear in her eyes over me getting my fingers chopped off now replaced with shame. "I, well—it was bad enough having to come here after getting fired from my job, but I just couldn't bring myself to admit that I'd been dumped too."

She'd been fired? But my brain quickly moved on to the next part of her confession.

"He dumped you?" Without another thought, I sank down onto the floor beside her. Sure, getting dumped was no fun, but I didn't understand what she had to be ashamed of.

She nodded, sniffed, then quickly swiped a hand across her cheek. "Yup, it was—it was pretty messy. But in the end, he said we just didn't work together. That I was 'too much.'" She made air quotes then gave a shaky, humorless laugh. "I think his family pressured him into it. They never thought Odd Audrey was good enough to be Mrs. Mercer Van Higgens the Third."

I cursed under my breath. My curiosity turned to pure irritation. "He sounds like a coward. And that he wasn't good enough for you."

Audrey scoffed lightly. "That's just what people tell someone after they get dumped to make them feel better . . ." She stared down at the back of her now bare left hand and breathed out a long sigh. "It feels good to finally tell someone. Well, someone around here—Penny knew."

"Wait—you haven't told anyone else? Not even your family? Why not?"

She shook her head. "I didn't want everyone to feel sorry for me—especially Tucker. You know how he is. He would have felt terrible for me, and I didn't want anything to wreck his and Melissa's big day. They earned it, you know?"

I nodded slowly, partly understanding—but not completely. "But his wedding's over now . . ."

She sighed again. "I know, I know. *I'm* the coward. But it was bad enough having to move back here with nothing. I felt like such a failure. First, I lost my job. I didn't want to admit I'd been jilted too." She paused. "I guess, I just—I just wanted to be someone different, you know? Not have everyone in this town see me as Odd Audrey."

I was silent for a few beats. I got it. And I felt like I at least owed it to her to admit it.

"Did Tucker tell you why Gwyneth and I broke up?" I slid my leg out on the floor in front of me and leaned my head back against the hard stone wall. Not the most comfortable of places to have a soul-baring conversation, but maybe that was the point.

"Not really." Audrey shook her head. "He just said that you realized she wasn't the right person for you."

I laughed, but there was little humor. "That's one way of putting it. Did he tell you *how* I realized it?"

She shook her head again.

I figured as much. Tucker was never one to talk smack about another person, no matter how much they deserved it.

I heaved in a deep breath. "She came on to Tucker one night—strong. I'll spare you the details, but let's just say, she laid it all on the table."

"No way—" Audrey gaped at me. "She didn't."

"Yup, sure did. Tucker turned her down flat, of course. I think it nearly killed him to have to tell me about it. But I'm pretty sure she was only ever with me as a way to try to get to him." My tone turned dry. "Being best friends with the great Tucker James has benefits, you know. Like the town beauty queen giving an average Joe the time of day." I ran a hand through my hair. "The worst part was that she barely even denied it—she just acted like it shouldn't even bother me. Like I should be so happy she was with me that it shouldn't matter that she came on to my best friend." I shook my head. "I ended things that night."

"I never thought she was good enough for you," Audrey said vehemently.

I laughed. "I thought that was just what people said when you get dumped to make you feel better."

"Well, in this case it sounds like *you* dumped her. Serves her right. So what was she doing here tonight?"

"I think she's trying to get me back." I sighed. "I thought she'd give up by now, but every once in a while, she makes an appearance—like she's hoping to show me what I'm missing or something."

"A lifetime of suspicion and misery?"

I laughed. "Something like that."

"I'm sorry she did that to you. You didn't deserve that."

I shrugged. Did anyone deserve the crummy things that happened to us? I gave a half smile. "A wise person once told me that we can't always control our circumstances. Sometimes we just have to make the best of what we have."

She laughed, then glanced down at her empty hand again. "I guess it's time I took my own advice." She flexed her fingers, then groaned. "I'm really not looking forward to telling my mom—she adored Mercer. I'm pretty sure he was the only thing I ever did in my life that she was actually proud of."

I frowned, hoping that was an exaggeration. But then I recalled what little I knew of Audrey's parents from Tucker and Penny. I knew Audrey had a rough relationship with her mom, that she was hard on her, but it was hard for me to believe. Tucker's mom was the nicest, most supportive mother I knew, and she was Audrey's mother's sister. But genetics didn't always pass on those traits.

As Audrey remained silent, I also recalled Gwyneth's cruel words that evening—that Audrey's engagement wouldn't last. I wondered if Audrey was thinking of them too.

Not that it mattered what Gwyneth thought, but at the same time, Audrey had a right to tell those closest to her when she saw fit. And for whatever reason, she didn't seem like she was ready yet.

And idea came to me.

"Wait here." I peeled myself off the ground and headed to the restaurant entrance, grabbing my massive set of keys out of my desk drawer on the way.

When I returned, I handed her a plastic cube wrapped in cellophane. "How'd I do?"

She laughed, peeled the wrapper off, and popped the lid open. Then she pulled out a fake diamond on a silver band. "It's almost identical to the one I had. Where did you get this?"

"The claw machine out front. That thing has been sitting there for ages. I think it was too small for the claw to properly grasp." I jerked my chin. "Go on, try it on."

She slipped it on her left hand, then wiggled her finger, testing. "It fits perfectly. Even better than my last one."

Satisfied, I nodded. "Then keep it. Tell everyone when you're ready. Your secret's safe with me."

Chapter 10

AUDREY

It had been a strange twenty-four hours. Between getting stuck with Jackson in the barn loft, Gwyneth showing up, me accidentally destroying my fake engagement ring, and Jackson giving me a replacement, I had a lot on my mind by the time I got home that evening.

I was ready for a long hot bubble bath and some peace and quiet, but that didn't seem to be in the cards for me when I walked into the kitchen.

"Audrey!" my mother greeted me with exuberance from her seat at the kitchen table. "I was hoping I would catch you tonight. How was work?"

"Good. I mean, I'm beat, but it's the good kind of beat. I think I'm really going to like this job. It's so—"

"That's wonderful, dear. You'll never guess who I ran into today."

"Who?" I tried not to feel hurt at my mother's lack of interest in my day. It was clear she had something else on her mind, and my shot at a bubble bath was probably better if I spent a minute or two indulging her.

"Clara's mother. You remember your friend Clara Perkins from school, right?"

"Yeah." I grabbed some sliced turkey and cheddar cheese from the fridge to fix myself a sandwich. Friend was a stretch. Clara had been part of Gwyneth's crowd, and the only interaction we really had was her calling me Odd Audrey along with the rest of Gwyneth's posse. But my mother had always liked to pretend that I was more popular than I was, so I didn't correct her.

"Well, her mother was telling me that when Clara got married, she had *two* dresses—a ceremony dress and a reception dress."

Uh-oh, I didn't like where this was going.

"Now, I know you already agreed to wear Mercer's mother's dress." My mother sniffed, clearly still sore that I had agreed to this without her approval. Not that it mattered now because I certainly wouldn't be wearing Mercer's mother's dress for anything. "But I see no reason why you can't get a reception dress. That way you can have one that's all your own."

"I don't know, Mom . . ." Even if my wedding was still on, the thought of having two wedding dresses seemed extravagant. I mean, you only wore it for one day, why shorten that to half a day?

"It's the perfect solution. You can still honor Mercer's mother by wearing her dress, and you and I can still go wedding dress shopping together." My mother's voice took on her martyr edge. "I only have one daughter. Are you really going to deny me the joy of wedding dress shopping?"

I swallowed, my guilt increasing. I had felt such relief after telling Jackson the truth today, maybe now was the time to tell my mother? Rip the Band-Aid off. There was really no reason not to, now that Tucker's wedding was over. I should have already done it.

I sucked in a deep breath. "The thing is, Mom—"

"After all, *I* never got to go wedding dress shopping. All my life I dreamed of a beautiful gown, but things being what they were . . ."

And my mom was off on her favorite tangent. How miserable her life had turned out because she had gotten pregnant with me and married my father in a quick ceremony—no frills, no fanfare. Pretty much my mother's worst nightmare.

"I know, Mom," I said, trying to steer her back to the present. "That must have been really hard for you but—"

"Of course, not that there would have been many options for me had I had the time to go to a boutique. They didn't have many options for pregnant brides in those days. And oh, what you did to my figure! People used to say I was destined for Hollywood with my perfect hourglass shape. The next Marilyn Monroe, they said. But after you, it was never the same . . ."

It was useless. My window had passed. My mother had already segued into her second favorite topic of conversation—how I had been disappointing her since before I was born. How her glory days had ended once I came along.

Had I been braver, I would have sucked it up and confessed anyway. After all, what was one more disappointment on top of so many? In a weird way, she might even be happy—it would give her one more thing to complain about.

But I didn't. Call it cowardice. Call it self-preservation. Call it a strange sort of mercy, letting my mother enjoy her vision of my soon-to-be fancy wedding that would allow her to live her dream vicariously through me for one more day.

The words of my confession stuck on my tongue. And when I finally did find my voice, it came out rigid, almost robotic. From years of practice saying what my mother wanted to hear—even while wishing I could say or do something else.

Yes, I invited everyone in my class to my birthday party. But Penny and two other girls were the only ones to show up.

Yes, I tried out for the lead in the school play. But due to my stage fright, I bombed every tryout and only ever got a part in the chorus, which was secretly a relief to me.

Yes, I made sure not to talk too much in front of Mercer's family. But it turned out they hadn't thought I was good enough for their son anyway.

"I guess we can consider a reception dress if that's what you really want." *But I won't be buying one because there isn't going to be a wedding.*

"Oh, Audrey, you won't regret it!" My mother clapped her hands together, instantly happy once more. "I'm telling you, it will make the perfect statement. Show everyone you're classy enough to honor family tradition by wearing Mercer's mother's dress—which of course is very important with a family like theirs." She could never keep the awe out of her voice when she talked about

Mercer or his family—their connections and their money.

One of the few things I had done right in her eyes was get a marriage proposal from Mercer. She was going to be so devastated when I told her the truth. Most likely, it would lead to a weeklong spiral of depression and anguish.

But for the moment, her mental health and my worth as a daughter were still intact. She prattled on. "But everyone will see you're still fashion-forward enough to wear a daring, modern style."

"I'm not really looking to 'prove' anything, Mom—"

"Nonsense. You need to make a statement. The society columns are bound to cover the wedding with Mercer's family's standing. I only wish you could get the same attention around here. But at least with the wedding being in Chicago, you will have all his important connections."

Click-clack went her perfectly manicured nails on her laptop touch pad and the screen flashed to life, revealing poofy, yet daring, princess wedding gowns—nothing like I would choose to wear. One of them had a see-through bodice and the other had a neckline plunging to almost the belly button. "Here are some of the styles I think you absolutely *must* try. This one is a Lazaro, and this one . . ." And she was off on another, much happier, tangent, secure in her dream of lace and tulle, fairy-tale weddings, and perfect daughters.

She'd been like this since before I was born—even naming me Audrey after the classy and beautiful Audrey Hepburn. But it was hard trying to live up to being an Audrey when most of the time you felt more like one of the Three Stooges.

But tonight, I listened and nodded numbly, throwing in a "Wow" or "So pretty" when appropriate.

Was there ever the perfect moment to break your mother's heart?

I didn't know. But still, I held out hope that I would find it—and soon.

But not tonight. She was just too happy.

CHAPTER 11

JACKSON

Audrey's not engaged.

Those three little words kept popping into my head the next few days at the most random times.

It was honestly annoying.

I'd be at my computer filling out an order and in between selecting cases of rolls and cartons of condiments, there it was again.

Audrey's not engaged.

If I didn't know better, I'd say it was panic. After all, wasn't that one of the reasons I'd agreed to hire her in the first place? No risk of repeating our awkward history if she were happily engaged to another man.

Only, turned out, she wasn't.

And I couldn't help but wonder if part of the reason she had been keeping it a secret was because she knew I wouldn't have wanted her to work for me if I'd found out.

But she had told me—me, and apparently, very few other people.

It was a bit strange being taken into Audrey's confidence. Even though we had grown up together, we'd never been close. But I'd meant what I said when I told her I'd keep her secret until she was ready to tell her family.

What she was waiting for, I wasn't sure. Did she hope maybe she and her fiancé would reconcile and she wouldn't have to tell them at all?

Whatever. It wasn't my job to worry about it. I would keep her secret, and as far as us working together, nothing would change. We were simply two professionals coexisting.

And whatever momentary pull I had felt toward her at the sink last night was irrelevant.

So why did my brain keep going back to those three words?

Audrey's not engaged.

I shut my computer down and rubbed my eyes. It had been a long day. And tomorrow would be another one. Usually that was a good thing. Filling my days with work kept me from thinking too much. But suddenly, all I seemed to be doing *was* thinking. I needed to go home and get some rest.

Audrey's not engaged.

I didn't care. All that mattered was that Audrey did her job, and that she and I remained professional.

The staff was gone for the night, so after flipping off the lights, I locked the restaurant doors and headed for the parking lot. My feet crunched against gravel, but I also heard the sound of music coming from the barn. I spied the soft glow of lights through the windows.

Strange. We hadn't had an event tonight. We had a show scheduled for tomorrow, but I was pretty sure the crew had finished setting up a while ago.

I turned my feet toward the barn and when I walked inside, everything was pretty much how I expected it.

Tables and chairs were set up around the stage. The lighting looked ready to go. The only thing out of place was the loud old-timey country music playing from the sound system, and the figure behind the bar, her back to me, robustly singing along as she stocked the straw and napkin caddies on the counter.

I smiled. Had I known Audrey could sing like that? She had a surprisingly soulful voice—rich, low, slightly husky with just a hint of twang. Although maybe it shouldn't have been a surprise, since she was related to Tucker. Her song choice reminded me of one he used to play on his guitar—it wasn't a top forty hit from the current country charts, that's for sure. It was an older song, slightly sad, with harmonica carrying the melody over the guitar, in between the singers. It was a duet, both a man and a woman.

Audrey kept right on singing with the female part, clearly lost in her own world as she stuffed the caddies spread out in front of her.

"I didn't realize there was a show tonight," I called out loudly, figuring I should make myself known before she turned and saw me standing there.

She shrieked, spun around, and straws flew out of her hand, scattering everywhere.

"Holy smokes!" She placed a hand to her chest. "You

almost gave me a heart attack."

"Sorry." I laughed, partly over her reprimand and partly over her chosen expression—it was as old-fashioned as her music, yet it suited her.

She muttered something, then walked to the end of the counter, hit a button on her phone, and the song stopped.

"I didn't mean to scare you." I crossed behind the bar and bent down to retrieve the scattered straws. "I was heading out for the night and was surprised to see you were still here. I thought the crew finished setting up ages ago."

"They did." Audrey knelt down beside me and began grabbing straws too. "I, uh, just wanted to double-check and make sure everything was in order."

I straightened, set a handful of paper-wrapped straws on the counter, and looked around. The place was spotless, and the bar shelf looked fully stocked. I opened the mini fridge underneath. That too. Then I checked the cupboards. Filled to the brim.

"You're good," I said. "I've never seen it look this great in here."

"Okay, good." She cleared away the straws. "I just didn't want to forget anything."

"You nervous about running your first show?"

"A little," she admitted, giving a sheepish smile.

"You've got nothing to worry about. Trust me, Tucker usually wasn't even here to get things ready—that's why we have the setup crew. He was more about the actual shows. Tending to the crowd, hearing the band, keeping things running smoothly. You've gone above and beyond."

"Okay, I hope so. I just really want to prove I can do

this job."

"Relax. You'll do great." I jerked my head toward the door. "Now get out of here and get some rest. Tomorrow will be a late night."

"Okay, thanks." She smiled and grabbed her phone and purse off the counter.

I chuckled to myself as I reached up to hit the lights. The last thing we needed was another workaholic like me around here.

"Hey, Jackson," Audrey called out, and I turned toward her.

"I've been meaning to ask you something."

"Sure. What is it?"

"Well, I'm just a bit confused. You guys are paying me a full-time salary, but the work—" She paused. "It doesn't seem to be full-time."

"Oh, is that all that's bothering you?" I hit the main lights, leaving the one by the entrance on. "That's because Tucker makes his own schedule. He's not really here full-time. He's still got his music. And you know, he likes to keep his evenings free to spend time with Melissa."

Audrey nodded. "That makes sense. I just—well, it feels like I'm being paid a full-time salary for not full-time work."

"That's between you and Tucker. He decided your pay."

She sighed, clearly unsatisfied with my answer.

I reached the entrance and motioned for her to go first, a smile on my lips. "You know, most people wouldn't complain about getting a full wage for part-time hours—especially during the summer."

Audrey stepped outside and placed a hand on her hip.

"I'm not some kid back from college. I want to work as much as I can and save as much as I can, so when Tucker comes back, I have enough money to figure out where I'm going next."

Right. Because Tucker was coming back and she was leaving.

"What *is* your plan after this?" When we'd hired her, the assumption was she'd be leaving in the fall to go back to Chicago and get married. But that wasn't happening anymore, so I wondered what her actual plan was. I flipped the last light switch and pulled the heavy barn doors shut behind me.

"I'm not sure, to be honest." Her shoulders slumped slightly, as if the decision was weighing on her. "I'm not going back to Chicago, that's for sure. I want a fresh start somewhere. Which is why I want to have enough saved to move, get an apartment, and have a little breathing room to look for a job I really like."

"Sounds like a good plan."

"Yeah, I think so." She brightened slightly. "Penny and I might even room together again once her book tour is done." Then her expression turned firm. "Which is why I want to work as much as I can now. And I certainly don't want to get preferential treatment because I'm Tucker's cousin."

"I get it." I brushed a hand against my bearded chin. "But you know Tucker. He's a generous guy, and he's got the means to pay you whatever he thought was fair—even for part-time work."

She crossed her arms. "How many hours a week do *you* work?"

"I dunno. Fifty, maybe sixty."

"What?" Audrey's eyes bulged. "How is that fair? I thought you guys were partners in this."

I chuckled. "It's not as bad as it sounds. I like being here—this is my passion project. Tucker's more of the investor."

"Tucker might be the investor, but I'm not."

"Look, if it bothers you that much, why don't you see if you can schedule some weekday shows? Maybe start an open mic night. Those are some things we've talked about doing to draw extra business, but Tucker really hasn't had time to focus on it."

"I could do that." Audrey's eyes lit up with interest. "In fact, I wanted to ask you what you thought about doing a karaoke night during the week. I think that would draw a great crowd."

I nodded. "That sounds real good. We'll have to coordinate the schedule though. I'm a little short on waitstaff at the moment. And down a bartender, so we don't want to book more than we can handle."

"You need a bartender? I have my bartender's license."

"For this state?"

"No, but it would just be an online class. My experience would carry over." Her voice turned excited. "Why don't you let me handle bartending for any of the extra events I set up?"

"You sure? You don't have to feel pressured to work more hours. Whatever you and Tucker agreed on is fine."

"Positive." She nodded definitively. "I want to stay busy."

I thought about it for a moment. "You'll make good money in tips too."

"Even better."

"All right, if that's what you want. Get me your license and we'll get you on the schedule."

CHAPTER 12

AUDREY

The Stonewall Barn was packed. Almost two weeks later, our first karaoke night was a hit. From the moment the doors had opened, we had a full house.

I was glad the turnout was good, considering it had been my idea. Also, tonight was my first night bartending. It had been a little while since I'd tended bar, but since we had a limited drink menu in the event barn, I was fairly confident I could handle all the orders.

And to be safe, Jackson had agreed to work the shift with me. I'd felt a little bad when I realized Jackson would be picking up another shift in order to help me tonight. But considering the only other bartender who had volunteered to work it was Randy, I was glad I'd be working with Jackson instead. Randy had trained me on a few day shifts at the bar, and while he was friendly, something about his manner, and what Brittany had said, put me on edge with him.

The way Jackson had easily agreed to fill tonight's role made me realize this wasn't an unusual occurrence for him. It seemed like any time there was a problem or a shift that needed to be covered, Jackson was most often the one filling it. He was certainly devoted to the restaurant, and I suspected that his estimate of fifty- to sixty-hour work weeks was actually a low one.

Although, Jackson working hard was really nothing new. He'd always been that way. Not even a year after Penny and her family had moved here, Jackson had gotten a job busing tables after school at the local diner during the dinner shift. He'd seemed so grown-up to me at the time, I didn't think much of it. But looking back, he was only fourteen. And most summers, he often took on more, working two, even sometimes three, part-time jobs.

Still, I wondered if Tucker knew how many hours his best friend put in on what had started as a joint venture for them.

But I had to admit, right now, I was grateful Jackson was here because the barn was packed.

We worked in a good rhythm together, him taking one end of the bar and me the other, although our paths crossed quite often. Such as now when Jackson crossed to my end and grabbed a mixer from the fridge.

"Don't look now," I said, "but you've got a visitor." I jerked my head toward where a familiar blonde had just taken a seat at Jackson's end of the bar. Gwyneth and a small group of her friends.

"Great," Jackson muttered, following my gaze. "She would pick tonight."

"Is that what you meant by her trying to show you what you're missing?" I grimaced for him as I watched Gwyneth making a show of enthusiastically greeting other patrons. With her dress tight enough to split the seams, she was all hugs and kisses. Air-blown kisses and winks to those who weren't lucky enough to be in her immediate sphere.

"Yep," Jackson replied calmly. "If it's slow, she tries to chat me up. If it's busy, she flirts with other guys."

"You've got to be kidding me." I slammed a glass full of ice on the counter so hard a couple of cubes flew out. Then I quickly dumped in a shot and topped it off with my soda gun. "You know what?" I slid the drink to my customer, then turned to Jackson. "You take this end. I've got her."

Without giving him a chance to respond, I stalked over to Gwyneth and her friends, pasted a huge smile on my face, and said, "What can I get you ladies tonight?"

Gwyneth scanned me up and down, nose wrinkling like she smelled something sour. "Jackson always takes care of me." She gave me a pointed look, all bitterness now masked by a fake sweet smile. "He knows what I like."

Gag me. "Jackson's busy at the moment. As you can see, we've got a full house. So get your order in now or enjoy waiting."

Gwyneth's friends told me their drinks, while Gwyneth remained stiff as a rock. "This is quite a turnout for *karaoke*"—she said it like a dirty word—"but I'll wait until Jackson has a minute." A pointed look. "I'm very patient."

"Suit yourself." I slid a drink her friend's way. "You

guys come to do some singing?"

Gwyneth scoffed. "Hardly. I wasn't aware that Jackson was turning this place into a dive bar."

"Yup, Thursday-night karaoke. Tell all your friends." With that I moved on to another customer not in her group. She'd had her chance to order.

It didn't take long for me to become swamped with other customers, and for Gwyneth to get up and saunter toward Jackson's end of the bar. When it was her turn, she leaned over, exposing ample cleavage, flashing Jackson a megawatt smile.

They were too far away for me to hear what she was saying, but Jackson didn't seem to give her much time for small talk. As he turned to grab a clean glass, I flashed him a look that said, *I'm sorry, I tried.*

He flashed his own back. *I know, thanks.*

Satisfied he knew I had his back, I returned my focus to work. It wasn't like I didn't think he could handle Gwyneth. I just hated what she had done to him. And that she had the nerve to show up here and act like he was going to take her back.

Sure enough, as the night wore on, Gwyneth made her way around the bar, chatting up every young, semi-attractive male in the place.

To Jackson's credit, he didn't seem bothered by it at all, but my annoyance only grew.

A good hour later, Gwyneth was back with her friends, and when I refilled one of their drinks, she turned her attention to me.

"So Audrey, this must be a dream come true for you, working here."

"It's a good job," I replied. "I really enjoy getting to

meet all the musicians we hire."

She gave a light laugh. "I meant working with Jackson. C'mon, the whole town knows how bad you used to have it for him. Although to be honest . . ." She blinked up at me with seemingly innocent eyes. "I was a little surprised he hired you. What exactly did you say you'd do for him on your application?"

Her entourage snickered behind her. One murmured a crass remark under her breath, earning even harder laughter from the crew.

"Tucker's actually the one who hired me," I said, calmly wiping down the counter. "You know, my cousin. Who's happily married now and on his honeymoon. With the love of his life." I paused. "You remember Melissa, right? She was a few years ahead of us in school." Was I rubbing it in that Tucker was officially off the market? Sure, but she deserved it.

Gwyneth pursed her lips. "Right. Melissa Ellis. The girl he pined over for years." Another hair swish. "So tell me, does stalking run in the family or is it just you and Tucker?"

I raised an eyebrow. "Kind of ironic that *you* bring up stalking."

"Look, *Odd*-rey"—her emphasis on the first part of my name was not coincidental—"I don't know what type of thing you think you have going on here, getting all cozy with Jackson, but it's not going to work." She sat up a little straighter, projecting confidence, although her words reeked of insecurity. "He's never going to be interested in a weirdo like you. Why don't you give it up, already?"

I planted both hands on the edge of the counter and

said calmly, "I don't know what you think your black widow spidey senses are telling you, but I'm here for one reason: to work. Now if you'll excuse me, I have customers to attend to." With that, I walked away, not missing the catty whispers directed at my back as I went.

Chapter 13

JACKSON

"Is Gwyneth bugging you?" I asked Audrey when she made it over to my side of the bar and began helping me clear glasses. "Because I can tell her to leave. Wouldn't be the first time I've had to. Although usually if I ignore her, she gets tired and gives up. Or finds someone else to set her sights on."

"I'm fine," Audrey said, tipping glasses upside down into the under-the-counter dishwasher. She shut it and hit the on button. "Nothing I haven't dealt with before. You can take the small town out of the mean girl, but you can't take the mean girl out of the small town."

"Uh . . . I'm not really sure that makes sense."

"Whatever." She swiped a rag from the sink and began wiping the counter. "You know what I mean."

"Yeah, I do." I grabbed a box from a cupboard under

the counter and began refilling straws and napkins.

"Honestly, I knew it would be like this coming back here." Audrey rubbed aggressively at a stubborn spot on the stone countertop. "Everyone's stuck in the past."

"So why *did* you come back?" I wasn't trying to be judgmental; I was simply curious. From what I'd heard from Penny, both she and Audrey had loved living together in Chicago.

"Our lease was up, money was tight, and I had to come back for Tucker's wedding anyway, so it seemed like a logical place to regroup." It was a basic regurgitation of what she'd told me before. But I got the feeling it wasn't the complete truth.

"Is that really the whole reason? I mean, I know you lost your job and needed money, but you know Penny would have covered your rent until you were back on your feet. What made you leave?"

Audrey stopped scrubbing and stared at me. Then she laughed. "You're the first person to call me out on it." She sighed. "I guess after messing things up so royally in Chicago, I started to believe that it was true—I am a screwup. A joke. A crazy can't-hold-down-a-job, can't-hold-a-man mess. That I'm not just down on my luck, I *am* the bad luck. So I thought if I could come back here and make it work, you know, flip the script, then maybe I wouldn't be so scared to figure out what I wanted next."

"Why would you be scared of that?"

She shrugged. "Because everything I've ever wanted has blown up in my face." She made an explosion gesture with her hands, adding sound effects to match. She shook her head with a smile. "So I figured, if I was going to reinvent myself, why not go back to the place it all started? Put Odd Audrey in the grave once and for all."

She resumed her busywork, scrubbing away, but the heightened color at the top of her cheeks clued me in to the fact that she was slightly embarrassed about what she'd revealed to me. But she shouldn't have been—not one bit.

"I get it. Trust me, it's hard work trying to break out of your own shadow, especially in a place like Halften. But if you want my advice . . ."

She didn't say she did, but she paused as if she was listening, so I went on.

"I don't think you need to put Odd Audrey in the grave at all. I think you just need to realize how special she is—and how boring this town would be without her. Because I, for one, am glad you came back. And for the record, you haven't screwed anything up." I waved a hand around me. "Heck, look at what you've done for the Inn. This place is hopping tonight—I've never had a Thursday night like this." I drew in a deep breath. "And as far as all the other things that blew up in your face, maybe that's because they weren't right for you. And maybe that was just the spark you needed to light a fire. Because you're not an explosion, Audrey Miller. You're a firecracker."

Audrey gaped at me, and I shut my mouth, not quite sure where that little speech had come from—maybe some of Audrey's outbursts were rubbing off on me. But I didn't regret saying it, even as I felt color rise to my own cheeks. I could see now how unfair this town—no, how unfair I—had been to her.

Sure, she was unpredictable, persistent, and at times, chaotic. But I had spent so long thinking of her as a nuisance, I had failed to notice one very important thing.

She was dazzling.

"You know, I—" Whatever Audrey was about to say was cut off by the MC's announcement.

"For our last performance of the night, I want to call Audrey to the stage."

I was relieved for the distraction. "You signed up to sing?"

"I didn't." Audrey's brow furrowed with confusion. "Maybe there's another Audrey here."

We both glanced around, but no one else jumped up to take the stage.

"Audrey?" the MC called again. "Do we have an Audrey Miller here tonight?" He paused as he read off the slip of paper in his hand. "It looks like she'll be wowing us with her rendition of Patsy Cline's 'Crazy' tonight."

An eruption of laughter exploded from the end of the bar, and I turned to see Gwyneth and her followers cackling away at what was clearly—to them—one big joke.

"That does it." I slammed my fist down on the counter. It was time to tell Gwyneth off once and for all. "And don't worry, I'll tell the MC there was a mistake."

"No, wait—" Audrey grabbed my arm, pulling me back. "I'll do it. I'll sing."

"What?" I stared at her. "Audrey, you don't have to. They're clearly making fun of you—"

"Exactly." She began untying the black apron around her waist, her eyes bright and alert. "But you know what, you're right."

"I am? About what?" She had lost me a little. Or maybe

it was just the anger I was feeling toward Gwyneth and her friends for picking on Audrey that was making it hard for me to focus.

She shoved her balled-up apron into my hands and started walking, then said over her shoulder, “It’s time to be a firecracker.”

CHAPTER 14

AUDREY

I had to hand it to Gwyneth. Her little joke was, in a way, perfect.

Odd Audrey singing a song about how crazy she is? Isn't that hilarious? And not only that, she's singing about loving a man she can never have. Ha, ha, ha.

That was Gwyneth's way of reminding me that Jackson would never want me the way I once wanted him—the way she thought I still did.

Of course, she hadn't actually expected me to sing it. It was supposed to be a big joke to her and her friends, and anyone else in the bar who knew who I was. Odd Audrey, requesting to sing a song and then being too chicken to actually do it. After all, she probably knew I had no desire to relive my theater tryouts from high school, where I stumbled over my audition and girls like Gwyneth got the lead role.

But the thing was, I was over it.

And after what Jackson had just reminded me of behind the bar, it had become clear, the only thing I could do was sing the song. To show that I didn't care. That Gwyneth, this town—and heck, even Jackson if Gwyneth thought he was going to think I was singing it about him—could all think what they wanted about me.

I was no longer the butt of their jokes, because I simply no longer cared.

And the joke could be on Gwyneth because she had actually chosen a song I knew and loved. One I had sung over and over again while in the shower, in the car, doing dishes, or while Tucker played the broken chords for me on his guitar.

So yes, I was crazy. Crazy enough to sing it in front of the whole town and not care what they thought.

So I strolled passed Gwyneth's group wordlessly, took the mic from the MC, whose name was Noah—I knew because I'd hired him and helped him set up earlier that night. Then I shut my eyes as the music began and took a deep breath.

It certainly wasn't perfect, but I let go and sang like I'd never sung before. Every long, soulful note was all mine, and I didn't let one of them go to waste.

And as the song progressed, I didn't just sing it, I felt it. I became it. It and Jackson were right. Why did I let myself worry? Worry about what everyone else thought of me? Worry about trying to make myself into someone I wasn't? I'd done that with Mercer and look how well it had turned out. It was time to stop worrying and start being.

Who cared if everyone in this town thought I was crazy? There were worse things to be.

And as I finished the song, holding the last long note at the end, I envisioned I was a firecracker bursting high and proud in the sky, until I faded with a final trill that fell like a waterfall of lights burning out into the night.

When I pulled the microphone from my lips and opened my eyes, the crowd erupted into a massive applause. The first person's eye I caught was Jackson's. He was still behind the bar where I had left him, but no longer looking confused. He clapped wildly with my apron still in his hands, then raised one arm and hollered my name.

A number of patrons had jumped to their feet and were doing the same, followed by whistles and hoots.

Slightly embarrassed from all the attention, I said a quick "thank you" into the microphone and handed it back to Noah.

"Give it up for one of the Stonewall Inn's very own, Audrey Miller!" he said.

When I slipped behind the bar again, I didn't miss Gwyneth glaring daggers at me, but I held my head high and kept walking.

"Audrey, that was amazing!" Jackson exclaimed once I reached his side. "I had no idea you could sing like that—okay, I had a little bit of an idea since I heard you the other night. But why aren't you on tour with Tucker instead of working here?"

I released a shaky laugh, the adrenaline in my system dying down now that I'd finished my performance. I took my apron from him and began retying it. "Trust me, my level of talent ends at small-town karaoke. Tucker's next level."

"I'm not so sure about that. Did you see the way Gwyneth's smirk fell when you started singing?"

"No." I laughed again. "I was too nervous to look at anyone. I had my eyes closed or stared at the wall."

"Well, trust me, it was priceless. You really put her in her place. And you know what—you just gave me an idea. Wait here."

"What are you doing?" I called after him, but he didn't answer, a fire in his step. He was a man on a mission.

I thought maybe he was heading over to Gwyneth to tell her to get lost, but he breezed right by her and bounded up to the stage. He chatted off to the side with Noah for a few moments. Noah nodded and handed the microphone to Jackson.

"Hey, Stonewall Inn, how are you all doing tonight?" Jackson said. "Thanks for coming out."

The crowd responded with cheers and clapping, letting us know they were happy to be here. All except Gwyneth, who only offered up a half-hearted clap of her fingertips. I guess the night was only fun when she was tormenting somebody.

"That's what I like to hear," Jackson said. "Now how about one more round of applause for our good friend Audrey."

The crowd responded enthusiastically, all except Gwyneth, who lifted her empty glass toward me, signaling that she needed a refill. I resisted the urge to roll my eyes as I made my way over. Apparently, she only wanted a drink from me if it was a way of putting me in my place.

Jackson went on. "Not only did Audrey put this whole

night together, but she just wowed us all with that amazing performance."

More enthusiastic cheers rang out and I was almost grateful that Gwyneth had put me to task. It distracted me from my embarrassment over the enthusiastic crowd.

"Now I know Noah said that was the last performance of the night, but I think you can all agree that Audrey needs to give us one more song."

What?

I dropped an orange garnish into Gwyneth's drink and looked up at Jackson in disbelief.

What was he thinking? I knew I had said I wanted to be a firecracker tonight, but that didn't mean I was ready to be the whole stinkin' Fourth of July fireworks show.

"What do you say, Audrey?" Jackson held out a hand, inviting me up. "Care to help me out with this final song? I know for a fact it's one you know."

I set Gwyneth's drink in front of her, not missing the death glare she shot me. Clearly, she wasn't any happier about Jackson singling me out than I was. The rest of the crowd, however, seemed to agree with Jackson, since another applause broke out cheering me on.

"Come on, Audrey." Jackson sent a teasing smile my way. "If you don't help me, I'll be forced to sing this whole song by myself, and I know you don't want to put all these people through that."

Despite myself, I laughed. He and Tucker had been best friends long enough that I had heard Jackson sing backup in Tucker's amateur days—it wasn't pretty.

With a shake of my head, I slipped my apron off once more and headed toward the stage. If Jackson was willing to purposely put himself through this humiliation, I guess the least I could do was humor him.

"What has gotten into you?" I said in his ear when I reached his side.

"You'll see." He grabbed my hand and helped me climb onstage, then handed me a second microphone. Noah let the music roll and the first strains of a slow country melody rang out, instantly familiar to me.

It was the song I had been singing the other week when Jackson had come across me in the barn stocking straws. I turned to him, surprised that he knew the song, and more so, that he remembered it.

He just smiled encouragingly and then took a deep breath, since the male part of the duet began first.

His voice was loud and clear, but he more talked than sang. The crowd offered some comical boos and heckling, which he seemed to take good-naturedly.

But when he got to the line about remembering green eyes and a rancher's daughter, Jackson looked directly at me, his own eyes steady and sincere. My heart jumped to my throat.

Suddenly, the feelings I had once had for him—the feelings I had once shoved deep down inside, never to see the light of day again—rose to the surface. I swallowed. This was bad. This was so, so bad.

I pulled my gaze away, turning it to the teleprompter with the lyrics flashing across it, even though I didn't need it to remember the words.

I only needed it to avoid looking at Jackson and having him look at me like *that* again.

I lightly pressed my fingers to my stomach, as if doing so could stop the butterflies that had emerged there. I pulled in a breath as the chorus began, although my part was mostly backing vocals at this point.

The musical intro to the second verse began and I inhaled slowly to calm myself, then took it away as the female part began. Despite the fluttery feeling in my stomach, my nerves had nothing to do with singing, and my voice filled the room smoothly and confidently.

As I finished the first line, I snuck another glance at Jackson. Although he had taken a step back to allow me to have my moment, his eyes were still fixed on me and he wore a proud, encouraging smile.

A flush crept up my cheeks, even as I sang fully and clearly. But this time I didn't turn away. Because as our eyes held, and as Jackson nodded slightly enough that I was likely the only one who noticed, I realized why he'd called me up here in the first place.

Not just to give me another chance to shine—although he was certainly doing that—but to send me, Gwyneth, and maybe all of Halften a message—that I wasn't someone to be messed with. That I had confidence. A voice. And that he admired me for it.

I returned his smile, even while singing, and his eyes crinkled at the edges as his smile deepened.

For the rest of the song, I didn't shy away. I turned and faced him, and he faced me, and we sang to each other. We had a strange sort of connection on that stage—almost an understanding—that something had shifted between us. That we saw each other as more than what the rest of the town saw us. Me, as Odd Audrey. And him as—what had he called himself the other day? An average Joe.

Please. There was nothing average about Jackson. I'd always known that. But while I knew I'd need to continue to guard my heart after this, for those few minutes, I let it be.

When the song ended, Jackson pulled me in for a brief side hug, then let go, and said into his mic, "The Amazing Audrey Miller, everyone."

Amazing Audrey. Now there was a nickname I never expected. And sure, it probably wouldn't stick, but I didn't care. Jackson thought it and that was enough for me.

"That was crazy," I said breathlessly as we hopped down from the stage and headed back toward the bar together.

Jackson just chuckled. "Yup."

It wasn't until I was slipping my apron on behind the bar that I noticed Gwyneth and her friends were gone. But I don't think Jackson or I had even realized when they'd left.

The rest of the night passed quickly. With karaoke done and only an hour left until close, customers began closing out their tabs and trickling out of the restaurant.

After locking the doors, Jackson turned to me. "You got everything else if I start counting down the register?"

"No problem." There were only a few closing tasks left.

Jackson typed his code into the computer and printed a slip. He whistled as he looked it over, then handed it to me. "We did good tonight. Really good. I've never had a Thursday night like this."

I looked at it, pleased to see all the zeros on the bottom line for the night's sales. "We had a great turnout."

"Thanks to your good idea." With that, Jackson opened the till and began counting down the register.

Pleased, I finished cleaning and restocking in no time.

After checking over the closing list one more time, I threw my dirty apron into the laundry basket. "All done here," I called over to Jackson.

"That's great," Jackson said back, but his words seemed absentminded.

"Is everything okay?" I walked over to where he frowned down at paper and bills stacked on the counter.

"The register's off." He looked up at me, brow creased. "By a lot."

"Really?"

"Yeah, I can't figure it out." He turned and opened the register once more, empty now that he'd taken the till tray out and ran his hand inside, as if searching for errant bills. Coming up empty-handed, he closed it.

I frowned too. "Maybe I rang something up wrong."

"Either one of us could have," Jackson said calmly. "I initially thought maybe some credit card sales were mistakenly run through as cash, but"—he held up a stack of receipts—"the credit card sales match up."

"Has this ever happened before?"

"Sure. It's not uncommon for a register to be off by a little. But I've never seen one off this much." He sighed and shoved everything into a leather bank envelope. "I'll go over it closer tomorrow. One of us probably hit a wrong button."

He didn't say it, but I knew it was probably me. I was the one training. And the one who had a knack for screwing up. "I'm sorry, Jackson."

"Hey." He looked up at me. "I'm not saying it's your fault. It could have been either of us."

"Sure, in theory, but I'm the one training. I probably messed something up."

He smiled kindly. "Then I'm sure if you did, I'll figure it out. Don't worry about it. It's not a big deal. I just want to figure out what happened, that's all."

"Hang on," I said suddenly, an idea striking me. "Let me count my tips. Maybe I accidentally pocketed some cash that was supposed to go in the register."

"Good idea." Jackson pulled out his own tips and began counting them as well.

I finished counting my stack and told him my number. His was close to it.

He shook his head. "That seems reasonable. I don't think we messed up on the tips."

I groaned and shoved my cash back into my purse. "How does that much money just disappear?"

"It doesn't. Not unless it was a computer error or someone took it."

I slung my purse across my body, then froze. "What if someone did take it? I mean, we were both up there singing tonight."

Jackson frowned, pondering this. "I guess it's possible. But the register is locked when it's closed. They'd need an employee code to get in."

"Does Gwyneth know your code?"

"Gwyneth?" Jackson seemed surprised by my accusation. "She might be a lot of things, but I don't think she's a thief."

"Maybe not . . ." I said slowly, although I recalled hearing that she'd gone through a shoplifting stint in high school. "But she seemed pretty annoyed tonight."

"You think she stole to get back at me?"

I shrugged. "I don't know. Isn't getting back at you kind of her game when she's here?" There was a good chance I was wrong, but all I knew was that Gwyneth and her friends had left sometime when Jackson and I were on stage singing.

"I guess it's possible. I'll check the surveillance footage. I'll let you know if anything turns up."

CHAPTER 15

AUDREY

A few weeks later, it felt like I had settled into a comfortable routine at the Stonewall Inn. Except for the missing money on the first karaoke night, things were running smoothly. We still didn't know for sure what had happened to it. Jackson had checked the surveillance footage and hadn't noticed anything off. I had a feeling I had typed something in wrong, but because I had still been training, Jackson had written it off as a casualty of the busy night.

I tried to take extra care at the register, and as far as I knew, there hadn't been any other issues.

Weekends were by far the busiest because that was when we had most of our shows scheduled. But Thursday karaoke night had become a hit, and Wednesday's open mic night was growing as well.

I usually took Sundays and Mondays off, but this Monday was a little different because we had the upcoming Fourth of July festival to prepare for. The restaurant would be closed that day, but the Stonewall Inn had a booth at the local festival and I had signed up to work a shift.

So instead of taking Monday off, I decided to take advantage of the quiet of the closed restaurant to get caught up on some scheduling and paperwork.

And I wasn't the only one. I passed Jackson in the parking lot on the way in, except he had headed up to the barn to get started prepping for the Fourth of July.

I told him to let me know if he needed any help pulling the large tent out of storage, then headed into the restaurant. When I reached the office, I was surprised to find Randy sitting in Jackson's spot at the desk in front of his computer.

"Hey, Audrey." He grinned widely, friendly as always.

"Hey, Randy." I sat down in my chair next to him, trying my best to be friendly back but it was a bit forced. Sometimes I felt that Randy was a little *too* friendly. The few times he'd trained me behind the bar, he'd stood close, even brushed up against me a time or two. But it was a tight space, so I hadn't said anything about it. Maybe it had been an accident and I was reading into nothing.

"So whatcha here for?" He turned his swivel chair to face me.

"Just working on scheduling," I said as I set my purse down by my feet and fired up my computer. "I figured today was a good day to do it with things being so busy with the holiday this week. What about you?"

"I'm doing the weekly liquor order. Jackson's got his hands so full around here, he asked me to do that for him." There was a hint of pride in his voice, like he appreciated the extra responsibility.

"That's great that you're able to help with that," I said and meant it. Despite the fact that Randy sometimes made me uncomfortable, he was a good worker and the customers seemed to like him. Plus, I was glad he was willing to take some things off Jackson's plate. "Jackson's definitely got a lot to do."

"I 'spect he'll make me the bar manager soon." The pride in his voice turned to arrogance. "I pick up alotta slack around here."

"That's exciting." I forced a smile, then turned my eyes back to my screen and pulled up the scheduling program. Hopefully, our small talk quota was met now and I could focus on work. Sharing this small office with Randy sure felt different than sharing it with Jackson.

"So, Audrey . . ." Randy didn't seem to take the hint that I was done chatting. "How come we never see that fiancé of yours around here?"

My skin prickled. Partly from guilt over the fact that Tucker's wedding was well over and I still hadn't come clean about my broken engagement to my family. Honestly, I'd been so busy working, I wasn't even home that much. But mostly I felt annoyed because it was really none of Randy's business. Still, I said, "He's got an internship in Chicago and he's taking the bar exam this month, so he's really busy right now." I kept my eyes focused on my screen. "And he's not from around here."

"That's convenient." Randy snickered and the

sardonic tone of his words gave me pause.

"Excuse me?"

"Sorry, it's just"—he looked apologetic, although I could tell he was anything but—"I knew a girl once who wore a fake engagement ring. Said it kept dudes from bothering her." He jerked his chin toward the ring on my finger.

Heat rose up my neck. Was Randy astute enough to have noticed that my rock was fake? Surely Jackson hadn't told him.

"Huh." I feigned disinterest with a shrug. "I've never heard of doing that before, but I guess that makes sense."

"Kind of a jerk move though, don't you think? I mean, not even giving a guy a chance?" He leaned back in his chair and placed his hands behind his head, his eyes narrowing at me.

"If a woman's not interested, she's not interested." I kept my voice level. "Now if you'll excuse me, I really need to get some work done."

Randy didn't take the hint. "What does your fiancé think about your sleepovers with the boss?"

I blinked, stopped typing, and faced him. "If you mean the night we got stuck in the hayloft, that was an accident and nothing happened—"

"Whatever you say, baby." He held up his hands, seemingly a gesture of innocence, but I wasn't fooled one bit. "No one could blame you for getting a little lonely with your fiancé in another city. But if the boss isn't keeping you satisfied, maybe I could—"

Immediately, I grabbed my purse and stood up. "You know what, I'm going to finish this later."

I made for the door, but Randy was closer, and in an

instant, he shot up out of his chair and blocked my way.

"What's the rush?" His eyes took on a dangerous gleam. "We were just gettin' to know each other."

"You better get out of my way, Randy." My voice was loud and firm, but I'm proud to say it didn't shake, despite the way my heart was racing right now, every alarm sounding in my brain. "Or so help me—" I plunged my hand into my purse, trying to find the pepper spray I'd kept in there ever since—

"Or what?" He sneered at me, taking a step closer. "You're going to tell your *fiancé*? You're nothing but a liar and a tease."

My fingers closed around the spray and I yanked it out, but Randy must have seen it coming because he grabbed my wrist and twisted it. I shouted in protest as the small canister clattered to the ground.

He swore at me, still yanking on my wrist and I shrieked against the pain, feeling like it might dislocate. Still, I struck him with my free hand and kicked my leg, connecting with his shin, while I screamed again.

"You little—" Another curse flew from his lips, but before he could retaliate, the office door swung open so hard it hit the opposite wall.

"What the— Get off of her!" Jackson barreled in and grabbed Randy by both arms, breaking his grip on me and yanking him away. I stumbled but caught myself before falling completely to the ground. Rubbing my wrist, I looked up in time to see Jackson holding both of Randy's arms behind him and shoving his shoulder against the wall.

"Are you insane?" he yelled in Randy's ear. "What is wrong with you?"

Randy's answer was a few more colorful phrases and curses directed at me. He fought against Jackson's grip, but it was no use. Jackson held him tighter, pushing him even harder against the wall.

"Are you okay?" Jackson asked me, even as he struggled to restrain Randy.

I managed to nod, even though it was far from the truth. Part of me felt disconnected, like I was watching the scene but not really part of it. It was too familiar—too much like last time. Yet also very different.

"Call the cops," Jackson managed to say while he wrestled Randy down to the ground. His simple directions snapped me out of my haze. With shaking hands, I snatched up my fallen purse and yanked out my phone.

CHAPTER 16

JACKSON

It felt like years between when the cops hauled Randy out of here in handcuffs and we finished giving our statements. Even though it was all necessary, I felt awful about how long Audrey had to spend telling her side of the story and filling out paperwork just to press charges.

Finally, the last cop left and it was just the two of us in the office.

"Audrey, I'm so sorry." I bent down and grabbed some of the items that had fallen off the desks in Randy's and my struggle. "I should have listened to my gut about that guy. I just honestly never thought he'd do something like this."

"It's not your fault." She hugged her arms around herself, still in her office chair. There was a vacant look in her eyes that worried me.

"Audrey, I know you went over this with the police, but I have to ask . . ." I sat down in the chair across from her, keeping my words calm even while panic rose in my chest. "Did he do anything to you that you didn't tell them about?"

"No, I told them everything."

"Okay." I relaxed a little, but not much. I couldn't get the echo of her scream out of my mind that I heard from out in the parking lot. The one that had me racing in here to find Randy with his hands on her. It was a good thing Audrey called the cops when she had because I wanted to kill him.

I ran a hand down my face. Why had I ever trusted that guy? I glanced at my computer where Randy had been working and made a mental note to change my passwords. Even though he wouldn't set foot in the Inn again on my watch, I wouldn't take any chances.

"I'm glad you filed a restraining order," I told Audrey, even though deep down it did little to ease my mind. "And please take as many days off as you need. Heck, I understand if you never want to come back here."

"I was fired from my last job," she said abruptly, looking up.

"You were?" I recalled her mentioning she had been let go, but I had assumed it was budget cuts or something. And I didn't understand why she was telling me this now. Did she think I was firing her? "I'm sorry."

She didn't acknowledge my condolences, just kept on talking, which made me keep quiet. Obviously, there was a reason she was going into this. "I was an event coordinator at one of the fancy hotels. It was a great job. I got to help plan exciting parties, fundraisers, meet important people . . . I loved it.

"One evening, I was meeting with a huge potential client to show them our event space. It was Mercer's dad's law firm, actually—they were the biggest firm in the area, and getting a contract with them for all their events would have been huge for the hotel. My manager was thrilled, and my colleague and I were told to pull out all the stops—pretty much anything to get them to sign with us. It seemed like it was going well—we had just finished showing them our banquet hall, when my colleague took the rest of the group out to the gardens.

"This one lawyer held me back, asking all these really specific questions about the hall. Then once we were alone, he, uh, made advances."

My eyebrows shot up. Suddenly, I knew exactly why she was telling this story.

"I slapped him as hard as I could and got the heck out of there, but the damage was done. He had all the say, and he complained to my boss about me." She glanced down at her hands. "When I explained what really happened, my boss didn't believe me."

"You're kidding."

She shook her head. "I even asked them to review the surveillance footage, but apparently, there was none. The system had 'conveniently' glitched." She shook her head. "I got fired."

"What? That's awful."

"The worst part was that the lawyer was my fiancé's dad's partner—pretty much the head honcho. When I told Mercer what happened, he was furious about it, but then a day later, he completely changed his tune."

"So he didn't believe you?"

"That's the thing. I think deep down he did—but he didn't want to. He wanted to pretend it didn't happen. And he wanted me to pretend too. I think it was his dad talking, but that's when I realized he was always going to pick his career over me."

"That's complete crap."

"He ended up accusing me of making it up. And then he broke up with me. Said I wasn't the right fit for his family or his career."

"Are you serious?"

She sighed. "The worst part was that he actually made me question if I had gotten things wrong."

I cursed loudly. "Audrey, listen to me. You did nothing wrong. Not then and not now. Your ex was clearly a coward. And Randy was a creep—I should have realized it sooner. I certainly never would have let him within ten feet of you if I thought he was going to do what he just did. And as far as your last job, they should be sued."

She shook her head. "I was just so happy to get out of there. To be done with it all. That's why I came back here. It was all such a mess, I just wanted to be somewhere familiar—somewhere safe."

It was on the tip of my tongue to tell her she was safe here—with me. But considering what had just happened, I didn't feel like I had done that good of a job at keeping her safe. I should never have let Randy's comments slide. I felt like a crummy boss, and what was worse, like a crummy friend.

So instead, I said, "I'm sorry that happened to you. But I'm glad you came back here."

"Thanks, Jackson." Her smile returned, not quite full

of its usual dazzle, but it was heartening just the same.

And it gave me an idea.

"Hey, you want to get outta here?"

"I never got my scheduling done." She glanced at her computer, frowning.

"Don't worry about it. I can cover that this week. I know someone who's dying to see you."

CHAPTER 17

AUDREY

"Mr. Darcy!" I caught sight of the familiar dog in the front yard the moment Jackson's truck pulled into his parents' driveway.

Once Jackson parked, I barreled out and raced over to greet Mr. Darcy, who did seem older and slower, but every bit as friendly as I remembered.

"He clearly hasn't forgotten you," Jackson said with a chuckle as he joined us.

"I thought you said Mr. Darcy lived with you." I glanced up at him while rubbing Mr. Darcy's shaggy fur.

"He does, but sometimes when I know I'll be working long shifts, I drop him off here first so he doesn't get lonely. Mom loves having him."

"Who wouldn't?" I returned my attention to Mr. Darcy, who barked happily, then licked my face.

Eventually Mr. Darcy calmed down and flopped into the grass, content to let me rub his belly. I glanced up at Jackson, who was kneeling on one knee in the grass beside me, a satisfied smile on his face.

"Thanks for bringing me here," I said and I meant it. It was exactly what I needed to get my mind off what had happened today. Things just felt simpler when you had a lovable ball of fur to distract you.

"No problem." Jackson's eyes crinkled as his smile deepened. "Honestly, ol' Darcy has been eager to see you. He's been extra antsy ever since I told him you were back in town. I think he missed you."

I laughed, picturing Jackson and Darcy having a conversation about me. "I missed him too."

"Jackson, you're back earlier than I expected," a voice called out from the front porch, followed by the sound of the screen door shutting. "Oh, Audrey! Is that you?"

I looked up and saw Jackson's mom hurrying down the front steps toward us.

"Hi, Mrs. Crowe." I stood just in time for her to wrap me in a hug. "It's good to see you again." The last time had been Tucker's wedding, but the day had been so busy, I hadn't had much time to talk to her.

"It's so good to see you too, dear." She pulled back and beamed at me. "I told Jackson he needed to bring you around one of these days. I'm glad he finally listened."

I laughed, while Jackson shrugged and said, "Ol' Darcy wasn't the only one who was impatient to see you."

"And your timing couldn't be better. I just got off the phone with Penny and she's coming for a visit."

"Really?" Despite how this day had started, it was getting better.

"Yes, one of her book signings was canceled, so she has enough of a break in her schedule to come home for a few days."

"That's great! Will she be here over the Fourth of July?" It was kind of a tradition for Penny and me to go to the Fourth of July festival together. Neither of us had made it last year, but maybe this year we would be able to.

"Unfortunately not." Mrs. Crowe shook her head. "She has a signing in Cincinnati on the fifth, but she thinks she'll be able to make it home the day after that and stay for a few days."

"That's great!" Even though it would be a bummer to do the festival without her, I would take what I could get. I hadn't anticipated seeing Penny at all this summer.

Mr. Darcy barked loudly three times in succession and we all laughed.

"He knows we're talking about Penny," I said.

"He's probably wondering why she's not here," Jackson said. "You two are pretty much a package deal."

"Be patient, old boy," I said to Mr. Darcy. "She'll be here in a few days. Don't worry, I miss her too."

"Audrey, dear, would you like to stay for dinner?" Mrs. Crowe asked.

"I'd love to," I said. "But I don't want to impose."

"Nonsense." Mrs. Crowe waved a hand. "I'll just see what I have in the kitchen to whip up."

"Don't worry," Jackson said. "I brought burgers from the restaurant. We can grill."

"Oh, Jackson, you spoil us," Mrs. Crowe scolded her son, but she looked relieved. "I'll go tell your father to start up the grill."

Once she was inside, Jackson headed for his truck, turning back to me with a tilted grin. "You were scared there for a minute, weren't you?"

"Of course not." I swiped my hair behind my ear. "I just didn't want your mom making a fuss over me."

He laughed. "Yeah, sure."

Okay, he had a point. As sweet and nurturing as Mrs. Crowe was, she was not known for her culinary skills. She was infamous for creating "casseroles" out of whatever she had lying around in the kitchen. Penny's dad did a lot of the cooking growing up, and come to think of it, so had Jackson.

"Is that why you started a restaurant?" I asked as he grabbed a paper sack out of the backseat of his truck. "Because you liked cooking so much?"

"Growing up, it was necessary for survival." He shrugged. "But yeah, I guess that was part of it. I like creating and trying new recipes."

"You must get that from your mom," I teased.

"Hey, I like to think mine are at least edible."

"They're great. Remember the pizzas we used to make? Those were so good." I thought back to Friday night sleepovers at Penny's house. We used to build our own pizzas, but Jackson had always been the one to make the homemade sauce and crusts they had on hand.

He nodded. "My grandma's recipe. I still use it at the restaurant." He lifted the sack in his hand. "I'll get these started in the house. Why don't you bring Darcy in the backyard?"

"Sure thing." I unclipped Darcy's collar from his leash and then whistled for him to follow me. I opened the gate of the fenced-in backyard, then waved when I saw

Jackson's dad standing by the grill. "Hi, Mr. Crowe."

"Hi there, Audrey," he called back. "I heard you were back in town."

I chatted with Mr. Crowe for a few minutes, then he looked up from the grill and said, "That should do it. Why don't you run in and see how those burgers are coming?"

"No problem." I crossed the yard to the back door and pulled it open. Once in the mudroom, I paused to take my sneakers off, an old habit, and heard Mrs. Crowe's voice float over from the kitchen.

"I'm so glad you brought a *nice* girl home for a change," she said.

"You're implying that I'm constantly bringing girls home for you and Dad to meet," came Jackson's dry and immediate reply. "Which I'm not."

"Well, no, I suppose not. But there was that Gwyneth . . ." It was clear from Mrs. Crowe's tone that she wasn't a fan. Who could blame her? I briefly wondered who else Jackson had brought home for his parents to meet over the years, but then reminded myself that it was none of my business.

"Besides, it's not like that," Jackson said. "Audrey wanted to see Darcy, and I knew you wanted to see her. We got done at the Inn early, so today seemed like a good day." I was glad he didn't say anything about the Randy incident. The last thing I wanted was for Mrs. Crowe to worry, and I didn't really want to think about it at the moment.

"Well, that's a shame." Mrs. Crowe's rueful response floated over, followed by the sound of a cupboard opening. "The two of you would make the cutest couple. And you know, I always thought Audrey had a thing for you."

I wasn't sure whether to laugh or groan. But I did neither because I didn't want either of them to know I had overheard this conversation. It was no surprise Mrs. Crowe knew about my former crush on Jackson—I had never been subtle. But it was kind of sweet to hear her admit that she actually thought we would work together.

"Mom," came Jackson's exasperated reply. Okay, I guess he didn't find it sweet. "That was years ago. And we work together now—it wouldn't be ethical."

"Oh, nonsense. You're both adults. Plenty of people work together and go on to have healthy relationships. You know, your father and I met when we were both working at that movie theater."

"That's different. I'm technically her boss."

"Well, I suppose that does complicate things a bit. But she's not going to be working for you forever. Maybe when the summer's over, you could—"

"She's engaged." Jackson's voice cut in firmly.

"Oh! Oh, dear me, that's right. I can't believe I forgot that! It must be because I've never met her fiancé. Have you? Is he nice?"

Jackson muttered some vague reply, while I bit my lip and glanced down at the ring on my left hand.

Right. I was still supposedly engaged. Why hadn't Jackson told her that from the start?

I twirled the ring—the one that was supposed to signify my commitment to Mercer, but honestly, made me think of Jackson more often than not whenever I looked at it. He had given it to me, after all.

Why did I suddenly have the urge to stuff it in my pocket, head into the kitchen, and wave my empty hand while saying, *Just kidding, I'm not engaged! So, you know, carry on. I'd really like to see how this conversation ends.*

But the next thing I heard was Jackson saying, "I better get these to Dad." His footsteps headed toward me.

Shoot.

I slipped my feet back into my tennis shoes, squashing the backs of them, and made a point of opening then slamming the door loudly, just as Jackson turned the corner of the mudroom.

"Hey," I said brightly, "your dad asked me to check how the burgers were coming."

"Got 'em right here." Jackson lifted the tray. "But why don't you help my mom gather the condiments." He made a face. "I just saw her pulling out chocolate sauce."

I couldn't help but laugh. "Sure."

I slipped my feet out of my tennis shoes, taking a step back, just as Jackson moved to pass behind me.

"Whoa—" His free hand fell to my waist as we collided and I twisted, bringing one hand up to help him steady the tray, while my other landed on his chest.

"Whoops, sorry," I said, tilting the tray back up so none of the burgers fell off. "Close one."

I lifted my gaze upward and found Jackson's eyes on me, not the tipping burgers.

"Yeah . . . close one." His reply was slow and husky, like his words were struggling to keep up with whatever was going through his brain. His eyes searched my face, then dropped and fixed on my lips. I swear his grip on my waist tightened, just for a second, like he wanted me there, like he was pulling me in.

My heartbeat turned erratic, while my muscles went slack.

Splat!

We broke apart, both our gazes dropping to the lone hamburger patty that had landed by our feet.

"Well, I guess that one's Darcy's." Jackson stooped and scooped it up, then without a glance back, pushed his way out the door and bounded down the porch steps.

CHAPTER 18

JACKSON

Nice going, I berated myself the moment I stepped outside. *Real smooth.*

But whether I was chastising myself for pulling Audrey into my arms or dropping raw meat at her feet, I wasn't entirely sure.

All I knew was I was a total hypocrite. I'd just gotten done scoffing at my mother's suggestion that I had feelings for Audrey, then I'd turned right around and tried to kiss her.

Okay, maybe I hadn't tried to kiss her, but I'd be lying if I said the thought hadn't crossed my mind.

Which was completely unprofessional, and I don't know, *wrong.*

She'd just gotten done dealing with one overly forward coworker today, she didn't need another one.

Regardless of if our collision had been accidental, the pull I'd felt toward her had been anything but. It felt natural.

Maybe it was because I'd been dying to take her in my arms ever since the Randy incident—and even more when she'd told me about what happened at her last job. Not to make a move, but just to hold her. To let her know she was safe. To let me know it.

But no, those feelings were crossing a line big time. A line as her boss and a line as her best friend's brother. Not to mention the fact that I'd once told her in no uncertain terms that I would never feel that way about her. Whatever feelings she had once had for me were trivial—kid's stuff. They'd surely faded away and allowed for her to feel real love—and real heartache—with her former fiancé.

A heartache that probably hadn't healed yet. How could it have? Their breakup was recent.

And any feelings that were growing on my end wouldn't be fair to her. What could I really offer her? She didn't want to stay in Halften. And even if she did, so what? I was a workaholic who needed a babysitter for his dog—a dog who wasn't even really his. She deserved more than that.

I set the tray of meat down by my dad, then mashed the fallen patty into a square instead of a circle and set it aside, asking my dad to cook it up last for Darcy. Then I headed back into the house to wash my hands.

I made a point to avoid the kitchen, where Audrey and my mom were chatting away. I headed for the hall bathroom, but I could still hear snippets of their conversation.

"Oh my, a lawyer!" my mom gushed. "How

prestigious. I bet he's so handsome."

I didn't hear Audrey's reply as I flipped the faucet on and began scrubbing my hands with soap.

Instead, my gaze flicked to the mirror above the sink, and as I met my own eyes, I heard Gwyneth's words on the night we'd broken up.

How could you really expect me to be happy with a glorified cook in a pathetic little town like this? I want more, Jackson. And you should too.

Right—any woman would. But that was the thing. I didn't have more to give.

We ate in the backyard at the picnic table, and whatever strange feelings I'd had in the house seemed to dissipate with the fresh, charcoal-infused air.

I sat across from Audrey and smiled as she chatted easily with my parents, and it was almost like going back in time. Just another meal that Audrey had joined as Penny's best friend. Only Penny wasn't here. And I'd never found myself hanging on to Audrey's every word before. Had she always been so funny? Were her eyes always that green and sparkly?

Okay, so maybe it wasn't exactly like old times. But that was on me, not her.

In some ways, it was like a weird role reversal. Family dinners with Audrey had once meant me pointedly ignoring her while she threw not-so-covert glances my way. Now, I was the one who couldn't keep my eyes off her, even when she and my mom started talking about the romantic subplot of Penny's latest book and my dad asked me about business at the restaurant.

Normally, I would have loved to tell him about how we had a new beer on tap for the summer and how I had just saved five percent on our beef orders by switching to a local supplier. But instead, I found myself more interested in hearing which of the men in Penny's latest fictional love triangle Audrey thought was more swoonworthy.

"Uh, it's good," I said when my dad repeated his question. "Real good, actually. Audrey's booked more summer shows in the barn than we've ever had. And she's started an open mic and karaoke night. Both have been hits."

"Is that so?"

"Yup." See? I could still talk business. Apparently, I just liked it a little more when I could talk about Audrey too.

To shut myself up, I took a big bite of my burger. Which was fine, because my dad turned his questions to Audrey, asking her how she liked running the shows.

"I love it." If I'd thought her eyes had lit up when she was talking about Penny's dreamy characters, it was nothing compared to the way they lit up now. "Getting to meet the musicians and see all the shows is amazing. I'm never bored. There's always something new."

I swallowed and smiled. Her words were genuine. It was no surprise since she really was doing great at her job besides a few little hiccups—the main one being the money that had gone missing the first karaoke night. I had never figured out for sure what happened, but since Audrey and I had both been working the register that night, I couldn't be certain it was anything she had done.

However, her drawer had come up short two times since, on nights she was working alone, which was a little more concerning. It wasn't as much as that first time, but it was enough that I had decided to do a little more register training with her. But I wasn't going to bring that up tonight.

That aside, she really was doing a fantastic job. The bands that she had found and scheduled on her own had been hits. And it made me happy to know that she didn't see the role as just biding her time, or filling in for Tucker. She gave it her all, even with it being temporary, and that was admirable.

Conversation the rest of the night passed easily, even over my mother's surprise dessert of ambrosia Jell-O salad. I was pretty sure there wasn't just fruit hidden in there.

I managed a few bites, but Audrey, champ that she was, finished her entire bowl. When we were driving back to the restaurant, I couldn't help but quip, "So I'm thinking of adding my mom's ambrosia salad to the dessert menu."

The look on her face said it all but I kept on going. "She has a lot of variations, so I might need you to test them all out. You game?"

"Stop." Audrey whacked my shoulder lightly, even as she laughed. "Seriously, I'm trying not to think about it."

"I can't believe you ate all that."

"I didn't want to hurt your mom's feelings! She's the nicest woman on the planet."

I chuckled. "You might be right, but still . . . it was over for me when I tasted the pine nuts."

"Is that what it was? I thought it was corn."

We both burst out laughing, and Darcy gave a few quick barks from the backseat, like he was in on the joke, which only made us laugh harder. It wasn't until I pulled into the parking lot and parked next to Audrey's car that our laughter died away. I could only assume that Audrey, like me, was thinking about what had happened today now that we were back at the restaurant.

"Thanks for that," Audrey said once we'd gotten out of the car. "Seriously. That was exactly what I needed."

"Good," I said with a nod.

"I loved seeing your parents." She knelt down and patted Darcy. "And I especially loved seeing you. Yes, I did." She stood and fished her keys out of her purse, jangling them in her hands as she faced me. "Well, have a good night."

"You too. Drive safe." I paused, feeling suddenly awkward. Maybe because with the moonlight and Audrey fidgeting with her keys, this felt strangely like the end of a date. Which it wasn't. But even as I told myself that, the thought of leaning in before Audrey got in her car popped into my head.

Ambrosia salad, I reminded myself, trying to fill my mind with unappealing thoughts instead. *With corn and pine nuts.*

It seemed to work. I took two huge steps back, tugging Darcy's lead with me. "See you tomorrow." Then I turned and started walking toward the back entrance.

"Are you seriously going in to do more work right now?" Audrey called after me.

I turned with a shrug. "Just a little office work. Won't take me long."

She shook her head. "You work too much."

"Force of habit, I guess."

"Why is that?" Audrey cocked her head to the side.

I shrugged again. Her question was valid. For as long as I could remember, I always had a reason to work extra hard. When we first started the restaurant, I told myself that was what I needed to do to get it off the ground—which was true. But things were running pretty smoothly now. Recently, the excuse I had used was that it took my mind off Gwyneth's and my messy breakup.

But the thing was, I hadn't even thought of Gwyneth in a while until she showed up here out of the blue. And even then, I was only annoyed, not heartbroken. So it wasn't like I really needed the distraction.

So what was it?

"I don't know," I said finally. "It's just what I've always done."

Audrey nodded slowly. "You worked a lot in high school. Like, a *lot*, lot. I never really realized it until now, but it was more than any kid I knew. Why was that?"

"You know we moved here because my dad lost his job, right? The factory he was working for closed and there weren't a whole lotta options where we were living, so we came here."

"Yeah, Penny told me that."

"Well, what she might not have told you was that Dad got a job with Ellis Manufacturing, but from the start, he wasn't making what he used to. He was supposed to get a raise after a year. In the meantime, my mom got a job at the high school, but it still wasn't enough. So I started working to help out."

"Really?" Audrey raised her eyebrows. "I didn't know

that."

"My parents, of course, didn't want me to. They wanted me to focus on school, but they finally caved when I said it would just be till Dad got his raise."

I scratched my head. "You probably know, but Ellis Manufacturing was already in trouble at that point. The raise never came. And a few years later, they folded, and my dad lost his job again, so things got even tighter . . ." I shrugged. "So I kept working, and at that point my parents knew how much we needed my income, so they didn't fight me. Anyway, we got by, but yeah . . . that's why I worked so hard."

"Penny never told me that."

I shook my head. "She didn't know. Not the extent of it, anyway. And I didn't want her too—I didn't want her thinking she had to do what I was doing. That would've been dumb. Penny's smart—she got good grades and had talent. We all wanted her to focus on that. And I'm glad she did."

"You have talent too."

I laughed. "Not the way she does. I wasn't book-smart—I'm still not. And I honestly liked working more than I liked being at school. Sure, I went on and got my business degree, but it was all the means to an end. From day one, when I started busing tables, I was really intrigued by how the restaurant business was run—margins are tight, you know. And it was kinda a game for me to see where there was waste, opportunities for improvement." I brushed a hand over Darcy's head, remembering. "The owner rarely took my advice. I don't think he trusted a teenager, but it got me thinking that one day I wanted to run a restaurant of my own. Do things my way. That became my goal, and once my parents were okay, I kept working hard to make it a reality."

"You're clearly doing a fantastic job."

"Thanks. But like I said, it's a tough business. Not a lotta room for error. It helps having Tucker as an investor, but I certainly don't want him sinking his money into a losing venture. I actually plan to buy him out in a few years once I get enough saved."

"Really? I didn't know that."

"Yeah, as long as things continue on an upward trend, it should be doable. But I guess that's why I work the way I do—it's what I know." I paused, then admitted, "And in the back of my mind, there's always a worry that it's not enough."

I'd never really told anyone that, except maybe Tucker. Not Penny. Not my parents. But it was a pressure that had started ever since I'd become a contributor to our household. Even now that I just had to worry about myself it was there. A mental pressure that, at times, felt physical, building in my chest, weighing me down. The only way I knew how to keep it at bay was to keep on working.

"I think that's really admirable the way you stepped up for your family." Audrey's brow creased as she studied me, as if seeing more behind my words than I was willing to admit. "But you're so much more than your job—than your business. I hope you don't forget that."

"Thanks," I said and I meant it. But there was still a part of me that didn't quite believe her. After all, to Gwyneth, that was the most important part of me, or at least the part of me that wasn't good enough. And it was who I'd been for so long—I wasn't sure I knew how to be anyone else.

But after Audrey got in her car, waved goodbye, and drove off, I walked into my empty restaurant, wondering for the first time if I could be.

CHAPTER 19

AUDREY

Halften's Hometown Fourth of July Festival is in full swing. Wish you were here!

I attached the picture I had just snapped of the carnival festivities, then sent my text to Penny.

Within a minute, she replied.

Wish I was too! Send a pic from the top of the Ferris wheel and don't forget to make a wish!

Don't worry, I won't forget. Want me to make a wish for your too? FYI since you are missing this, you owe me a round through the haunted house at the fall festival. <GIF of evil clown laughing>

<Terrified emoji> No way! You know how I feel about the haunted house!! But yes to the wish. Please wish that I get my next book written before my deadline. I love being on tour but I'm so far behind on my writing. It's hard to find inspo in hotels.

Done! And don't worry, you can always find some inspo in the haunted house. I can see it now: Penelope Crowe, Renowned Fantasy Romance Author Finds Her Inner Stephen King.

Penny replied with a GIF of a judgmental baby shaking its head.

I laughed and pocketed my phone, then made my way through the fairgrounds. It was the same place that Halften held their winter and fall festivals, and while each event held its own special attraction, today was the one time of year when Halften turned into a full-on carnival, with a large selection of fairground rides and games.

I smiled as I passed by a white-and-red-striped tent where the bicycle-decorating contest was currently underway. Every year, the kids of Halften were invited to decorate their bikes and participate in the Fourth of July parade. It had been one of Penny's and my favorite parts about the holiday growing up. I almost pulled out my phone again and snapped a few pictures to send her, but held off when I saw who was in charge of judging the contest.

Our former classmate Camden Clarke. Gone were the days of him needing to be tutored by Penny—last year, he had been elected mayor of Halften. Much to my surprise and Penny's disgust.

I'd never gotten around to confronting Camden that night at the Jorgens' party. But it turned out that Camden standing Penny up was the least of her problems with him.

Time might heal old wounds, but it seemed to only grow grudges, at least in this case. Penny still hated Camden Clarke, and she would not be happy to be sent a picture of him smiling and schmoozing the crowd in his festive red-white-and-blue tie.

Nope, I wasn't about to taint Penny's memories of bike decorating at the Fourth of July festival.

Growing up, it was my favorite of all the festivals, and I was excited to be back for the first time after a few years away.

The only downside was that Penny wasn't here with me. This was my first time attending without her, but since she was due to arrive back in town the day after tomorrow, I focused on that instead. Maybe we'd even be able to figure out where we wanted to move once her book tour was over and the summer was up. She could write anywhere, and I just needed to find a permanent job somewhere.

The thought niggled at my mind that I should be putting in more of an effort with my job search, but between my full shifts at the Inn and taking time to enjoy summer in my hometown, I hadn't been that motivated in my job search. In fact, my mother's criticism was the only thing that had really prompted me in my searches so far. I loved being home, but I did not like living at home. So that would be one good thing when Tucker returned and I had to say goodbye to Halften again.

Next week, I promised myself, I would buckle down and search for my next permanent role. Today, I was going to enjoy the holiday. And the day after tomorrow, the time I would spend with Penny. Jackson had been nice enough to give me time off while she was in town, and I looked forward to having a mini vacation.

Today, I had worked the morning shift at the Stonewall Inn food tent for the festival, and now, a little past three p.m., I had plans to meet up with my friend Caleb, and his girlfriend, Victoria. It wouldn't be the same as spending the day with Penny, but I was excited to have an old, and new, friend to hang out with.

"Hey," Caleb greeted me when I met up with his group in the music tent. "Your grouchy old boss finally let you off, huh?"

"You're one to talk . . ." Caleb's younger sister, Kelsey, rolled her eyes. "You're way grouchier than Jackson."

I laughed because it was true. And since Kelsey and Caleb were Melissa's siblings, I assumed they had gotten to know Jackson through Tucker.

"Fine." Even Caleb knew better than to argue with his sister on that point. "But he's still old."

"You'd better not let Melissa hear you say that," Kelsey said. It was a fair point, since Jackson was the same age as her, four years older than us.

I pulled up a chair next to Victoria and sat down. "My non-grouchy, young boss kindly let me take the morning shift so I could enjoy the festival after. How long have you guys been here?"

I unwrapped my sub that I had bought from another food vendor as Kelsey filled me in on what they had done at the festival so far. When she and Caleb got into a good-natured argument about whether we should do rides or check out the vendors next, Victoria leaned closer to me and asked, "So how are things with you and your non-grouchy boss, anyway?"

"Good, I think." I wasn't put off by her question since I had filled her in on Jackson's and my history at Tucker's wedding.

"You think?"

I swallowed a bite of my food. "Yeah, I mean, overall they've been good. I really like my job, it's just . . ." I searched for the right words to explain it. "Working with Jackson is harder than I thought."

"Old feelings popping up?" Victoria grimaced, but her gaze was sympathetic.

"Maybe . . . kinda." I shook my head. "I don't know, sometimes it feels like we're having a moment, but then he's right back to being all business." I could have sworn that Jackson had a six-feet-apart-from-me rule the rest of the evening at his parents' after we collided in the mudroom.

"What kind of moments?"

"It might be nothing." I briefly filled her in on what had happened with Gwyneth at karaoke night, how Jackson had stopped Randy, and then how he'd taken me to his parents' house for dinner afterward.

"Sounds like he came to your rescue," said Kelsey, who had joined in on our conversation while her boyfriend, Rob, and Caleb went to get drinks. She sighed. "How romantic."

"But as your employer, he may have just been trying to protect you from trouble," Victoria reasoned. "I think the question you need to ask yourself is what do you want? Are you willing for things to get messy at work by pursuing something more with him? And what are your plans when the summer ends?"

I bit my lip, trying to find the answers to her questions, when Kelsey piped up.

"I think we should head to the Stonewall tent so I can see him interact with you." Kelsey leaned back in her chair, full of confidence. "I'm an excellent judge of unrequited love."

"Is that how you missed that your brother's best friend was in love with you for ten years?" Victoria quipped.

Kelsey waved a hand. "Rob was different. I couldn't see it for myself, but I can see it for other people." She pointed at Victoria. "After all, I was right about you and Caleb."

"No way," I said with a laugh. "We are not going by the Stonewall tent so you can stare at Jackson. I still have to work with him, you know."

"Spoilsport," Kelsey grumbled.

"Whatever you decide," Victoria said, "you can't go wrong if you're honest with him. Trust me on that one."

"Ha!" Kelsey scoffed. "This from the woman who had a fake relationship with my brother for weeks before admitting how she really felt."

Victoria's face colored slightly, a strange look on her because she usually seemed so calm and collected. "Like I said, trust me. I learned the hard way."

"Okay, I really need the full story on that one," I said with a laugh.

Kelsey didn't hesitate to launch into the details of Victoria and Caleb's at-one-time fake relationship, while Victoria inserted comments and clarifications here and there, probably trying to make the situation seem less ridiculous.

I listened intently, transfixed and happy for the

distraction.

While I didn't doubt that Victoria had given me good advice, I also didn't quite know what to do with it.

I'd been honest with Jackson about my feelings for him once before, and it had nearly wrecked me. I wasn't sure I was brave enough to do it again.

As dusk approached that evening, I excused myself from my friends to head toward the rides. I still hadn't gone on the Ferris wheel, and I wanted to make good on my promise to Penny.

On my way, I passed by the food vendors and noticed the Stonewall Inn tent was closed. Jackson was the only one behind the small booth, taking down equipment and filling boxes.

"Where is everyone?" I asked as I approached.

"We sold out, so I let 'em all go so they could enjoy the rest of the night. Fireworks should be starting soon."

"Want some help packing things up?" I stepped behind the counter and grabbed a discarded apron, then slipped it on.

"You sure?" Jackson glanced up from the boxes he was stacking. "I thought you were meeting your friends."

"I already did." I began winding the cord from a slow cooker we had used earlier. "I might meet up with them again for fireworks, but I just needed to do something first. Kind of a festival tradition."

"What tradition is that? Getting more work in?" Jackson grinned. "You're as bad as me."

"No." I laughed. "Although, I honestly don't mind. You should've had a few people help so you could get done early too."

"It's fine. I'll probably just head back to the Inn once I get all this packed up anyway."

"Jackson Crowe." I stopped cleaning and placed one hand on my hip, pointing a ladle at him. "Do you mean to tell me that you plan to leave without enjoying the festival at all? How unpatriotic of you."

Now he laughed. "What can I say, I'm a workaholic and I'm beat."

"*Bore*-ring." I rolled my eyes. "C'mon, there must be one thing you look forward to about the Fourth of July festival. It's the best day of the year."

Jackson stopped for a minute and stared out across the bright colored lights. "There is one thing . . ." A grin spread across his face and he scratched his chin. "When we were kids, our parents used to kick off the festival by taking Penny and me to get those twisted chocolate and vanilla soft-serve cones." He shook his head. "I swear, no ice cream ever tasted as good as that."

"That settles it." I picked up the boxes I had packed up and loaded them into the back of Jackson's open truck, which was pulled up behind the booth. "The minute we're done here, we're getting soft-serve cones."

Jackson raised his brows at me, but his grin didn't leave his face. "All right, you've got it." He slid some boxes into the truck beside mine. "So I told you my festival tradition. What's yours?"

"Oh, it's kind of silly." I paused for a moment, wondering if Penny would care if I told her brother about our festival tradition.

"Sillier than a grown man wanting to get twisted ice-cream cones? Good, then tell me so I stop feeling so stupid."

I laughed. "Fine. But it's Penny's and my tradition, so you have to promise not to make fun of her about it."

"I promise." He grinned. "I have enough other things to make fun of her about anyway."

I took a deep breath. "Every year, Penny and I ride the Ferris wheel together, and when it gets to the top, we make a wish. I can't even remember how we started doing it, but it always makes the fair more fun."

Jackson was silent for a moment, like he was thinking, and I wondered if he was trying to find something to say that wouldn't count as making fun of us.

"That's not silly," Jackson finally said, surprising me. "That's a great tradition. In fact"—he slid the final box into place and slammed the truck shut—"next stop, ice cream and the Ferris wheel."

CHAPTER 20

JACKSON

"Whoever thought of these was a genius," Audrey said as I handed her a paper-wrapped cone piled high with a lopsided twist of ice cream.

"Why's that?" I took my own from the teen behind the counter and we started walking again. The oppressive heat of the afternoon had waned now that the sun was dipping closer toward the horizon. Even though there were tons of people milling about, not being confined behind the Stonewall Inn's booth felt freeing.

"Because you don't have to pick between chocolate and vanilla." Audrey licked her ice cream. "Pure genius."

I laughed and took a large bite of mine. A familiar yet almost forgotten sweetness filled my mouth. "Wow, I haven't had one of these in years."

"Why not?" Audrey regarded me curiously.

"Dunno. I just haven't."

"Well, now that you run the Stonewall Inn booth, you really have no excuse. You're here every year anyway. And just think, someday you can take your kids here and start the tradition over." Audrey smiled to herself as she took another lick.

I, on the other hand, dipped my head. It was a nice idea, but something about it seemed foreign to me—out of my reach.

I'd always assumed I'd have a family someday, yet it also didn't seem feasible with how much time I spent working.

But wasn't that how I wanted it? No time for distractions—no time for anything else. I had thought so. But for the first time in a long time, I was starting to realize how empty my life had truly become.

"I've always ridden the Ferris wheel," Audrey went on, "at least, every year I've been here. It would be a crime not to. But this will be the first year I've done it without Penny." Her words were casual but I sensed a bit of sadness behind them.

"You guys did everything together . . ." It was true. Penny and Audrey were inseparable growing up, sometimes annoyingly so. But they certainly had a bond. Penny and I were close enough, in a teasing, big brother and little sister sort of way, but our relationship wasn't always very deep. Audrey certainly knew her better than I did. "Is it weird being apart so long?"

"Kind of. Especially being back here. But, you know, it's good. All part of growing up. We knew things were going to change and this year would be our last time living together. I mean, I was going to get married and I couldn't very well bring Penny with me."

I chuckled. "No, I guess not."

"And even though that fell through, Penny's got a big life all her own." She paused. "You know, when Mercer broke up with me and I lost my job, Penny invited me to go on her book tour with her. She said it would be a grand adventure. And I almost did."

"But you chose to come back here instead?"

"Yeah, traveling the country doesn't sound that glamorous when you have no funds to do it. And I wasn't about to let Penny foot the bill for me—even though I know she would have. Heck, I think she was ready to make up some phony position for me so her publisher would be on board."

"Like what?" I snickered. "Her emotional support animal? She could have gotten you one of those cute vests."

Audrey shoved my shoulder and I laughed harder, then sobered. "For what it's worth, I totally get it. I know a thing or two about having a best friend who's famous, remember?"

"I guess you do." Audrey chuckled softly and then she was silent as if it were just occurring to her this thing we had in common. "It's weird, isn't it?"

"Super weird." I nodded. "Like how everyone sees them differently, but to you, they're just the same person you've always known and loved. But still, it changes things. People treat them differently. They even treat you differently."

"Totally. And you're so happy for them, but sometimes it feels like their life is moving a million miles an hour and yours . . ." She paused as if searching for the right words.

"Just stopped," I finished for her.

"Exactly." Audrey tilted her head, looking at me with a new understanding. "You know, I never could really quite put it into words before. And I've never been jealous of Penny. I know she's worked so hard for everything she has, and she totally deserves it. But I think that's why I chose to come back here. To try to do something on my own. I didn't want people to think I was just coasting off Penny's success."

"I get it." I threw my paper wrapper in the trash. "Believe me, I get it. Even now, I know people think that Tucker just bought the restaurant because I wanted him to. That the only reason I have it is because of him."

"That's ridiculous!" Audrey frowned, looking angry on my behalf, but the dot of chocolate ice cream on her nose made her lose some of her fierceness. "Tucker told me how you put everything you have into that place."

I shrugged. "It is partly true. I mean, I wouldn't have gotten financing without his portion. But yeah, it changes the way people see you."

"Is that why you work as hard as you do? All the hours you put in." She paused. "You're trying to prove you deserve it?"

"That's part of it, I guess. The other part, well, like you said, I want something of my own." We started walking again, heading toward the rides. "And as long as I have the restaurant to focus on, I don't have to think about all the other messy stuff."

It was more than I had admitted to anyone. Not even Tucker knew how much of my work was due to me hiding. But there it was.

"Oh, I get it," Audrey said, her tone judgment-free. "Why do you think I asked for more hours? Less time to think about my failed engagement. And getting fired."

"And cheating exes," I said.

"And figuring out what the heck I'm going to do once this summer's over."

"And deciding when you're going to start living again."

Audrey nodded slowly, then finally she stopped and faced me. "Jackson, will you make a deal with me?"

I narrowed my eyes, slightly suspicious. "What kind of deal?"

"If I promise to deal with some of the messiness in my life this summer, will you deal with some of yours?" Audrey stared up at me with unsure, yet hopeful, eyes. Like she wasn't sure how I was going to react to her request, yet she knew she had to make it. For both our sakes. She held out a tentative hand.

I took it. "I can't promise results, but I promise I'll try."

"Good." A wide smile broke out across her face as she pumped my hand enthusiastically. "It's a deal. Oh, and look"—she pointed—"I can see the Ferris wheel. We better hurry before they shut it down for the night!" Instead of letting go of my hand, she used it to pull me forward as we broke into a run.

CHAPTER 21

AUDREY

"We made it," I said between panting breaths as Jackson and I climbed the metal stairs leading up to the Ferris wheel platform.

"Barely," the attendant said unenthusiastically. "This is the last ride of the night."

Jackson pulled out his wallet and tried to hand the attendant some bills, but the worker just pointed to the sign and said, "Tickets only."

"Don't worry." I reached into the back pocket of my denim skirt. "I still have some from earlier. And besides, you bought ice cream."

Once we were seated in the metal car, Jackson pulled the bar from over our heads across our laps.

"Thanks." I draped an arm across it and settled happily against the seat, ignoring the discomfort of the metal at my back. "I'm glad we made it in time." I wouldn't have wanted to tell Penny I hadn't fulfilled my promise because I'd gotten too distracted eating ice cream with her brother. Penny had long ago discouraged me when it came to Jackson, stating that "if he doesn't see how awesome you are, that's his problem."

But the thing was, being with Jackson tonight hadn't felt like living out my childhood crush fantasies, but really, just talking to a friend. Someone who got me.

"So how exactly does this wish thing work?" Jackson asked as our cart began its climb, only to stop shortly after with a jerk as the attendant loaded the next group.

"It's simple," I said. "You wait till we get to the top and then you make a wish. Since you're a newbie, you might want to use this time to think about what you're going to wish for."

"To be honest, the only wish I'm thinking about making is that this thing stays in one piece till we make it to the ground." Jackson craned his neck, looking over the side while our cart swayed, now halfway up. "Have you ever stopped to think about how old this thing is? Who do you think is in charge of setting it up?" He pointed to a slightly rusty cable above our heads. "And I really hope that's not what's holding us up."

"That's a waste of a perfectly good wish." I crossed my arms in mock indignation. "*Obviously* this thing is held together with magic. Otherwise it wouldn't be able to grant wishes."

"Okay, you want me to be a believer." Jackson chuckled. "Tell me about a wish that *actually* came true."

"Do you remember the year your parents got Penny Mr. Darcy for her birthday?"

"Yeah."

"Ferris wheel wish."

"No way." His jaw dropped. "I always wondered how she talked them into that. You know, I asked for a dog for years before I finally gave up. They always said we couldn't because of my dad's allergies."

I laughed. "Well, there you go. You should have just come straight to the source." I patted the edge of the Ferris wheel car.

Jackson rolled his eyes. "I'm sure the fact that Penny was a straight-A honors student with extra credit for days—unlike me—had nothing to do with it. I'm still not convinced. What else?"

"Well, the majority of Penny's other wishes were to be a best-selling author someday." I spread my hands. "I think the fact that she's on a nationwide book tour at the moment proves my point."

He laughed. "Sure, nothing to do with the fact that she's a total nerd and basically spent more time living in books growing up than she did in the real world."

I smacked his arm. "I'm not doubting her talent, I'm just saying, it's proof."

"All you've told me about are Penny's wishes." Jackson fixed me with his gaze. "What about yours? You have any that came true?"

I tried not to squirm in my seat. The truth was, the vast majority of my wishes usually had something to do with the very man sitting beside me. That Jackson would be my first kiss. That he'd fall in love with me. That we'd get married someday and live happily ever after.

Not very progressive of me, I know. But as a romance-obsessed girl with an impossible crush and none of

Penny's talent for weaving magical stories, I had a one-track, unimaginative mind.

Obviously, none of those wishes had come true. In fact, the only Jackson wish that had come true was the one I made the Fourth of July after the disastrous Jorgens' party: That I would get over Jackson once and for all.

Up until a few days ago, I would have confidently said that wish had certainly come true. Never mind the backsliding I had experienced the past few weeks. It was nothing that a little distance wouldn't cure once my stint in Halften was done.

But obviously, I wasn't about to tell him that wish either.

"The same year Penny wished for Mr. Darcy, I wished for a kitten," I said.

"You had a cat growing up? I didn't know that."

"Well, not exactly, but that Christmas, my parents did get me one of those Tamagotchi electronic pets. And it was a kitten."

Jackson laughed. "Nice try. There's no way that counts."

"Hey, it was my fault for not being specific." I laughed too. "Okay, fine . . ." I paused, then figured what the heck. My reputation as a Ferris-wheel-wish-believing woman was on the line. I took a deep breath. "The last time Penny and I were here together, I wished that Mercer would ask me to marry him. And he did." I looked down at my hands. "Again, I guess I should have been more specific."

When I glanced up, I found Jackson studying me with a frown on his face, and I knew I had killed the lighthearted mood.

"What?" I gave a half-hearted shrug. "It still counts."

Jackson just shook his head. "All you've done is convince me that this so-called wish-granting Ferris wheel has a dark sense of humor. Be careful what you wish for and all that."

"Whatever. Hey, look, we're at the top. Now's our chance." I sat up straighter in my seat and called out into the summer evening air, "This wish is for Penny! Penny wishes that she gets inspiration to write her next book before her deadline."

Jackson snickered. "Penny has the lamest wishes."

I elbowed him in the side and finished my wish by shouting, "Thank you!"

Jackson laughed next to me. "Thank you?"

"What? I figured it doesn't hurt to be polite."

Jackson just kept laughing as we began our descent.

"All right, I got Penny's done," I said. "The next one is all yours."

"Fine. I'll give it a shot."

"Yay!" I clapped my hands with enthusiasm, happy I still had someone to share this tradition with. Although Penny was never so hard to convince.

Just before we crested the top again, I said to Jackson, "All right, give it all you got."

Jackson shut his eyes and just sat there. I paused, wondering if he was trying to think of something. After we reached the peak and started back down again, he opened his eyes.

"You took too long," I admonished. "Now you have to wait for next time."

"No I didn't. I closed my eyes and made a wish."

"That's not how it works. You have to say it out loud."

"Everyone knows if you say a wish out loud it won't

come true."

"That's birthday wishes. Ferris wheel wishes you have to say out loud."

"Says who?"

"Me."

Jackson chuckled. "I'll take my chances. But I'll tell you what, if it comes true, I'll let you know. Then you can add an amendment to Ferris-wheel wish rules. And if it makes you feel better"—He tipped his chin up and called into the sky, "Thank you!" Then he turned to me with a smirk. "Better?"

I just shook my head. "Don't blame me when your wish doesn't come true. All right"—we climbed upward again—"my turn."

I closed my eyes for a brief second, but when we crested the top, I sucked in a deep breath and called out, "I wish that I would find my dream job this year." I had to admit, it was a little more awkward doing this with Jackson than it had been with Penny. But tradition was tradition, and more than ever, I wanted my wish to come true. I cleared my throat. "Thank you."

I released a long breath and settled back into my seat. Mission accomplished. That ought to help my job search next week.

"That was a good wish," Jackson said.

I nodded. "I've got a good feeling about this year." And I did. Hopefully the Keeper of the Ferris Wheel Wishes would see how much I had grown, since my wish hadn't involved a man this year. I had learned my lesson in that regard—no more wishes about love. Penny had it right all along.

"So . . . what *did* you wish for?" I asked.

"Nope, sorry. I already told you it's against the rules to tell."

"It is not!" Who did he think he was, adding rules to *my* wish-making process?

"Okay, fine, but it's against my rules."

"Fair enough." If he had truly wished for something he really wanted, I could understand his desire to keep it a secret. Even though part of me was a bit disappointed that he didn't feel comfortable enough to share it with me. But then again, he was my boss and I was just his little sister's best friend. Probably best if we kept some boundaries.

When we reached the top again, I took a moment to really admire the view. It was beautiful. The colored lights from the other rides and game booths on the ground. The setting sun, the last of its colors dipping below the horizon, reminding me of the sunset Jackson and I had watched in the hayloft. And not too far off, the packed green hill on the outskirts of the fairgrounds where most people had already gathered to watch the fireworks.

"It's kind of a shame this is the last run of the night," I said, turning back to look at the Ferris wheel. "This would be a great place to watch the fireworks from. It always gets so crowded on the hill."

"You planning on watching the fireworks?" Jackson asked.

"Of course." And then Jackson finished the last part of my sentence with me. "Tradition."

I laughed. "Exactly."

"So"—he shifted in the seat beside me—"I may have lied before when I said I didn't have a Fourth of July tradition. I actually kind of do—besides the ice cream thing."

"Oh, do tell!"

He scratched his head for a moment. "I have a really great spot where I like to watch the fireworks. It's super peaceful."

"Really? Where is it?"

He shook his head. "I can't tell you that."

"What?" I feigned indignation. "After I shared with you how to get your wish granted." I looked up at the sky and shouted, "Don't you dare grant his wish now!"

Jackson chuckled. "Instead of telling you, how about I show you?"

CHAPTER 22

JACKSON

As we walked back through the fairgrounds, I felt suddenly unsure. Atop the Ferris wheel I had been so certain. I couldn't share my wish with Audrey—how could I when it wasn't something I even fully understood myself? But my fireworks spot? That I could do.

But now, with two feet firmly on the ground as we made our way back toward my truck, things felt different. Heavier.

The various sets of eyes that fell on us as we passed through the crowd didn't help. Sure, the throng had thinned out now that most people had already gone to the hill to claim their firework-watching spot, but some of the familiar faces with questioning eyes made me ask my own question.

What were we doing together? Everyone in Halften

was probably wondering. How much more oddly had they looked at us when we had raced through the crowd hand in hand on the way to the Ferris wheel? Funny, I had been so caught up at the time that I hadn't even noticed.

But now?

Audrey was supposedly still engaged to another man. And me? I was the workaholic town bachelor. What could the two of us possibly have in common?

It turned out, more than we thought.

And that was the crazy thing. I had spent so much of my life trying to avoid Audrey that I'd never actually gotten to know her. And now that I was, well, it just made me want to know her more. Spend more time with her.

Which was why I was doing things like eating ice cream cones, riding Ferris wheels, and inviting her to watch the fireworks with me.

And making stupid wishes about how I didn't want her to leave.

But she was leaving. That much was certain. She'd practically wished it herself. Her job with me was temporary. And so was her time in Halften. She'd come here for one purpose—to pick the pieces up and make a new plan for herself.

What on earth could I possibly have to offer her?

And more so, even if I did have something real to offer her, why would she want it?

I mean, she was still wearing another man's ring. Kind of. Technically, I had given it to her. But what it represented? A link to a man I was fairly certain she wasn't over yet.

So yeah, in other words, my timing was less than epic.

Which was for the best. My life revolved around cooking food, placing orders, keeping drinks full, and booking other people's happily ever afters. Not making my own.

It certainly wasn't about making silly wishes that would never come true.

But just for tonight, I wanted it to be.

And so when we reached my truck, I unlocked it and held the passenger door open.

"So this mystery spot isn't on the fairgrounds . . ." Audrey said as she jumped up, eyes dancing. "Interesting."

"You cracked the first clue, Watson." I climbed in next to her and fired the engine. Based on the level of the dipping sun in the sky, I'd say we had a little more than ten minutes before the fireworks show started, which would be just about perfect.

When I pulled into the Stonewall Inn's parking lot a few minutes later, Audrey let out a laugh. "Okay, now I think you're full of it. You just brought me here to do more work, didn't you?"

"Nope." I grinned. "Believe it or not, you finally convinced me to take a night off."

"Ha. I'll believe that when I see it."

"This way." I grabbed my keys and instead of heading for the Inn, I strode toward the event barn, which was all closed up. I unlocked the main door, but once inside, I headed toward the side.

"So back when this place was still owned by the Cartwrights, the barn was just used for storage. It was pretty run-down."

"I remember," Audrey said. "Penny used to say it was

haunted. She made up this story about the ghost of a handsome farmhand who died when he was kicked by a horse before he was able to elope with his sweetheart on a rainy evening. It was very tragic."

"Of course she did." I shook my head and laughed over the ridiculously morbid story. "No wonder she didn't date till college. She was too busy mooning over fictional dead farm boys."

"Anyway"—I held the ladder and motioned for Audrey to climb up—"I used to sneak in here as a kid, and one Fourth of July, I discovered the hayloft is the best place to watch the fireworks."

"You're kidding!" Audrey began climbing, then stopped. "But wait—you remember what happened the last time we were up here, don't you? Did you close the barn door?"

"Yes, and don't worry. I installed a bolt to keep the ladder in place. We won't get stranded."

"Okay, if you're certain. I don't want to have to eat olives and pickles for dinner again." She began climbing once more.

When she reached the top, I followed after. Then I crossed the wood floor and threw open the huge window. Immediately, a gentle breeze cooled the stuffy space.

Audrey joined me at the window and drew in a deep, awe-filled breath. "It's just as pretty as I remember."

In the dusk, it truly was.

"Wait here." I crossed to the corner and opened the box of tablecloths. I grabbed the top one and draped it across my shoulder, then hoisted a huge box and brought it to the window. I spread the tablecloth on the ground, then centered the box in the middle so we could lean against it for a backrest. It was the same setup that Audrey had made when we'd watched the sunset. "Have a seat. I'll be right back."

A few minutes and a few trips later, I returned just as the first golden firework burst across the sky.

"It's starting!" Audrey called to me as I reached the top of the ladder. I joined her and set down a camping lantern, which I left off so we could properly enjoy the fireworks. Then I reached for one of the bottles of ice-cold lemonade that I had brought up moments ago, along with big bowl of popcorn for us to share.

Another firework burst across the sky, this one bright red. "We can see them perfectly," Audrey said, taking a handful of popcorn. "I can't believe I didn't know about this. This has to be the best firework spot in all of Halften."

"I know." I laughed lightly, my eyes glued to the sky as a stream of green and gold Roman candles erupted then trickled down like waterfalls. "I've thought about turning this space into a deck and opening it up for business, but I don't know . . . there's a part of me that just doesn't want to share it."

"Thanks for sharing it with me."

"You're welcome." I smiled. "I hope I can trust you not to blab about my Fourth of July tradition."

"You can." She nodded solemnly. "I take Fourth of July traditions very seriously."

I laughed. "I noticed."

We watched the colors for a few moments in silence until Audrey broke it.

"Did you ever bring Gwyneth here?" Her words were slow, casual, but I sensed a weight to them all the same.

"No." A laugh escaped me. I couldn't help it. The thought of Gwyneth climbing that ladder in her fancy high-heeled shoes and sitting on a slightly dusty floor eating popcorn was truly comical. Just one of many signs that we were never truly compatible, but I'd been too stupid at the time to see it.

"No," I said again. "The last Fourth of July we were together, she wanted to spend it with a crowd of her friends at the festival. She liked being places where she could be the center of attention."

"I spent last Fourth of July at Mercer's country club." Audrey wrinkled her nose. "It was black tie and all the food was really tiny, so I was hungry by the end of the night. And I wore heels, so my feet really hurt. There were fireworks over the golf course, but I like this much better."

"Me too." It wasn't like I'd spent last year at Mercer's country club, but what I meant was that I liked this Fourth of July better than any other I'd ever had.

And when I tore my eyes from the flashing colors to glance at Audrey, her lips turned up in a smile and she nodded, so I think she understood.

I smiled too, and I was about to look back at the fireworks when I saw them reflected in her green eyes, which in a way, was even more spectacular.

"What?" Her gaze found mine and her smile turned shy. "Do I have popcorn all over me?" She wiped the back of her hand across her lips. "I swear, it gets everywhere." She began dusting off her shirt.

"No." I laughed softly and grabbed her hand gently, wanting her to look at me. And was rewarded when her dazzling eyes met mine again. "I was just thinking . . ."

But the thing was, I wasn't thinking. I couldn't have been or I wouldn't have done what I did next.

Because instead of finishing my sentence, I curled my free hand into her hair, leaned forward, and pressed my lips to hers.

CHAPTER 23

AUDREY

The moment Jackson's lips brushed mine, I gasped. I know, not the smoothest, but it was hard not to be surprised when the man who had once claimed he would never want to kiss me was doing just that.

He pulled back immediately, no doubt worried he'd crossed a line, or that I was upset with him. As he moved away, my eyelids fluttered open. I met his eyes, full of heat and then disappointment, like he thought I was rejecting him.

Nuh-uh.

I shut my eyes, and my words came out breathless. "Do that again."

He didn't hesitate. His lips met mine once more, full of fervor, much more confident now that I'd made my wishes known.

And it was like a wish come true. Literally, for I had wished for this on a Fourth of July years ago. Only it wasn't my first kiss, but hey, I wasn't complaining.

It wasn't my first kiss, but it was good enough to be my last. My heart just might stop here and now, and Penny could write a story about me dying in this barn like her fictional farmhand heartthrob.

As Jackson's lips moved across mine, his hands moved just as tenderly. One steadied me, laced into my hair as it cradled the back of my head. The other wove around my back, pulling me closer.

I happily complied, reaching up and grabbing a handful of his T-shirt, just as our kiss turned deeper.

Holy smokes, the man could kiss! If he kept this up, I had a feeling we'd miss the entirety of the fireworks show, but hey, there was always next year. And I had to say, I appreciated the slow, careful way his lips moved against mine.

With Mercer, I'd always gotten the feeling that he was in a hurry anytime he kissed me—like he had somewhere else he needed to be, better things to do.

Somewhere in the distance, I heard the crack and pop of the fireworks out the window, but the sense was dull compared to the way my other senses were awakening.

Mainly touch as Jackson's lips caressed mine, gentle one second, insistent the next, like he was both savoring the moment and living it to the fullest. My fingers splayed across his chest as he tugged me closer still, revealing the firmness of the muscles beneath his shirt. I pressed my palm flat, and skated my other hand up to his cheek, feeling the softness and prickle of his stubble depending on which way I stroked.

Scent followed as I took in the mixture of the comforting aroma of wooden beams around us and the lingering trace of Jackson's fresh soap and cologne, only known to me now because I was tangled up with him so closely.

Smell gave way to taste from the perfect blend of salted popcorn and tangy lemonade on both our lips, and I knew, unlike most people, I wouldn't think of a movie theater when I thought popcorn, but I'd always be brought to this magical moment.

Sight was a momentary flash as I pulled back just enough to catch my breath and caught the reflection of multicolored fireworks bursting in the sky in Jackson's heavy eyes as they flashed open, then closed when I leaned toward him again

And finally, sound caused fresh heat to ignite my core when our lips met, and a satisfied groan rumbled from the back of Jackson's throat, as if he was pleased I wasn't ending our kiss. His enthusiasm elicited a soft, contented sigh from me.

I'm not sure how long we would have stayed that way, lost in discovering each other, if not for the jarring sound of voices below us that ripped us apart.

Two very close voices. And very familiar.

For a moment, Jackson and I stared at each other, frozen, listening over our own heavy breaths as footsteps landed on the barn floor below, heading toward the loft. The only light in the sky came from the sporadic bursts of fireworks in the distance, illuminating Jackson's shocked face, which I could only assume was a complete mirror of mine.

Jackson was the first to snap out of it. He muttered

what sounded like a curse under his breath—not exactly what a girl wants to hear after receiving the best kiss of her life. But also not surprising considering who was about to walk in on us.

Jackson turned and flipped the switch on the lantern he had brought up here. Right. Because its soft, romantic glow made this situation any less suspicious.

Still, I tried to do my part by quickly combing my fingers through my mussed-up hair and pressing my lips together, hoping they didn't look as swollen as they felt.

A voice called out Jackson's name, rising up from the loft's ladder, and Jackson quickly responded with "Up here!"

"I thought we'd find you here." Tucker's face appeared over the edge, then he climbed into the loft.

"Hey, Tucker," I called out and waved, hoping my voice didn't sound as shaky as my heartbeat.

"Audrey?" Tucker turned from where he was giving Melissa a hand as she climbed up into the loft after him. "I wasn't expecting to find you here."

"Yeah, Jackson and I loaded everything up and brought it back here after the festival. He mentioned this was a great place to watch the fireworks, so I wanted to check it out." I sat casually on top of the cardboard box Jackson had shoved in front of the loft window, but my words sounded guilty to my own ears.

Chill out, I commanded myself. *You don't have anything to feel guilty about.*

Except for the fact that I just kissed Tucker's best friend. My boss. Oh, and Tucker also still thought I was engaged to another man. Yikes, this could get messy fast.

"What are you guys doing here?" I figured changing

the subject was the best course of action at this point. "Aren't you supposed to still be on your honeymoon?"

"Yeah, we decided to take a quick detour before our next stop." Tucker grinned at Melissa, who put her arm around his waist.

"Turns out I'm more of a homebody than I thought." She laughed. "Traveling the world is amazing, but I really started missing Halften."

Tucker laughed too. "And she couldn't stop talking about the Fourth of July festival. Finally, we decided to cut Ireland a little short and try to make it back in time."

"Which we would have if our flights hadn't gotten delayed."

"We made it to town just before the fireworks started, and instead of dealing with the parking and crowds at the festival, I suggested we watch them from here." Tucker turned to Jackson. "I hope that's okay."

"Yeah, of course." Jackson pointed to our spot by the window. "Make yourself comfortable. I'll grab some more popcorn and drinks."

Jackson hurried down the ladder and part of me wanted to follow after him. After what just happened, I really felt like we needed to talk. But at the same time, I didn't want to call any more attention to our awkwardness. So instead, I grabbed another box and settled in next to Melissa.

"Nothing is better than this." Melissa snuggled into Tucker's arm and gave a satisfied sigh, while Tucker kissed the top of her head.

"So Audrey," Tucker said. "You and Jackson seem like you're getting along well. That's great."

"Yeah, it is." My words came out a little stiff. I hoped

Tucker didn't guess just *how* well we'd been getting along.

"He's kept me updated on some of the changes you've made—the extra shows and events you've booked. That's awesome." Tucker grinned. "I knew you'd be a natural at it."

"Thanks." I relaxed a little at his words. "I really do love it."

"Well, don't worry, I'm not here to butt in—we're still on vacation."

From there, the conversation turned to how long he and Melissa planned on staying until they headed off to their next destination, and what they had done on their trip so far.

When Jackson returned, he took a seat on the ground next to Tucker—as far away from me as possible. Which was probably for the best. But still, there was a part of me that missed the closeness we had shared earlier this evening. Before Tucker and Melissa arrived, bringing with them the reality of our situation.

That Jackson was my boss and I shouldn't be feeling these things about him.

That even though my role here was temporary, so were my plans to stay in Halften. The last thing we should be doing was starting something we couldn't finish.

And that stupid lie that I had told about still being engaged, now weighing heavier on my shoulders by the minute. Now seemed as good a time as any to come clean to Tucker and Melissa, yet I still couldn't force myself to say the words.

Why? Because if I brought it up now, would Jackson think it was because I was expecting him to define whatever it was that was going on between us? Which was what, exactly?

I didn't come back here with plans of falling for my former crush. The one who once said he would never want to kiss me. Yet, five minutes ago, he was doing just that. So what exactly did that mean?

All these questions were still swirling in my mind when the big finale started. Firework after firework burst into the sky in a massive frenzy, reminding me a lot of my frantic mind.

By the end of it, Melissa and Tucker were cheering and clapping, but I was still staring at the dark night sky, my vision slightly blurred from the bright colors there moments ago.

Jackson had called me a firecracker at one point, and now more than ever, I felt like one.

Because at some point, every firecracker burns out.

CHAPTER 24

JACKSON

I'm stupid, stupid, stupid.

Did I really just make a move on Audrey? What was I thinking?

Real professional, man.

And her being my employee was just the tip of the iceberg of why kissing her was a bad idea.

How about the fact that she was practically my best friend's little sister?

Or that she just ended a relationship and the last thing I needed was to be her rebound?

Or that she was leaving town soon and I was collecting dust here by the minute?

The list went on.

"Kelsey just responded." Melissa held up her phone. "They're all still at the festival. Wanna go there next?"

"Why not?" Tucker pulled her to her feet, chuckling. "This is one of the few days of the year Halften has a nightlife." He turned to Audrey, then me. "You guys wanna come?"

"I will for a little," Audrey said. "My car's still there." She twisted her hands together. "Can I get a ride?"

"Sure thing. Jackson?"

Despite my better judgment, I found myself nodding. "Yeah, let me just unload the truck real quick."

"Lemme help." Tucker followed after me as I headed for the ladder. "It'll make me feel better about being such a slacker around here."

I laughed. Despite his horrible timing, it was good to have him back. "Yeah, you are."

Once Tucker and I had caught up a bit and were dropping the last of the boxes in the kitchen, Tucker asked, "Hey, is everything okay with you and Audrey?"

"Yeah." I did my best not to seem too put off by his question. "Why wouldn't it be?"

"I don't know. The vibe between you guys seemed weird tonight."

"What kind of weird?"

"I dunno." Tucker laughed. "Don't get me wrong, I was happy to see you guys getting along, but I was honestly surprised to see you together. And the air just seemed kind of . . ."

Confusing?

"Off." Tucker finished his sentence. Yeah, that was one word for it.

"We both worked a long shift in a hot, stuffy booth at the fair today. That'll make anyone feel off."

"Yeah, good point." Tucker laughed, then turned

serious. "So you're not mad at me for hiring her. I mean, I know she's never been your favorite person, but I just knew she'd be great in the role."

"No, I'm not mad. Business has been great. Honestly, I underestimated her."

Tucker nodded. "I think everyone in Halften always has. But I had a feeling you two would work well together. So everything's cool?"

For a moment, I considered fessing up. Talking to Tucker as my best friend and not as the co-owner of the restaurant. Because despite business being good, everything else certainly didn't feel cool between me and Audrey. Especially not now that I'd kissed her.

But how could I admit that without him thinking I was a complete slimeball for making a move on an engaged woman? Or coming clean to him completely about Audrey not being engaged anymore. But then what did that make me? Besides telling the secret I promised her I'd keep, I'd be the guy who moved in when she was on the rebound. Yeah, that wasn't much better.

I'd messed up. Messed up big-time. And while I knew I could count on Tucker, this wasn't a mess he could clean up. It was all on me.

And one thing was certain.

Work was about to get a whole lot more awkward.

As we made our way through the festival again, the air seemed to have shifted.

Before when it was just Audrey and me, things felt

easier. Freer. The night air was alive with possibility.

Now as we trailed behind Melissa and Tucker, it was the complete opposite.

Maybe it was the massive amount of space between Audrey and me, made more apparent by Tucker and Melissa holding hands in front of us. While we had done the same thing earlier in the evening, although for a different reason, now it was a reminder that such closeness was entirely off-limits.

We reached the tent where Kelsey told us to meet them, and Tucker and Melissa slipped inside. Just before Audrey followed, I reached out and grabbed her hand.

"Audrey, wait a minute." I let go of her quickly once she stopped. "Can we talk?"

"Sure, yeah." She scuffed her sandal into the dirt. "That's probably a good idea."

"About what happened tonight . . ." I raked a hand through my hair, trying to find the right words, the silence making it apparent that I had no clue what I wanted to say.

Should I apologize? Maybe, but deep down, I wasn't sure I regretted it.

Should I fess up and tell her how confused I felt? Maybe, although there was a part of me that felt like a total jerk for kissing her on a whim. That's not something you do with your employee—or your sister's best friend. You only cross that line if you're sure the risk is worth it, and right now I wasn't sure of anything.

Should I ask her how she felt about it? Maybe, but what if it was entirely different than how I felt? What if she wanted more than I was able to give? What if she wanted less?

Before I could settle on any of those options, Audrey filled the silence for me.

"It was a mistake."

I shut my mouth, then found myself nodding even before I fully processed her words.

"I mean," she continued, "you and Tucker did me a huge favor hiring me, and the last thing I want to do is mess that up. I really need this job—"

More nodding from me, while I instantly felt like the lowest scum on the planet. How could I have moved in on her like that? Especially knowing what happened at her last job? And after what happened with Randy?

I could only imagine what she thought of me right now.

It didn't matter that working with her felt like a partnership. And it didn't matter that she was there to fill in for Tucker and that he was technically the one who hired her—she was still my employee. My name was still on her paychecks.

Shame flooded me. What if she only kissed me back because she thought she'd lose her job if she didn't?

"Audrey, I'm so sorry." I finally found my words and they were full of regret. "I never meant to put you in a hard position. I promise you, nothing that happened between us will affect your job."

Her cheeks colored as she dropped her gaze. "Can we just, you know . . . forget it ever happened?"

"Yes—absolutely." I held up a hand. "In fact, it's already forgotten."

"Thanks." Her shoulders finally relaxed, and without another word, she turned and slipped into the tent.

I stood rooted in place for another minute, trying to

ground myself before I went in there and faced everyone.

In addition to feeling like a complete jerk, I'd now made myself a total liar.

Because despite what I just promised Audrey, I knew there was no way I'd be forgetting that kiss anytime soon.

CHAPTER 25

AUDREY

If I'd thought my first day working at the Inn with Jackson was awkward, it was nothing like showing up for my shift the next afternoon.

It didn't help that I was scheduled to work the evening shift inside the restaurant bar that night and Jackson was who I was relieving when I started.

"Hey," I said as I walked behind the bar and slid my purse under the counter.

"Hey," Jackson replied, looking up from where he was rolling silverware. Was it just my imagination or did his eyes light up for a second when he saw me, only to immediately dim?

"Busy day?" I tried to keep my voice light as I punched my employee code into the computer to clock in.

"Nah, super dead. It's the day after a holiday. Everybody's probably taking it easy after a late night."

"Right." I slipped my apron on, really wishing he hadn't mentioned last night—that was the last thing either of us needed to think about. Hadn't he agreed that we should be forgetting about that?

"Tonight might be busier for you though," he went on.

The dishwasher clicked off and Jackson opened it. I turned to it too, eager to have a task to keep me busy.

Jackson must have had the same idea because as soon as the steam cleared, he reached toward the glasses inside. Our hands brushed and I immediately pulled back.

"Hot," I said quickly, feeling like an idiot for jumping away from his touch. "The glass, I mean. It was hot—from the dishwasher."

Please. Stop. Talking.

"Yeah," Jackson replied, but he easily picked up the glass and began drying it with a towel.

I stepped away and turned my attention to the garnish tray. I could restock that and leave him to the dishes to avoid any more accidental hand brushes. In addition to making me babble like an idiot, it also made me think of his hands all over me last night.

Pressed against my back.

Brushing my shoulders.

Caressing my cheek.

"Well, I'll get out of your hair." Jackson closed the now-empty dishwasher and draped the towel across the handle.

Running through my hair. . .

I squeezed my eyes shut. Seriously, was he doing this on purpose?

"See you later," I said cheerfully—too cheerfully. Could he tell it was forced? I held my breath as he slipped past me to leave the bar. The last thing I needed was to inhale his intoxicating scent, the one that had made me practically dizzy last evening.

The minute the door swung closed behind Jackson, I exhaled, long and slow.

Okay, crisis averted. I bent down and grabbed a jar of maraschino cherries from the fridge. With any luck, I wouldn't see him for the rest of the evening—

"Okay, girl, spill," a loud voice called over. "What is going on?"

I was so startled, I yelped and almost sent the cherry jar flying.

"Geeze, Brittany! You almost gave me heart failure." I looked up to find Brittany eyeing me from the serving window that connected the bar to the kitchen. It was convenient for the waitstaff to pick up any drinks for their tables. And apparently, for some waitstaff to sneak up on the bartenders.

Brittany cocked a well-shaped eyebrow. "*I* almost did? Are you sure you don't mean our fearless leader?"

"What are you talking about?" I didn't meet her gaze, instead I focused on refilling the maraschino cherries.

"C'mon. What was that? What is going on between you two?"

"Nothing."

"Oh really? That's not what I heard." She dipped her head closer and lowered her voice, whether for the sake of being discreet or being dramatic, I wasn't quite sure.

"I heard you two were seen holding hands yesterday at the Fourth of July festival."

A genuine laugh escaped me. Leave it to the rumor mill to thoroughly distort that. "It wasn't that kind of hand-holding. I was just pulling him through the crowd."

"Uh-huh. Well, when Melissa and Tucker stopped by this morning, she mentioned they dropped in on you and Jackson here last night. Alone. Watching the fireworks together." She smirked. "I wonder what your fiancé would think about that."

"We were just unloading the truck." This excuse did not come so easily. Unfortunately, Brittany was getting warmer, much like my face.

"Really? In the hayloft? In the dark?" When I didn't respond, she went on. "Maybe I'd buy your innocent act if I didn't just witness *that*"—she waved a hand—"between the two of you."

"What? There's nothing between us—"

"Oh, please. That man wants you. Bad. And by the shade of your face it's obvious you want him too. What I want to know"—she reached through the window and plucked a cherry off the tray and chewed thoughtfully—"is how you did it. I mean, I'm not sure if I'm impressed or jealous. Okay, I'm definitely jealous, but—"

"There's nothing to be jealous or impressed about." I crossed my arms, my denial building. "There is nothing going on between Jackson and me."

"Okay, yeah . . . sure." For someone who was offering up a lot of affirmations, she didn't seem to be agreeing with me. In fact, she laughed. "You want my advice, honey, save your innocent act for Jackson." She eyed me up and down. "I'm assuming that's what it is about you that he likes so much, anyway. But seriously, you'd better figure out what you want—and fast. Because trust me, when word of this spreads, I'm not the only waitress who's going to be put out that he picked you over them—especially when you've apparently already got your hooks in some hot lawyer. It's slim pickings around here. Why should you have two men when the rest of us have none?" With that, she flipped her hair and strolled off.

I dropped my head in my hands and groaned.

Great—just great. It was bad enough trying to deal with the emotional aftermath of Jackson's and my kiss, but having to worry that the rest of the staff was going to be on to us soon was not an extra problem I needed. I certainly had no intention of getting into a catfight with any of the other waitresses, like Brittany had suggested.

And the thought that I was some two-timer trying to carry on with two men at once was absolutely ridiculous. I had half a mind to march into the back and set the record straight for Brittany—and anyone else who thought I was trying to cheat on my so-called fiancé—that my man-count was zero, not two. But if I called attention to my fake engagement now, would it just make it seem even more like I was after Jackson?

It was just another reason why my being here—my being with Jackson—was a terrible idea. He'd worked hard to be the kind of boss his staff could respect. One who didn't do casual flings with his employees. Now after one careless evening with me, was that all ruined?

I'd like to say I managed to put all those conflicting thoughts out of my mind that night, but the truth was, I was working on autopilot. Every conversation with customers felt forced. Every laugh, fake. And every drink poured, a blur.

It wasn't until after close when I opened the register to place the money in a deposit bag, did I snap out of my self-indulgent-Jackson-induced wallowing stupor.

Blinking, I pulled the metal drawer open as far as it would go and stared.

It was empty.

CHAPTER 26

JACKSON

The till was empty, just like Audrey had said when she'd texted me after close. I'd hurried back to the restaurant, having only been gone for a few hours.

I stared at the empty register. Something bigger was obviously going on here. Miscounted change was one thing—but a completely empty register at the end of the evening? This couldn't be explained away as coincidental. What had started as a small problem had grown into a bigger one.

And even though it was just one part of the restaurant and one register, the bar made up a good portion of our profits. One night of loss, I could handle, but if this kept up?

I saw more than an empty register.

I saw bills that couldn't be paid. Staff we couldn't

afford to keep. Struggling to stay afloat—I was supposed to be paying Tucker back, not adding to my debt. I saw our doors closing for good.

And as if that weren't enough, my brain flashed with other images as well. Old ones. Unreasonable ones, but still the fear was real.

I saw searching through the cupboards to find whatever we had to stretch one pound of ground beef into two meals instead of one. I saw Penny wearing my hand-me-down clothes instead of the latest styles that all her classmates wore. I saw putting another Band-Aid on our clunker car because we didn't have the funds to properly fix it. I saw lying to my classmates about what I'd gotten for Christmas because I didn't want to admit that I'd only gotten a used pair of winter boots—a necessity—to their snowboards and smartphones.

I shook my head quickly and slammed the till shut. No, this wasn't that. This wasn't going back to my childhood. Nowhere near it. But still, my voice came out tight.

"What happened?"

"I don't know, Jackson, I swear." Audrey twisted her hands together, looking just as dumbfounded as I felt. "The bar was empty and I went in the back for a bit. Then when it came time to shut the register down, I opened it and found this."

"How long were you gone?"

"Maybe about ten minutes." She bit her lip, thinking. "Brittany asked me to help her take out an order in the dining room. She had a group of eighteen."

I nodded slowly, taking this information in, while a headache built at the back of my skull. "Is it possible you left the register open?"

"I—I don't know." Audrey paused, clearly thinking hard about it. Finally, her shoulders shrugged and then slumped. "Maybe."

"I appreciate your honesty." And I really did. Yet my next words were out of my mouth before I could think about it. "Unfortunately, this isn't the first time your register's been off."

"What do you mean?" Her eyes rounded. "Are you talking about that karaoke night?"

"Not just that—I don't know what happened that night. But your register has come up short a few other times."

"It has? Why didn't you tell me?" She took a step back. "Wait—did you think I was *stealing* from you?"

"No, of course not." And, I didn't. Not really. But why hadn't I addressed the issue? If it were any other employee, I surely would have by now. So why hadn't I with her?

"It just—it wasn't that much." I shrugged. "And you were doing such a good job with everything else, it didn't seem like a big deal. But now—"

"I get it," Audrey said, a slight tremble in her voice. "You didn't bother because you think I'm careless. That it was just part of me being a screwup." She puffed out a breath. "And you're probably right. I mean, how else could this have happened? Maybe I *didn't* shut the register all the way—"

"But maybe you did. Look, I'm not saying any of it is your fault. It's just weird, that's all. Let's check the surveillance before we jump to conclusions."

"Okay."

We were both silent as we walked back to the office together and I pulled up the grainy surveillance footage from the bar from earlier tonight. There was Audrey serving a few customers. I sped it up to get closer to the end of the night.

The only positive about this situation was that we were both too engrossed in the footage to revisit any of the awkwardness between us from earlier.

"There's my last customer cashing out." Audrey pointed to the screen, so I stopped the fast-forward.

On-screen, Audrey opened the register and gave the customer his change. Even in the blurry footage, I could see a full cash drawer. Audrey shut it behind her, then turned back to the counter and cleared a few glasses.

"Looks like you shut the drawer," I said.

"Yeah." There was relief in her voice.

"When did you help Brittany with her order?" I asked.

"Pretty soon after that," Audrey said.

The screen jumped and then Audrey was back in the same spot, now wiping down the bar.

"Hang on." I rewound the clip, taking note of the time stamp on the bottom.

At 10:32 p.m. Audrey cleared the glasses. At 10:47 p.m., she was suddenly wiping down the counter.

I hit rewind again. Same thing.

I ran a hand through my hair. "Fifteen minutes of footage is missing. If I didn't know to look for it, I wouldn't have even thought you'd left."

Audrey leaned forward as I rewound the clip again. "Did someone delete it?"

"Either that, or we had a very ill-timed glitch." Or convenient, depending on how you looked at it.

What Audrey had told me about her last job came to mind. The last time her integrity had been questioned.

I asked them to review the surveillance footage, but there was none. The system had 'conveniently' glitched.

Unbidden, a question came to mind.

What were the chances that the last two places Audrey worked had security footage coincidentally wiped from the cameras? My stomach turned even as I thought it. No, I didn't believe it.

But she was the common factor here.

"Great." Audrey threw her hands in the air as she slumped back in her chair. "So we've got nothing."

I turned to her. "We'll figure this out. In the meantime, you have a few days off, which is probably for the best. Don't say anything to anyone else about this. Act like nothing is wrong. I'll see if I can glean anything from the rest of the staff."

"Do you think someone's trying to frame me?"

"It sure looks that way." I had no doubt that when I rewatched the footage from the first karaoke night that I'd find a chunk of time missing from that too. "Which is why I think it's best if we act like nothing's wrong."

"Okay . . ." Audrey said slowly.

"Look, this isn't the first time I've dealt with employee theft. And it won't be the last." Which was true. But it was the first time that I had no idea who the real culprit was. "Try not to let it bother you. Enjoy your time off. We'll regroup when you're back on Tuesday."

"If you're sure . . ." Audrey stood. "Jackson, I really am sorry. I can't help but feel if I had been more careful, more aware, this wouldn't have happened."

"Don't beat yourself up over it." I stood too and

opened the office door. "C'mon, I'll walk you out." If someone around here did have it out for Audrey, the last thing I wanted was for her to be out in the parking lot at night alone.

After seeing Audrey off, I went back inside the restaurant, but I headed to the bar instead of the office. I typed my master code into the computer touch screen and then brought up the login files. Based on the missing camera footage, I knew exactly what I was looking for.

Sure enough, there was only one login to the register between those missing fifteen minutes. At 10:36 p.m., the register had been opened.

And according to the employee code, Audrey was the one who'd done it.

With a sigh, I took a shot of the screen and time stamp with my phone, then shut the computer down.

I had a lot to think about.

Either someone was going to great lengths to set Audrey up or she was lying to me.

Chapter 27

AUDREY

I woke up the next morning and immediately buried my face into my pillow as if that would somehow erase the memory of the vivid dream I just had.

A dream of Jackson kissing me.

Shocker, I know.

And now that I thought about it, my entire night was filled with dreams of Jackson kissing me. The location of each one changed, but the gritty details were the same.

Jackson kissing me in the cooler at work. Jackson kissing me on the Ferris wheel. Jackson kissing me before we rode off into the sunset on two spotted cows—I'm not quite sure what prompted that one. What could I say? Dreams were weird. But needless to say, there was definitely a trend going on.

I was such a hypocrite. I'd asked Jackson to forget

anything had happened between us, but apparently my subconscious wanted it to live rent-free in my head.

I groaned and then threw my covers off, climbing out of bed.

Whatever. I was a strong, independent woman and my subconscious could relive that kiss until the cows came home. It didn't change anything.

Darn, now I was thinking about that last dream again—was Jackson wearing a cowboy hat? That was a good look on him.

Anyway, I could—and would—completely push Jackson out of my mind today. Luck was on my side, at least, because for the first time in ages, I had three whole days off.

That meant three days completely free of Jackson.

And the timing couldn't have been better, between what had happened on the Fourth of July and the missing money from my register last night.

My stomach soured as I thought about the empty register. What did it mean? Was someone really trying to set me up? Or had I simply been careless? I certainly hadn't been in a good headspace at work yesterday. But still, the missing surveillance footage was too strange to be ignored. That couldn't simply have been a coincidence.

I thought about what Brittany had said about being jealous of me—about the other waitresses being jealous now that everyone suspected something was going on between me and Jackson. Was that jealousy enough to prompt someone to try to get me fired?

Even as I pondered it, another worse thought came to my head. What if it was Jackson's way of getting rid of me? Now that things had blown up between us, what if he wanted an excuse to let me go that wouldn't make him look like the bad guy in front of Tucker?

I shook my head, dismissing the thought almost as quickly as it came. Jackson wouldn't do that. Not something so underhanded and awful.

But still my unease grew. Whatever was going on, things were getting increasingly more complicated at work. The summer wasn't over yet, but maybe all of this was a sign that I needed to leave sooner rather than later. Even if the matter of the money got sorted out, there was still the matter of my heart. And the truth was, every second I spent with Jackson seemed to put me at risk of losing it to him—again.

And that was the complete opposite of what I had come back here to accomplish this summer.

Kissing him in the hayloft had been a mistake—even he admitted it. Once I had said it, he was practically tripping over himself to reassure me that he was not looking for anything more. Just like I had expected—our kiss had been a whim.

And it wasn't our fault—it was the fireworks. And the Ferris wheel. And everything about that night that made the evening feel so magical, so full of possibilities.

Until reality hit hard and we remembered all the reasons why nothing was possible between us.

Because Jackson didn't feel that way about me.

And—I told myself sternly—I didn't feel that way about him.

And we worked together.

And I was leaving town soon.

And . . . well, I was out of ands, but I knew if I dug deep enough, I'd find a million more.

Jackson and I were never meant to be more than awkward acquaintances. Despite having found some common ground recently, we would never work in the long run. I was his little sister's flighty friend, and he was my adolescent fantasy that had died a long time ago—we didn't have anything real to base a relationship on.

I just needed a little time to get my head on straight and everything would get back to normal. What better way to start than with my three days off? Maybe that was all I needed to go through a Jackson detox.

"It's about time you were getting up," my mom said cheerfully to me as I walked into the kitchen. "I was just about to wake you."

I glanced at the time, seeing it was about twenty minutes to ten. Okay, yeah, I had slept half the morning away, but I'd also had a late night.

"It's okay, Penny said she wouldn't get into town till around noon," I said, grabbing a box of cereal out of the cupboard.

"Oh, I hope she makes it in time," my mother went on. "Our appointment is at eleven."

"What appointment?" I looked at my mother suspiciously. She seemed way too happy this morning.

She giggled. "Well, I was going to wait until everyone got here to surprise you, but I may as well tell you now. We're going wedding dress shopping today!"

"What?" My jaw dropped, and the cereal I was pouring overflowed and spilled out onto the counter. "What are you talking about? No, we aren't."

"Yes, we are!" She clapped her hands together. "I made an appointment last week and your grandma and Aunt Christine are coming. Oh, and Melissa since she's back in town. And when you told me Penny was coming back for a few days, I invited her too. I left her a message yesterday. I hope she got it . . ."

My mom droned on about her plans of bridal grandeur, but I tuned her out as I frantically grabbed my charging phone off the kitchen counter.

Sure enough, I had five missed calls from Penny. And several text messages.

Red alert! one of them read. *Your mom called me last night and left a message. She's planning on surprising you with wedding dress shopping today. Have you really not told her yet?? I'm leaving now to offer my moral support, but man, this is going to be a disaster.*

I swallowed thickly. A disaster was right.

"Mom—" Before I could fess up, fake sickness, or do anything to stop the onslaught of well-wishes and phony bridal bliss that was headed my way today, the doorbell rang.

"Oh! That's probably Christine." She rushed out of the kitchen, and the next thing I knew she was greeting Tucker's mom and my sweet eighty-nine-year-old grandmother at the door.

I groaned and buried my face in my hands.

Talk about the opposite of saved by the bell.

CHAPTER 28

JACKSON

The bell above the door dinged as I stepped into the Blushing Bridal Boutique. The place was hopping, which wasn't a surprise, given it was a holiday weekend. Plenty of people were probably still off of work, with relatives in town visiting and eager to do family things like shop for wedding dresses.

As I crossed the rose-patterned carpet, I felt the same unease I always did when stepping into this place. I wasn't sure if it was all the pink, or all the flowers, or all the white, but something about it made me feel as out of place as a bull in a china shop. A grungy bull in a china shop. I glanced down at my slightly worn jeans with a splattering or two of grease on the thighs.

"Hey, Lorelei," I greeted the shop owner when I reached the counter and set the large paper bag down.

"Got your lunch order right here."

"Wonderful. Vivian, please." Lorelei picked the bag up and handed it to another employee, who immediately whisked it away to the back room. I resisted the urge to chuckle. No doubt Lorelei didn't want the hearty smell of homestyle cooking to infringe on the too-sweet rose scent that seemed to hang in the air of this place. Although, I thought the savory smells were an improvement.

"Thank you, Jackson." Lorelei handed me a tip, which I knew from past experience would be generous. "As always, we appreciate your punctuality."

"Anytime." I shoved the bills in my pocket with a nod. "Hey, is it okay if I refill these brochures for the Stonewall Inn while I'm here?"

"Of course!" Lorelei nodded her approval. "They've been flying off the rack ever since the Ellis-James wedding took place there. All my brides seem to want to book the venue." She sniffed. "Even if it is a barn."

I resisted the urge to laugh as I thanked her. Lorelei might be a bit of a snob, but deep down, I knew she was also a softy who appreciated her employees and showed it by treating them to lunch once a month, hence her reoccurring order with the Stonewall Inn.

I headed toward the entrance where a rack of various wedding paraphernalia was displayed under a bulletin board with an assortment of posters and notices of Halften news. Local events, lost pets, items for sale, but none of that caught my attention.

Instead, I glanced at a bridal party around the corner *oohing* and *ahhing* over a bride decked out in a white dress. I wouldn't have looked twice, if not for the familiar head of red hair above the sea of white.

Audrey?

I blinked, wondering if maybe what happened between us the other night was causing me to see things. I'd honestly been trying not to think about her all morning. Trying not to relive the heat of our kiss and the un-July-like coldness that seemed to have taken its place ever since.

But it was Audrey, all right.

In a wedding dress. Standing on a little stage while a small group of women gazed up at her with adoration. I recognized Tucker's mom, Christine Wiley, among them, as well as Audrey's mother and Melissa.

Despite myself, I stared. What was Audrey doing trying on wedding dresses when she wasn't even engaged anymore?

Even though I knew she had her reasons for not wanting to tell her family about her broken engagement, this seemed like taking it too far. How much worse was it going to be to tell the truth if she'd already picked out a wedding dress?

Then another even more uncomfortable thought lodged itself into my mind.

Did Audrey and her fiancé get back together? The thought made my mouth go dry and I forced a swallow.

No, that was ridiculous. She would have told me, right?

Although, would she? We were coworkers, not friends. Honestly, I wasn't sure what we were anymore. Sometime over the past few weeks, we had started sharing personal things with each other. But maybe Audrey had sensed my shifting feelings and had been searching for a way to let me down easy that she and

Mercer had gotten back together.

Maybe that's why she was so adamant that our kiss had been a mistake?

Had I kissed an engaged woman?

A real-engaged, not a fake-engaged, woman?

It seemed laughable that I even had to make that distinction, but here we were.

As the thought settled, I hated it and searched for a sign it wasn't true. I studied Audrey, trying to catch a glimpse of her left hand. Was she wearing a different ring than the one I gave her?

But I couldn't tell because her left hand was buried in the flowing skirt that she lifted as she turned one way and then the other, modeling the dress for her family while they clapped and crooned.

Who could blame them?

Audrey looked absolutely breathtaking. For a moment, I forgot all about searching for her ring and just took her in. Heat flooded my chest, much like it had moments before I'd pulled her into my arms the other night and kissed her.

The dress flattered her perfectly. It was simple, yet elegant. Not one of those horrendously poofy things where the bride had to walk sideways just to get through the door.

The bodice was a crisscross pattern of silk that dipped into a heart above her chest, and the skirt hugged her curves perfectly while flaring out in a dramatic swoosh at the bottom.

She ran her hands down the front of the dress, and as she spread her fingers, I caught sight of a not very brilliant, yet very familiar ring.

I almost gave a sigh of relief, until my heart picked up its pace for an entirely different reason.

Audrey was standing here in a wedding dress while wearing *my* ring.

I should have been horrified, but the thought flared a weird sort of pride in my chest. And for a split second, I imagined it wasn't all make believe. I envisioned myself crossing the salon and taking her into my arms as if I had the right to.

"Okay, as entertaining as it is to wait and see how long you stand there staring at her like an idiot, I actually have to get through." A familiar, slightly sarcastic voice behind me made me almost shoot out of my skin.

I turned and faced my sister, Penny, who simply smirked. "Wow, someone's jumpy."

Even though I was surprised to see my sister, I was also relieved. She was bound to have answers. I grabbed her arm and pulled her to the side so we were completely out of view—and most importantly—out of earshot. "Why is Audrey trying on wedding dresses when she's not even engaged?" I whispered harshly.

"Wow, calm down. I know it seems kind of crazy, but it's not her fault. She was ambushed. Her mother made the appointment and planned it as a surprise."

"You obviously knew about it. Why didn't you tell her?"

"Because I only found out about it late last night after my event ended." Penny placed a defensive hand on her hip. "Audrey's mom left me a message. I guess she only found out yesterday that I was going to be in town and decided to invite me for Audrey's 'big day.' Anyway, I did try to warn Audrey, but at that point, it was too late.

She'd already been bombarded. I think finding out that I was coming was the only thing that saved her from having a panic attack."

"Why didn't she just tell everyone then, before coming here? That was the perfect opportunity if she had her whole family there."

"Have you seen her grandma?" Penny pointed a finger toward the group who was no longer in our line of vision. "She's, like, a hundred. Do you really think she wanted to risk giving her a heart attack?"

I opened my mouth to say more but Penny wasn't done. "Besides, why do you care? And what are you even doing here? I highly doubt you were invited."

"I wasn't. I was dropping off an order and then I was refilling these." I held up the stack of brochures for the Stonewall Inn event barn and pointed to the rack.

"I'll help." Penny snatched the brochures, grabbed the first one off the stack, plucked a stray thumbtack off the bulletin board and pierced it through the flyer—right over the top of a now-outdated ad showcasing Camden Clarke's smiling face.

Mayor Clarke invites you to Halften's Hometown Fourth of July Festival! Those words disappeared under the rustically charming image of the Stonewall Inn's event barn, fully decked out for a wedding.

"Perfect." Penny grinned at her handiwork, stuffed the remaining brochures into their spot on the rack, then brushed her hands together. "Your work here is done."

"You could probably go to jail for defacing our beloved mayor," I said with a snicker, not missing the way Penny had positioned the tack so it would have made a hole in Camden Clarke's head under my brochure. Even though I didn't understand why Penny hated her former classmate—now our mayor—her wrath always made for good entertainment.

She just snorted. "And you could go to jail for stalking women in bridal shops and drooling over them."

"I was *not* drooling—"

"Uh-huh." Penny's voice was dubious as she eyed me critically. "What's gotten into you? What do you care if Audrey's family thinks she's engaged?"

"I care because I care about Aud . . ."

Audrey's name died on my lips the moment she rounded the corner and exclaimed, "Penny! You're here." She shrieked and pulled her friend in for a tight hug.

I took a large step back and stood there awkwardly while the best friends greeted each other. I considered sneaking out the door while I had the chance, but Audrey let go of Penny and faced me with a confused look on her face.

"Jackson? What are you doing here?"

"I was dropping off an order and refilling these," I said again, almost robotically, then pointed to the brochures stacked neatly in the rack.

"Oh, gosh, you must think I'm completely insane." Audrey smoothed one hand down the white skirt of the wedding dress she was still wearing, while placing the other to her forehead. "I promise, this is not what it looks like—" Her cheeks turned as pink as the walls, making her look like she could be the bridal store's mascot.

I couldn't blame her for being flustered. Things had been weird between us ever since the Fourth. Add in the missing money from the restaurant—which I still hadn't gotten to the bottom of—and now me showing up while she fake-shopped for wedding dresses, and it seemed we were doomed to never again have a boring moment between us.

"Relax." I tried to lighten the situation. "Penny told me how it was a misunderstanding." I dropped my voice. "But seriously, Audrey, you've got to tell everyone the truth."

"I know." Guilt filled her eyes. "And trust me, I will. I just can't do it here."

"Don't worry, I have a plan." Penny held up a few clear garment bags draped across one arm that I only noticed now. One of the dresses inside was a light shade of pink dusted with sparkles and another seemed to be sporting a lot of ruffles. "I intercepted Lorelei just in time. I picked out the ugliest dresses I could find and told her you were dead set on trying them on. And when you do, I'm going to pretend to love them. Hopefully I can cause enough contention that you won't be pressured into picking a dress today."

"Thank you, you're the best." Audrey collapsed into Penny for another hug, clearly grateful for her friend's plan to put her in ugly dresses and cause a fight with her family.

"Good luck with that." I shook my head. "I doubt anyone is going to buy that now that they've seen her in this." I pointed to the dress Audrey was wearing. It was perfect for her. I admired her for one more second, then looked up to find both girls staring at me.

"I mean"—I rubbed the back of my neck—"I heard the way they were all going crazy over that dress."

Audrey gazed down at the dress and sighed. "I really do love this dress . . . I almost wish I hadn't tried it on."

Her voice was tinged with sadness, and I couldn't help but wonder how this day was making her feel. It couldn't be fun trying on wedding dresses knowing you weren't going to get a chance to wear one. Or was it the fact that she wasn't marrying Mercer that filled her voice with that wistful longing?

"It's just a dress." I shrugged, trying to make her feel better. "You'd look just as beautiful in any of the other ones in this store."

I heard the words as they left my mouth and I knew how they sounded, yet somehow, I didn't regret them. Not when Audrey's mouth dropped for a split second and then spread into a small smile. The blush tinging her cheeks was the perfect shade. My heart warmed at the sight and I didn't bother to look at Penny, who was probably staring at me like I'd lost my mind again. Let her. All I cared about in this moment was Audrey knowing she was enough just as she was.

"What's the holdup?" A new, slightly annoyed voice caused Audrey to jump and me to turn.

"Nothing, Mom." Audrey stepped away from me. "Penny just got here and she got the other dresses from Lorelei."

"Yup, got 'em right here, Mrs. Miller," Penny said brightly, holding up the garment bags.

"Wonderful." Mrs. Miller's creased brow softened. "So glad you could make it, Penny. And . . ." She turned to me and her smile dropped.

"Jackson just gave me a ride," Penny said, then began shooing me away with her hands, like I was some kind of stray dog. "Thanks, Jackson, you can go now."

I shot her a puzzled look, wondering why she'd lied

about that, when Penny gave me a look of her own. One that said, *You're not helping things.*

Right. I guess the last thing Audrey's mom wanted to see was another man ogling her daughter in her wedding dress. Not that I was ogling, but I had made Audrey blush. Yeah, I had definitely overstayed my welcome.

"No problem." I waved a hand and headed for the door. "Have fun."

Once outside, I took a deep breath and shook my head. Of all the days for Lorelei to place a lunch order.

CHAPTER 29

JACKSON

"What the heck is going on with you and Audrey?" Penny attacked me with the question the moment I walked into our parents' living room that night. The accusation in her tone made me instantly regret taking the night off of work for a family dinner, even if I hadn't seen my little sister in months.

"Nothing," I said quickly, but she just raised her eyebrows at me. So I tried to be more convincing. "Nothing's going on. I don't even know what you're talking about."

"Don't play dumb." Penny eyed me as she sank down on the sofa. "What was that earlier?" She lowered her voice in what I could only assume was supposed to be an imitation of me. "*Oh, Audrey, you'd look beautiful no matter what you wear.*"

"I did not say that." I frowned. "You're exaggerating."

"Whatever. Close enough. And don't even get me started on the way you were staring at her when I walked in." Each of her next words was followed by a dramatic pause. "So. Much. Longing."

I scoffed this time because there was no other way to respond to her suggestion. "You must have been imagining things."

"Nuh-uh. Have you forgotten what I do for a living? Romance is kind of my thing. And I know when someone is pining."

"I was *not* pining. I was just confused by why she was trying on wedding dresses when she claims she's no longer engaged."

"Is that jealousy I hear?" Penny's voice turned singsong. "Wow, it's worse than I thought."

"Whatever you think, it's not that," I shot back immediately, although my words sounded dishonest to my own ears.

Penny shifted on the couch and inclined her head, like she was weighing just how much of my bluff to call me on. Finally, she settled on an innocent question. "Seriously, though, how has it been working with her at the restaurant? I was honestly shocked when I found out you'd offered her a job there."

I scratched the back of my neck. "Technically, Tucker offered her the job."

"Sure, but you must've had a say in it." She spread a hand. "So how's it going?"

"Good—great, actually. I mean, she's really improved business for the event side of things. And she knows her stuff. She brings an enthusiasm to everything she does that's just . . ." My words trailed off, not quite able to find the right word to fully encompass all that was Audrey.

Penny nodded. "I know what you mean. When she decides to do something, she gives it her all. She's always been like that. And I can tell she really likes working there. She was talking about it a bunch today." Penny's brow wrinkled. "Although she said something about missing money. She seemed really worried about that."

I raked a hand through my hair. "Yeah, her register's been short a few times. At first, I didn't think much of it. Mistakes happen, especially when it's busy, but it's kind of become a thing."

Penny's eyes widened. "You don't really think she's stealing from you, do you?"

"No." I shook my head. And I meant it. The more I thought about it, the more convinced I was. "Audrey's not a thief." There weren't a lot of things I was certain of right now, but deep in my heart, I knew that was the truth.

"Of course she's not." Penny's words held the same certainty as mine. "But I can tell she's really worried she made a mistake."

"That seemed like the logical explanation at first. But now"—I shook my head—"it seems like too much to just be a mistake."

"You think someone's trying to set her up?"

"I'm not really sure what I think yet. But we'll figure it out."

"I'm sure you will," Penny said with confidence, more than I felt. "So work's good then?"

"Yeah, work's good."

Penny draped her arms over the top of the couch and

looked up at me expectantly. "Are you going to tell me what *else* is going on, or do I have to force it out of Audrey the next time I see her?" She looked smug. "We tell each other everything, you know."

"You're really making me regret taking the night off to come over and see you." I should have known she wouldn't let it go—and that business at the restaurant wasn't really what she was prying about. And while a part of me wanted to shut it down and leave the room, the other part of me wanted her opinion. After all, she probably knew Audrey better than anyone.

So I sank down on the couch next to her.

Penny grinned, but when I didn't say anything else, she placed her hands behind her head, leaning back against the couch. "I'm waiting. And don't worry, I have aaaaallll night."

"Fine, okay." I sat forward, forearms resting on my thighs as I stared at the ground. "Something happened between us, but it doesn't matter because it was a mistake."

"Hold up. *What* happened, exactly?"

"I may have kissed her. On the Fourth of July."

"Wait—*you* kissed *her*? She didn't attack you like she did at that party before graduation?"

"You know about that?"

She rolled her eyes. "Like I said, we tell each other everything. So *you* kissed her?"

"Yes, I kissed her. But she kissed me back."

"And?"

"We got interrupted." I threw my hands in the air. "And then things got weird. She said it was a mistake—"

"Was it?"

"I guess." I looked down at my hands. "I don't know."

Penny sighed. "So let me get this straight. You kissed the girl who used to have a massive crush on you and who also just got out of a super-serious relationship? And then you let her think it was 'a mistake'?"

"I didn't say that. She did."

"Of course she did if she thought you were backpedaling! You're such an idiot. Look, just answer me this, do you want something more with her?"

"I . . . I—" My shoulders dropped along with my tone, my next word coming out in a gravelly whisper. "Yes."

Instantly, I knew it was true. Despite all the reasons I'd been telling myself it was a bad idea. All the excuses I'd been making. Deep down, they weren't enough to stop me from wanting to take a shot with her. To see if we had what it took to be something more—something amazing.

"Yes," I said again, louder. "I do. I at least want to try."

"Wow." Penny was silent for a moment, as if digesting my confession.

I couldn't blame her. I would've had a hard time believing it myself a few months ago, but here we were.

She finally found her voice again. "If that's really how you feel, you need to tell her straight up. Audrey is way too vulnerable right now to get messed around—"

"I wasn't just messing around." My words came out defensive. Not because of Penny, but because it made me wonder if that was what Audrey thought—that I'd just been messing around with her. The thought turned my stomach. No wonder she'd backed away. I felt like such an idiot.

"Okay." Penny regarded me for a moment, and I resisted the urge to cringe. She seemed to be weighing my inner turmoil with that so-called sixth sense she had. Her tone softened. "I believe you. And I know things haven't been easy for you since the whole Gwyneth fiasco, but listen to me. You need to be careful with Audrey. You already broke her heart once—"

I opened my mouth to protest, but she held up her hand, cutting me off.

"And I'm not saying that was your fault. But if you do it again? This time, it will be." She exhaled deeply. "She was just betrayed by Mercer. If you hurt her too . . ." She shook her head, but I got the picture. A person could only handle so much disappointment before they stopped letting themselves get hurt in the first place.

"Is she still in love with him?" I asked softly.

"Mercer? I don't know."

I managed a small laugh. "I thought you guys told each other everything."

"We do. But her and Mercer?" Penny spread her hands and shrugged. "I could never really read them as a couple. On the surface, things seemed great, but underneath, it always seemed like something wasn't working."

I nodded slowly. That sounded like me and Gwyneth. Although maybe I was the only one who had really thought we worked, even on the surface.

"If I do go for it with Audrey . . . What if—" I swallowed slowly, then forced myself to ask the question. "What if I'm not enough for her?"

There it was. The real reason behind all my excuses. The real reason behind why I threw myself into my work, leaving room for nothing else. The real reason I hadn't dated since Gwyneth. The real reason, deep down, that I thought she had made a move on Tucker.

"Oh, Jackson," Penny's voice turned soft and full of sadness. "Is that really what you think?"

I shrugged. I didn't want her pity. But if I was going to go for it with Audrey, I did want to know if she thought I had a shot.

"Listen to me," Penny went on. "Gwyneth wasn't enough for herself. That's why she did what she did. Nothing you could've done would've changed that."

"But if I do this, if I ask Audrey to be with me, I'll be asking her to stay in Halften, to give up on her dreams."

"How do you know that *isn't* her dream?" Penny asked softly, and when I didn't answer, she stood up and squeezed my shoulder. "Talk to her. You'll be glad you did."

With that, Penny left the room to go help our parents with dinner, although really, I knew she was giving me some time alone to think.

So I did. I thought long and hard about Audrey and all the ways she had changed things since she blew back to town.

The hard things, like how she challenged me and made me realize that for too long I'd been surviving, but not really living.

The good things, like how she pulled me out of my comfort zone and given me the best Fourth of July I'd had in years.

Even the things I didn't quite understand, like how when I thought about the future, it seemed dull without her.

And as I thought, a crazy idea came to me.

In that moment, I knew exactly what I needed to do.

CHAPTER 30

AUDREY

The day after wedding dress shopping, I was grateful I had another day off of work. I needed a breather—from Jackson, from everything, really—to clear my head.

I spent the day with Penny, and to my surprise, she didn't mention Jackson's and my weird behavior in the bridal shop. Maybe she hadn't noticed, or more likely, she was choosing to not get involved. Which was probably for the best.

We had a carefree day spent catching up in our favorite spots in town. It was exactly what I needed.

After parting ways early that evening because Penny had to leave first thing in the morning, my head felt clearer than it had in a while.

Maybe it was the wedding-dress-shop fiasco.

Maybe it was reconnecting with Penny.

Maybe it was having a few days off and finally taking the time to clear my head.

Whatever it was, that night as I entered my parents' kitchen, I knew it was time.

"Hey, Mom, can I talk to you?" I asked as I hovered in the doorway.

"Of course, princess. In fact, your timing couldn't be better. I was just going through the wedding dress pictures, and I really think once you take a step back, you'll realize the first dress was the clear winner." She shook her head. "Honestly, if Penny hadn't filled your head with those ridiculous styles, I think we could have placed an order."

"Penny was just being a good friend, Mom."

"Oh, honey." Her tone turned condescending. "I think we can all agree that telling your best friend to wear this on her wedding day"—she pointed to a picture of me on her computer wearing the dress I'd mentally dubbed the Frilly Lizard—"is not being a good friend."

I wanted to laugh, but tears leaked out of my eyes. "You're right, it's hideous. That's why Penny picked it."

My mom gaped at me. "She was trying to sabotage you?" She shook her head. "I should have known. She's clearly jealous. After all, Mercer *is* quite the catch—"

"No, she wasn't trying to sabotage me. She knew I couldn't pick a dress yesterday because"—I sucked in a deep breath—"there's not going to be a wedding, Mom. Not for me and Mercer—we called it off."

"What?" She gasped, a hand flying to her chest. "Why would you do that? Oh, Audrey, this isn't about that Jackson boy again, is it? I knew you working for him was a bad idea—"

"No, Mom, it had nothing to do with Jackson. We broke up before I even came back here. In Chicago."

"I don't understand . . . why would you break up with Mercer?" If I had told my mother that I had plans to assassinate Santa Claus, she couldn't have been more appalled.

"I didn't break up with Mercer, Mom. He broke up with me."

"Oh, Audrey. What did you do?" Instantly, the dots connected in her eyes. Of course, I hadn't broken up with Mercer—I'd scared him off, just like she'd always feared. Not giving me time to answer, she started talking again, almost frantically, holding on to the hope that it could be fixed. "Surely, it must all be a misunderstanding. You two are perfect for each other."

"That's the thing, Mom, we're *not*. I'm not perfect for him and he's definitely not perfect for me."

"Don't be absurd." My mother's tone turned harsh. "Mercer is handsome, rich, successful, well traveled . . ." She went into a long list of Mercer's finer qualities, many of which stemmed from his money and family connections.

"I'm not denying that," I said. "But I don't care about those things. He wasn't the perfect guy for me. He was the guy that you wanted for me. That's why Mercer realized we were wrong for each other before I did." I swallowed. "I was so worried about disappointing you, I didn't want to admit what I really wanted."

"So your failed engagement is *my* fault?" Her voice took on an icy edge.

"No, of course not. I accept full responsibility for it. I'm just trying to explain to you what happened. How I let it get so far." I paused and looked her in the eye. "And even though I was sad to see it end . . . I wasn't sad that it ended."

My mom was silent for a moment, then she shut her laptop screen with a snap. "Well, I guess all my hard work was for nothing."

"Mom, really, it's for the best—"

"Oh, Audrey, don't be stupid. You'll never find anyone as wonderful as Mercer. Never." She stood and regarded me coolly. "But maybe it *was* for the best. Because you clearly didn't deserve him."

There it was. The truth I had always expected. That my mom truly thought that a proposal from Mercer was the best thing I had ever accomplished in my life. That in her eyes, he was worth more than me.

I sat there stunned for a moment, doused by the ice of her words.

"You're right." Finally, I found my voice but my words came out quietly, although they grew in strength. "I didn't deserve him. I deserve better. Better than someone who was always going to pick his career over me. Better than someone who wasn't man enough to have my back when it really mattered. Better than chasing after a dream that wasn't even mine in the first place."

"What does that have to do with anything?" my mother spat back. "What are you even talking about?"

I held up a hand. "It doesn't matter." And it didn't. Even though my mother didn't have the whole story, it wouldn't have changed anything if she did. She would have chosen the side of influence, money, and power—just like Mercer had.

I stood and looked my mother square in the eye. "I

deserve more than what Mercer was willing to offer me. I made my choice. You can either accept that or you can't." I lifted a shoulder. "I'll be fine either way."

And for once, I meant it. After all these years of trying to placate my mother. Trying to fix all her broken dreams. Trying to be someone I would never be—I was finally done.

My mother's mouth dropped open and she stared at me like she didn't know me. Which, I guess, was fair—she didn't know this version of me. I'd never really stood up to her before. Never told her that I didn't need her approval.

"I'll give you some time to think about it," I said softly.

And then I turned and walked away.

The next day was about the opposite of the day before. Penny left town again, and part of me had wanted to beg to join her for the last part of her book tour.

Anything seemed better than sticking around here and getting the cold shoulder from my mother.

As I ate breakfast that morning, I heard my mother crying dramatically into her phone from her bedroom—apparently, she was spreading the bad news about Mercer's and my breakup to the rest of the family. By the way she was carrying on, it seemed like she had made her choice and she was still Team Mercer all the way.

With a sigh, I washed my bowl in the sink, then grabbed my laptop bag and headed to my car. I wasn't sure how I was going to spend my day, but I knew I wasn't going to stay at home. My mother and I needed space from each other, that much was certain.

I almost wished I was scheduled to work, but it was Monday and the restaurant was closed. I could have gone in anyway and worked on some scheduling, but part of me wasn't ready to face Jackson yet. Plus, he had asked me to lay low these past few days to give him time to sort out what had happened with the missing money. And as curious as I was to find out if he had discovered anything about that, I was also worried what it meant if he hadn't.

But mostly, I wasn't sure I was ready to spend time in the office with him, just the two of us.

I'd told him our kiss was a mistake, but the thing was, I was starting to think this whole summer had been a mistake. A long, uncomfortable detour that I would have been better off not taking.

I spent the day at a coffee shop, searching for jobs and even applying for a few, but nothing truly sparked my interest—at least not when I compared it to what I was doing now.

With a sigh, I shut my laptop.

My time in Halften was meant to be a temporary regrouping, but instead I'd grown attached to a job and a man that were never meant to be mine.

I logged in to my bank account, heartened when I saw the fruits of my hard work in dollars and cents. At least one thing hadn't been a waste. If I did decide to join Penny for the last part of her tour, she wouldn't have to pay my way.

With the coffee shop closing for the day, I packed up my things and headed for home.

I was relieved to see that my dad's car was in the

driveway when I pulled up—and that my mom's wasn't.

But I was most surprised to see a familiar black truck parked off to the side. And even more surprised to see Jackson sitting on our front porch swing.

CHAPTER 31

JACKSON

"Jackson?" Audrey shut her car door and furrowed her brow as she headed up the front walk toward me. "What are you doing here? Did you find out what happened to the money?"

"That is part of what I want to talk to you about. And a few other things . . ." I stood, hoping I didn't look as nervous as I felt. "I thought it would be better to do in person. Do you have a minute?"

"Sure." She stepped up onto the porch, her green eyes unable to hide her curiosity. "Is here okay?"

"Sure." I followed her as she sat on the porch swing, although half of me wondered if it would be better if we took a walk. I had built up a lot of nervous energy sitting here waiting for her for the last half hour. At least her dad had answered the door, and he'd been friendlier to me than her mother had been at the bridal shop.

"So what's up?" Audrey settled her hands on the top of her jean shorts, seemingly relaxed, but her eyes held questions.

"So here's the thing—" I wiped my own hands on my jean legs, trying to decide what to lead with. Penny had given me a lot to think on, but she certainly hadn't given me a road map on how to move forward with it. "I did something, and I think it's good, but now I'm a little worried maybe I should have talked to you first."

"Oh?" Audrey tilted her head and lifted her brow.

"Yeah, I mean, I wasn't trying to go over your head or anything, I just felt like I needed all the facts in place before I—" My words were cut off by the sound of an engine and tires coming up the gravel driveway. Both Audrey and I turned in the direction of headlights, still not quite bright in the dusk.

"What the—" Audrey stood up quickly, then said, "Hang on a sec."

"No problem. Take your time." I was kind of relieved to have a breather. Maybe now I could get my thoughts in better order.

As she bounded down the porch, the car engine died and the door opened.

A young man stepped out and Audrey stopped in her tracks, so abruptly I wondered if something was wrong.

"Mercer?" The name on her lips hit me like a ton of bricks.

Even though I knew who he was, I stared. What was her ex doing here?

"Hey, Audrey." Mercer strode forward. "I hope I didn't catch you at a bad time."

"I'm just so surprised to see you." Audrey still hadn't moved, staring as if in a daze. "What's going on?"

It was the million-dollar question that I knew the answer to, even if Audrey didn't.

Mercer glanced up at me, then back at Audrey, looking uncomfortable that he had an audience. "I just really need to talk to you."

"I'll give you guys a minute." I stood up and headed down the steps. My movement seemed to snap Audrey out of her Mercer-induced stupor.

"Wait, Jackson." Audrey looked from me to Mercer, clearly unsure how she got into a situation where she needed to have two big conversations with two different guys.

"It's okay." I held my hands up and managed a smile as I passed by, letting her know I wasn't offended. "I'll catch you later."

"Mercer Van Higgens." Mercer held out his hand as I neared him on my way to my truck, clearly raised too well to let a little awkwardness stop him from properly introducing himself. Or maybe he was as curious about me as I was about him.

"Jackson." I accepted his handshake but said nothing else. The guy was all polish, slicked-back hair, shiny leather shoes, pressed dress pants and crisp polo with a fancy logo. He was built like he knew his way around the gym and smelled like his cologne cost more than all the clothes on my back combined.

"Jackson's my, uh . . ." Audrey stepped in, clearly feeling like she needed to be polite too. But her words trailed away as if she was searching for the right way to introduce me to her ex.

"Her boss," I said, helping her out. No need to make this any more awkward than it already was.

"Uh, right." Audrey went with it, tucking a lock of hair behind her ear.

"That's great." Mercer's charm was suddenly reinstated. "I'm so glad you were able to find a job here after, well, you know . . ."

"Yeah, it's been good."

"Can't wait to hear all about it." Mercer gestured with his hand toward the porch, and I took that as my official cue to go.

"See you tomorrow at work," I said to Audrey, managing a smile. "We can talk then."

"Okay, great." Audrey smiled too, although hers looked a bit sheepish. I wondered how much she guessed about my intent coming here, but it really didn't matter now.

If Mercer was here, one thing was obvious. I was too late. A dude didn't drive up from Chicago to talk to his ex unless he wanted her back. Even I knew that, as unromantic and out of touch with relationships as I was.

After I started my truck and headed down the driveway, I caught a glimpse in my rearview mirror of Audrey and Mercer settling themselves on the porch swing, like some weird cast change in a play.

Understudy, out.

Leading man, in.

Because if Audrey was still holding on to feelings for Mercer, it looked like all her dreams were about to come true.

CHAPTER 32

AUDREY

As I settled myself back on the porch swing with Mercer, I got a weird sense of déjà vu, having just sat there with Jackson.

But somehow, it felt all wrong.

I had no idea what Jackson had been about to tell me. I assumed it was something to do with the missing money and the restaurant, but he'd said that was only part of it. And he'd seemed nervous. Had he also come to talk about whatever had been growing between us?

Either way, I had no space in my brain to worry about it now.

Because Mercer was here. On my doorstep. Weeks after ending things and changing our lives forever.

I waited for my heart to skip a beat. To get excited. Or even to get angry, considering how things had ended.

Yet I felt nothing.

And suddenly, I knew everything I'd told my mom last night about Mercer and me not being right for each other—about me being in love with the idea of him, but not really him—was one hundred percent accurate.

Because here he was, sitting in front of me, the possibility of him wanting to reconcile concretely in front of me.

And my heart longed for nothing but for the man who'd just left to turn back around and take Mercer's place on this porch swing.

This knowledge made me want to breathe a sigh of relief and scream in frustration at the same time.

But I couldn't do either, because I needed to deal with the man sitting in front of me. And even though he had betrayed me weeks ago, I racked my brain searching for ideas of how to let him down easy.

"You look good," Mercer said, but even through his compliment, his nerves showed. He was not here to make small talk and we both knew it.

"Thanks. You look good too."

"Thanks." He smiled, and opened his mouth to say more, but unfortunately, mine beat him to it.

"I mean that in a non-fiancée type of way, of course." My mouth started going, trying to cover up the awkwardness the way it liked to, even though it usually just tended to add to it. "You look good, but just like platonically good. I mean, I'm assuming work is going well?"

"Yeah, it's great, actually. I've been—"

Even though I knew I should let him go on about his latest feats working for the sleazy lawyer who tried to feel me up, I couldn't take it anymore.

"Mercer, I'm so sorry, but I can't marry you!"

"What?" He blinked at me, clearly confused. Which I guess was fair. He hadn't even gotten to the groveling I-made-a-mistake-please-give-us-another-chance part of his speech yet.

I swallowed. Took a deep breath. And tried again. "I mean, I know why you're here, and while it's sweet of you to try to win me back—even after you were a complete coward—I'm sorry. This time apart made me realize that you were right. We aren't right for each other."

"I'm not here to ask you to take me back." Mercer stared at me like I was a visitor from another planet. And like he wasn't too happy about me calling him a coward. "Is that why you think I came?"

I swiped a wave of hair behind my ear. "Well, yeah, I just assumed. I mean why else would you show up here when you're supposed to be taking your bar exam in a week." A nervous laugh escaped me. "I mean, if you just wanted to check up on how I was doing, you could have called."

Mercer shook his head impatiently, his too-strong cologne wafting toward me. "This is why." He pulled his phone out of his pocket, then handed it to me.

I perused the screen, reading the message on one of the popular social media apps that I had all but abandoned when I'd had to crawl back home with my tail between my legs. I mean, not much to highlight when you get fired, dumped, and have to move back in with your parents all in the same month.

Mercer, the message read.

I'm not sure if you will get this since you don't know me, but I thought it was only right to make you aware of the situation.

I'm worried about Audrey Miller, who I believe is your former fiancée. She has returned to her hometown and seems to be living in a delusion. She is continuing to plan your wedding and is telling everyone that the two of you are still engaged.

Although her mental state has always been questionable, I fear that your breakup may have sent her over the edge. I worry the longer she lives in this delusion that she may become a danger to herself, you, or those in your life.

The words in front of me swam, and my lungs didn't seem to be taking in quite enough air. But the true knife to my heart wasn't the message itself, but rather the name signed underneath and the profile picture associated with it in the top left corner.

Sincerely,
Jackson Crowe

CHAPTER 33

AUDREY

"Audrey, you know we broke up, right?" Mercer's pitying, yet slightly fearful, words prodded me out of my shock and caused me to tear my eyes away from the screen.

"Yes, of course. That isn't what it sounds like." I practically threw the phone back at him, wanting to get the ugly words out of my sight.

"So you haven't been going around telling everyone that we're still engaged?" There was more disbelief in Mercer's voice than relief. And I couldn't help but notice that he was sitting on the edge of the swing, about as far away as he could get from me—like he was afraid I might lose it at any moment and start attacking him. Considering he had a good seventy pounds on me, he really was kind of a coward.

"Well, I was—" I said. "I mean, I did. Just for a time, but it's not why you think—"

"Audrey." Mercer's tone turned admonishing. "You know that's crazy, right?"

Crazy.

There it was again. The word I couldn't get away from, especially not here.

But to know after everything we'd gone through, everything we'd shared recently, that was really what Jackson thought of me?

Her mental state has always been questionable . . .

"Audrey?" Mercer's worried question brought me back to the moment.

"Sorry." I gave my head a quick shake, banishing all thoughts of Jackson. At least for now. I needed to deal with the issue at hand—which meant convincing Mercer he wasn't dealing with a grade-A crazy ex-girlfriend, despite the evidence he had supporting it. "Look, I promise I am not delusional. I am fully aware of and support our breakup."

"You do?" Mercer seemed taken aback, like he couldn't believe I had just said that.

"I do." I nodded, hoping he could see my sincerity. "And the only reason I didn't tell everyone about our breakup right away was because I didn't want everyone feeling sorry for me at my cousin's wedding. And I was hoping to spread the bad news out a bit." I sucked in a deep breath. "To be honest, I was mainly worried about disappointing my mom—you know how much she's always loved you."

Mercer's face softened. "Your mother is lovely."

I resisted the urge to laugh as the strange thought

popped into my head that Mercer and my mother would have made a better couple than he and I ever did.

I stood. "Yeah, well, do us both a favor and get out of here before she comes home and sees you. She'll definitely jump to the same conclusion as I did that you came here to reconcile, and I don't know if she could stand the shock of losing you twice in one week." I pictured my mom pulling up the drive, racing from the car, and grabbing on to Mercer's leg, sobbing, while begging him not to go.

"Right. Of course." Mercer stood up quickly. "The last thing I want is to cause more confusion."

I laughed wearily. "You and me both."

"So Audrey." Mercer paused on the top porch step. "We're good?"

"Yeah, we're good. Look, I'll even prove it to you." I pulled my phone out of my pocket, swiped back and forth on the screen a few times, then pulled up my own long-neglected social media profile. With the click of a few buttons, I made Mercer's and my breakup official. Where my relationship status had just said "Engaged" moments ago—although Mercer's name and profile link had disappeared from it the day after he had dumped me—now it said "Single."

"See? I know we aren't engaged." I held my phone out to him. "And I'm officially back on the market." I held a hand up to my ear. "If you listen hard, you can hear all the single men in Halften locking their doors as we speak."

Mercer gave an awkward laugh—granted, he had never really appreciated my sense of humor. "Now, I'm sure that's not true."

"Well"—I tapped my phone against my palm, trying not to grit my teeth—"there is one man I can think of who better, if he knows what's good for him."

Mercer's eyes widened slightly, so I quickly added, "Don't worry, it's not you." I waved a hand. "Go and live your life. I promise you won't find me hiding in your backseat or staking out your place."

"Well, that is a relief . . ." He tugged at his collar. "I have, uh, actually started seeing someone."

"Really?" I paused, waiting to see if this news stung at all—it didn't. "I'm happy for you."

"Thanks. It's new, but I've got a good feeling about it."

"That's great." Suddenly, Mercer's impromptu visit made a lot more sense. Nothing could kill a new relationship faster than a crazy ex popping out of the shadows.

"Take care, Audrey." With his mind at ease, Mercer hopped back in his shiny sports car and, within seconds, was on his way.

I returned to the porch swing, this time alone, and sank onto it heavily. Leaning back, I gazed up at the evening sky, which had turned dark in between Jackson's and Mercer's visits.

Much like my heart.

As much as I didn't want to believe it, I had seen the proof myself.

And the more I thought about it, I wondered if Jackson had even been about to admit it. Hadn't he said that he'd gone over my head about something? I had thought he'd been about to say something about how he was handling the missing money situation, not that he'd summoned my ex back to town and made me look like a complete idiot.

But the facts didn't lie.

Your secret's safe with me, Jackson had said.

Clearly only until he decided he couldn't be bothered to keep it anymore.

But one question remained.

Why?

Did Jackson really think I was unhinged? Was this his way of "babysitting" me because he didn't think I could be trusted to handle the truth myself?

Or did he think I was a liar who had stolen from him, and instead of firing me over it, he pulled this to get me to leave on my own accord?

Or was he simply sending me a message? He'd already said our kiss was a mistake. Was this his way of adding to it? Sorry, Audrey, but I don't do crazy.

I didn't know.

But one thing was certain. I was tired of being a spectator in my own life. Sitting back and letting others take control—my mom, Mercer, and now by the look of things, even Jackson.

No more.

Come tomorrow, I knew exactly what I had to do.

"Hey, kiddo." My dad found me an hour later, still sitting out on the porch swing, watching the fireflies.

"Hey, Dad." I smiled as he sat down next to me. My dad's nickname for me was one of the things I loved about him. Just kiddo, not princess or superstar like my mother. No expectations or pretense. I was just his daughter, and for that reason alone, he loved me and was proud of me.

"Your mother was in quite a state this morning," he said as he stared out at the summer evening.

I grimaced. "I know and I'm sorry . . . I'm assuming she told you about me and Mercer."

He nodded. "Can't say I was surprised."

"Really?"

Another nod. "I wondered about that boy . . ." He was silent for a moment, as if recalling his wonderings. "I know your mother thought he hung the moon, but I was never certain he was the one for you. Too weak-minded."

I couldn't help but laugh. "He's almost a lawyer, Dad. He's got a reputation for having a quick mind and being persuasive."

"Oh, I don't doubt he can talk his way around a courtroom. But I mean when it came down to the nitty-gritty. Were you going to be able to count on him then? Or was it always going to be whatever sounded the best to the rest of the world?"

I nodded slowly, understanding what he meant. "You're right. When it came down to the nitty-gritty, he couldn't walk the walk."

My dad slapped a hand on his dusty work coveralls. "Well, I'm sorry to hear that. A father never wants his daughter to go through heartbreak. But I'd rather you go through a quick and painful heartbreak and realize he's not the one for you, than a slow one and realize it too late."

"Thanks, Dad. Me too." I wondered if he was speaking from experience with life with my mother. Not that he ever complained about her to me. But I couldn't imagine life with her was any easier for him than it was for me.

Both of us were a disappointment to her in her own way. My dad had just managed to handle it better, it seemed.

"Do you think Mom will ever forgive me?" I asked quietly.

"There's nothing to forgive." He paused, then sighed. "She's always wanted the world for you. And there's nothing wrong with that—she just needs to realize that you've got your own life. That it's not her world you're living in. And you're just as entitled to make your own mistakes as the rest of us."

I nodded slowly. All I had ever wanted was the freedom to make my own mistakes. Was that what I had finally done, coming back to Halften? Well, it certainly seemed like I'd made plenty of mistakes. But as my father's words sank in, I knew I was finally ready to face them.

"Don't worry about your mother." My father patted my knee once. "She'll get over it. Not without a bit of bluster, but it's not your job to weather her storms. Remember that."

"Thanks, Dad." I gave him a quick side hug. "I'll try to. Where is she?"

"At your Aunt Christine's. She's always been the best one to talk her off a ledge."

I nodded, knowing it was true.

"Now what's this about that Crowe boy coming calling for you tonight?" my dad asked.

I almost laughed, both at my father's description of Jackson as a "boy" and the fact that he referred to him coming to talk to me as "calling." But the momentary humor died on my lips. "He wasn't calling, Dad. He just wanted to talk to me. He did something stupid, and I think maybe he wanted to apologize—or warn me. I'm not sure, but to be honest, I'm not very happy with him right now."

"Is that so . . ." He rocked the porch swing gently. "Well, if he comes calling again, you might want to send him my way. I know a thing or two about appeasing the wrath of an angry Miller woman."

"Dad!" I reprimanded him, mainly for his insinuation that my being angry with Jackson was the same as my mother being angry with him.

"Men do stupid things sometimes, Audrey. It's in our genetic code." He held up a calloused finger. "But when things get tough, you've got to take a good hard look and ask yourself if he's really someone you can count on."

I glanced down at my hands, noting the faint tan line on my left hand from where I had once worn Mercer's ring, and then Jackson's. Both men had left a mark on my heart. Both had hurt me at one point. But was my dad right? Was the difference between them that Jackson was someone I could count on, even when things got messy? Before I had seen that message, I had been starting to think so. But now? I wasn't so sure.

And since Mercer had interrupted us before Jackson had a chance to explain himself, I was more confused than ever. All I knew was I wasn't sure my heart was strong enough to risk getting hurt again.

"Thanks, Dad. I'll think about that."

He patted my knee again, then stood up. "I better go see how your mother's holding up now that she's had a full day to digest that you won't be marrying into royalty."

I laughed. "That sounds like a good idea."

CHAPTER 34

JACKSON

"Knock, knock." Audrey's voice caused my head to snap up from my paperwork early the next morning.

She tapped on the doorframe outside my open office. "Got a minute, Boss Man?"

"Audrey." My mouth went a little dry at the sight of her, but I tried my best to maintain my composure. *Boss Man?* I hadn't heard that in a while. I sensed irritation behind the words, and I wondered if she was referring to my introduction to Mercer last night.

Had it bothered her? How else was I supposed to introduce myself? *The man who kissed your ex-fiancée and can't stop thinking about her?* Yeah, that wouldn't have been awkward at all.

"Of course." I saved and closed the files I had been

working on. "Please, come in."

"Thanks." Her word was terse as she walked inside. Yup, she was definitely miffed about something. But still, she hesitated, keeping her hand on the door. "Is it okay if I close this? I'd like to talk privately, but if you aren't comfortable with that . . ."

I stared at her for a moment, confused. Was she asking that because of what happened between us on the Fourth of July? Was she afraid I was going to kiss her again if we were behind closed doors? Did she think *I* was afraid of that?

"No, go right ahead. Whatever you feel comfortable with." I gestured to the chair in front of me, determined to treat this like any other business meeting. "Have a seat."

"Thanks." She clicked the door shut behind her and slid into the seat across from me. "Don't worry, this won't take long. I just wanted to give you this." She pulled out a sheet of paper from the folder in her hand and pushed it toward me.

"What's this?" I grabbed it but before I could peruse it, Audrey answered.

"My two weeks' notice."

"What?" My brows shot upward. I cleared my throat, trying to cover my surprise. "Did you get a new job?"

"No, not yet, but I'm looking. Regardless, I think it's time. I mean, it's for the best . . . considering the circumstances."

"I see." My heart dropped. "So you and Mercer got back together then?" Of course she'd need to quit if she was planning on moving back to Chicago and picking up where she left off with him.

"No, of course not." Her eyes widened. "Is that really what you think happened?"

"I just assumed that was why he was there—"

"That's why you sent him that message? Hoping he would take me back?" She laughed but there was no humor behind it. "Are you really that desperate to be rid of me? Were you worried what Tucker would say if you fired me?"

"What? No—wait, what are you talking about? What message?"

She threw her hands in the air. "You messaged Mercer and told him that I was unhinged because I thought he and I were still engaged!"

"What?" Never in all my years of interacting with Audrey was I more lost than I was now—and that was saying something. "What are you talking about? No, I didn't."

"Jackson, come on." She scoffed. "I saw it. The message came from your profile."

"Audrey, I swear to you—" I leaned across the table, wishing that I hadn't started this conversation like a business meeting so I would be close enough to take her hands in mine. Maybe it wouldn't help, but I had the urge to physically impress the sincerity of my words upon her. "I did not send Mercer any message. How could I? I don't even know him."

"But—" For the first time since she'd walked in this morning, her icy, angry exterior seemed to crack. "But I saw it," she whispered.

"Hold on." I grabbed my phone off my desk. I clicked into the social media app that I hadn't used for almost a year. Sure enough, after a minute of searching, the message that Audrey had mentioned popped up clear as day under my sent history.

I cursed under my breath. And again when I read it in its entirety.

"You really thought I sent this?" I handed my phone to her.

Audrey's face turned red, no doubt embarrassed to have to read the terrible words she thought I had written about her again. "Are you saying you didn't? It came from your profile. What was I supposed to think?"

"No, I swear I didn't." I sighed, knowing how it must have looked to her. "It must have been Gwyneth." Gently, I took my phone back from Audrey. "She's the one who set this profile up for me in the first place. When we started dating. She said I needed it to be relevant. I think she couldn't stand not being able to tag me in pictures."

Audrey clapped a hand over her mouth.

"She must still have my password. I never changed it. I haven't even used the stupid thing since we broke up."

"Jackson, I'm so sorry. I shouldn't have assumed."

"It's not your fault." I scrolled through the app trying to find a way to delete the dumb thing for good, but that didn't seem to be an option. "Why is there no way for me to delete this?"

"You'll probably have to google it. The tech companies purposely make it really hard for you to delete them. They don't like losing users."

"It's like Gwyneth in mobile form," I muttered under my breath, then set my phone down to deal with it later. I had more important things to worry about at the moment.

I picked Audrey's two weeks' notice up and scanned

it, then I glanced at her. "Do you really want to quit?"

"I did, but . . ." She bit her lip, her gaze falling away. Then she threw her hands in the air. "I don't know, maybe it's still for the best. I mean, I'm obviously not good for your business. There's still the whole matter of the missing money. And"—she lowered her voice—"we probably shouldn't work together anymore considering what happened"—she paused—"on the Fourth of July."

I leaned back in my chair, rubbing my eyes. What a mess everything had become. The only question was, could it be fixed? "So, you and Mercer aren't back together?"

"No." She gave an awkward laugh. "The only reason he came to see me was to have me fitted for a straitjacket. He definitely wasn't looking to get back together. Which was good, because neither was I."

"You're not?" This was the information I needed to know. The information that would decide my next move. Was she possibly ready to move on? Or was she still in love with Mercer?

"Definitely not. I realized a lot about Mercer's and my relationship these past few weeks. And seeing him again last night just solidified it—we aren't right for each other. We never were. And I finally told my mom the truth about our breakup."

"You did?" My heart lifted with hope. "How was that?"

"Awful, honestly, but it was for the best. I should have done it sooner. I also left a message for Tucker and told him everything too. So, you officially don't have to cover for me anymore. Oh, and"—she reached into her pocket and pulled out the fake engagement ring I had given her—"I wanted to give this back to you. Obviously, I don't need it anymore."

I took the ring from her and twirled it in my fingers, studying it for a moment, trying to fight the smile spreading across my face. "You know what, keep it." I dropped it back into her hand.

"Are you sure? Don't you want to put it back in the machine?"

"Nah." I shrugged. "I'd rather you hang on to it. I mean, I don't expect you to wear it or anything, but maybe you can put it in a box somewhere and when you see it, you'll think, *That's that tacky ring from Jackson. He sure has bad taste, but he had my back that summer.* Because I do, you know." I held her gaze, hoping to erase any doubt she had about me. "I have your back."

"Okay," she said softly, a blush creeping up her cheeks as she tore her gaze from mine and slipped the ring back in her pocket. "Thanks, I guess." She bit her lip, like she was pondering this. And I let her. After weeks of confusion, I finally knew where I stood. Now I needed to know where she did.

"But wait—" She looked up, still puzzled. "What did you come to my house to talk to me about the other night?"

I sucked in a deep breath. I'd come to talk to her about a lot of things that night. But now with her on the brink of quitting, I wasn't sure how much I should throw at her. Her faith in me had been shaken, and as much as I wanted to tell her she could trust me, I knew it would take more than that.

I couldn't push her—I wouldn't. As much as I wanted to lay it all out in front of her right here and now, I knew her trust was fragile. Words wouldn't cut it here. Not after what she'd gone through with Mercer. Not after how I'd acted since the Fourth of July.

So instead of trying to convince her that she could trust me—that I was all in and she could have every confidence in me—I started with the simplest thing.

"I wanted to talk to you about the missing money. I actually have a plan to get to the bottom of that, but in order for it to work, I'd need you to finish out your two weeks here. Are you okay with that?"

She nodded. "Of course. I don't want to leave you short-staffed."

"I appreciate that." I smiled, confidence resurging.

Two weeks were all we needed.

CHAPTER 35

AUDREY

A few nights later, I was behind the bar, working one of my last bartending shifts.

Was it weird that I was going to miss this place? Admittedly, I enjoyed running the event-venue side of things more than I did working as a bartender, but ever since I'd given my two weeks' notice to Jackson, I'd found myself feeling strangely sentimental about this place.

About this place or about the owner? my pesky mind prodded.

Okay, so it had a point. But, I reasoned, it wasn't entirely my fault.

Unlike last week, Jackson had not been making himself scarce. In fact, I could have sworn he was seeking me out, spending more time with me at work than ever before. Sure, some of it was business related, but there were also moments when we'd get caught up in conversations that had nothing to do with work.

Was he, like me, grieving that my days here were numbered? Or was he simply trying to make my transition easier by showing there were no hard feelings between us?

I didn't know. But I did know that my feelings for him were only getting stronger by the minute. And as much as I was growing to hate the thought of leaving, I knew a clean break—and time apart—was the only thing that was going to let my heart move on from him.

With a firm resolve for the fiftieth time that night to push Jackson out of my mind, I cashed out my final customers, shut the register drawer firmly, and wished them a good night. Then I filled the dishwasher with glasses, turned it on, and peeked inside the fridge to see what I needed to restock from the cooler.

I had just finished my mental list, when the back door swung open and Brittany poked her head in.

"Hey, Audrey, would you mind running food with me? I've got that big group again." She rolled her eyes. "Who knew the bingo crowd would be such night owls. I mean, they're old. Aren't they supposed to be home falling asleep during the evening news?"

"Yeah, no problem." I followed her out the door, stopping a second to look back and ensure that I'd fully shut the register and the bar was, indeed, empty.

"Thanks." Brittany strolled back to the kitchen and began loading up a tray. "I was hoping to get out early tonight." She flashed a grin. "Got a date. How 'bout you? Any fun plans?" She flashed a mischievous grin my way.

"Nah." I placed a side of fries on my tray. "I'm calling

it a night after this."

"*Bore*-ring," Brittany called out in a singsong voice as we headed for the dining room with our full loads. "There's more to life than work, ya know." She wiggled her eyebrows. "Even hot bosses. How's that going, by the way?"

I shook my head. "It's not. Like I said before, there's nothing going on between us."

"If you say so." Brittany smirked, but luckily didn't say anything else as we reached her table and began handing out plates.

My quick food run ended up taking close to fifteen minutes, since I had to run back to the kitchen and correct two wrong sides.

"Hey, Monty," I said. "The burger and wrap were supposed to have onion rings, not fries."

"Sorry, I'll get those to ya in a sec." I heard the sizzle of fried grease, and a few minutes later, Monty slid the correct order my way.

"Thanks." I snatched the two plates up and headed back to the dining room, where Brittany was chatting animatedly with her customers.

I smiled to myself as I placed the correct sides in front of the patrons. Who knew Brittany had such a soft spot for the bingo crowd?

By the time I reentered the bar, it was still empty. It didn't look like anyone had been in since I left, but wanting to be sure, I punched my code into the register and the till slid open.

Empty.

Just like last week.

I snapped a picture with my phone, slammed the

register shut, then shot a quick text to Jackson with the picture and a simple caption.

Struck again.

His reply was almost immediate.

Be right there.

Ten minutes later, Jackson entered through the bar door and locked it behind him since it was closing time anyway.

"Let's check the footage," he said.

"Sounds good."

But we didn't head straight to the office. No, Jackson grabbed a chair and set it underneath one of the wall vents, pulled a screwdriver out of his pocket, then unfastened the grate.

A minute later, he held up the memory card from the camera he had planted there. "Let's see what we got."

I had to admit, when he'd told me his plan to figure out what was going on, I wasn't certain that the thief would strike again. But Jackson had kept quiet about the incident to the other staff, and he had asked me to do the same. That, along with staying silent about my resignation, had been enough for whoever was behind the missing money to steal again.

We headed to the office together, and we watched the footage in silence as Jackson skipped ahead to the end of the night.

Finally, I held up a finger. "Stop." I pointed to the screen. "Those were my last customers. I left the bar soon after this."

Jackson stopped the tape once the customers left, and we watched in silence as I paused my cleanup to turn my head and chat with an unseen person in the doorway.

"That was Brittany," I said. "She asked me to run food with her again."

"Just like last week." Jackson nodded and kept his eyes fixed on-screen.

We watched nothing for a few minutes, and then a figure entered and darted behind the counter, dressed in black pants and a dark gray hoodie sweatshirt. He wore gloves and moved swiftly, purposefully. He typed a code in the computer—no doubt the records would show it was mine—then the drawer slid open, and he began stuffing cash into a bag.

"Got him." Jackson paused the video the moment the thief turned his head, clearly showing his face.

I gasped. "It's Randy."

"I suspected as much," Jackson said grimly.

"You did?"

"Brittany actually helped quite a bit."

"Brittany? How? She wasn't involved, was she?"

Jackson shook my head. "No, but I actually suspected her at one point when you said she was the one who stalled you from going back to the bar the night the register was emptied. But before I could ask her about that, she came to me. She said that she had seen Monty and Randy in the parking lot one night after work. Since she knew that Randy wasn't supposed to be anywhere near here, she let me know."

Jackson leaned back in his office chair and scratched his chin thoughtfully. "And that's when I remembered

Randy put Monty as a reference on his job application. They were friends, or at least acquaintances. So I pulled it up and sure enough, there it was. Their link. And another thought came to me."

Jackson swiveled his chair to face me. "Randy was the last person I hired before you. He seemed like a great employee at first—taking on extra shifts, going above and beyond. I thought he was just a hard worker, but now, I'm pretty sure he was biding his time and waiting for the right opportunity."

"The right opportunity for what?"

"To steal and get away with it. He couldn't do it right away because it would be too obvious because he was the new guy. So he waited until I hired someone else—you—and then started. That way it would seem like you were the one behind it." Jackson shook his head. "When I fired him, I changed his code and mine, but I didn't think to change yours. But he trained you a few times, so I'm sure he saw you type your code into the computer."

I nodded. "I'm sure he did. He was always hanging over my shoulder."

"Even after he was fired, all he had to do was have Monty tell him your schedule and alert him when you were busy in the back helping Brittany."

"Two of the orders I ran with Brittany tonight were wrong. I wouldn't be surprised if Monty did that on purpose to stall me."

"And then once you weren't in the back, Randy probably told Monty how to wipe the cameras. But Randy's mistake was getting too greedy. A few swiped bills here and there could fall through the cracks, but the entire register? He probably was hoping you'd get fired."

"In addition to stealing from you, he could get back at me."

"Exactly." Jackson pulled out his phone. "I'm sure Randy's parole officer will find this interesting. Not only his theft, but also violating his restraining order."

"Crazy night, huh?" Jackson said when he joined me in the office again after walking the cops out that night.

"You could say that." I stood and grabbed my purse. It was late and the rest of the staff had left. Now that the excitement of catching Randy had worn off and the restaurant was silent, I was more aware than ever of Jackson's proximity.

"Hopefully things will calm down around here now . . ." Jackson shoved his hands in his pockets and leaned against the wall.

"If they don't, you could always make Mr. Darcy the official guard dog of the Inn," I said, trying to keep the situation light. "He could scare off any other potential thieves."

"That old bag of bones?" Jackson laughed. "He'd most likely invite them in for a cup of tea, thanks to you and Penny trying to instill such good manners into him."

I laughed. "Well, someone had to."

"Speaking of manners . . ." Jackson ran a hand through his hair and shifted his feet. "I just want to say that I'm sorry."

His nervousness was contagious and I swallowed. "For what?"

"For how I handled things after the Fourth." He stopped fidgeting, his eyes turning soft and steady. "I'm sorry if I made you doubt yourself—or me."

"Thanks." The word almost stuck in my throat as I recalled my father's words. About how I needed to figure out if Jackson was someone I could truly count on. I now knew for certain.

We had both made our share of mistakes this summer—heck, maybe even the entire time we'd known each other. But one thing was certain. I no longer doubted that Jackson had my back. That he was someone I could count on, regardless of the fact that we would soon be going our separate ways.

"Well, I guess there's only one thing left for me to do," Jackson went on.

"What's that?"

"Since I have you here, I should give you your letter of recommendation." He moved toward the filing cabinet in the corner.

"Oh, no, that's okay. You don't need to do that. I mean, I don't really feel like I deserve it since I'm not even staying my agreed-upon three months."

"Of course I do. That was one of the things you and Tucker agreed on when he hired you. Hang on." He turned around and rummaged through a stack of papers. "I've been working on it."

"Okay, thanks."

"If you don't mind me asking," Jackson said over his shoulder as he continued searching. "Are you sure there's nothing I can do to change your mind?"

What a loaded question.

But instead of really answering it, I licked my lips.

"Look, us working together was a bad idea from the start. Deep down, we both knew that."

Jackson shut the filing cabinet drawer softly, then turned and faced me. He held up a sheet of paper. "I found it."

"Great. Thanks." I held out my hand, but he didn't give it to me.

"Why don't I read it to you? That way if you want any changes, I can do that for you now."

"That's okay. I'm sure whatever you wrote is fine—"

But Jackson just cleared his throat. "To whom it may concern: Audrey Miller is an exemplary employee. Despite what you may have heard about her, she is professional, organized, passionate about her work, and overall, an amazing person—"

"Jackson," I began with a smile.

"Hang on." He held up a hand. "I'm not done. There are some who might say that Audrey Miller is"—he made air quotes—"'too much' and I would like to set the record straight and say that is absolutely true. She is too much. She's too confident to sit there and get stepped on by jerks who think they can treat her like a piece of meat. She's too talented to do anything but give her all, throwing her entire heart into the things she cares about. And she's too bright—way too bright. So much that you better step on back and let her shine because nothing and no one is going to stand in her way."

He dropped the paper on the desk between us and took a step toward me.

My mouth dropped when I saw the sheet was blank.

"Jackson . . ." I said again, this time uncertain. Where was he going with this?

"Just hear me out, Audrey, please." His eyes held mine. "I need to say this. I should have ages ago."

I nodded slowly and he took that as his cue, his voice stronger now.

"You're too much, Audrey, and that's a good thing. A good thing for anyone who is lucky enough to be in your orbit. So much that when you're around, I can't look away, and I don't know what I'm going to do when you're gone. Because now that I've had a glimpse of all that, I realize how empty my life is going to be without you."

Before I could say anything, he rushed on. "Before you leave, there's one thing you should know. I already talked to Tucker—that's the other thing I came over to talk to you about the other night. I was straight with him and told him this place needs a full-time music and event manager, and he couldn't agree more. He wants to be a silent partner from here on out—to have time to focus on his music again and start a family. And we both agreed you're the right woman to take his place. We want to offer you a full-time, permanent comanager position, if you're interested." He shook his head. "Then Mercer showed up, and you gave your two weeks' notice, and I thought maybe that wasn't what you wanted."

Jackson crossed to the front of the desk and took my hands in his. "And that's fine. Look, take the job or leave it. I want you to do whatever makes you happy. And if this isn't the role for you, I support you moving on one hundred percent. But what I am asking is that you'll give *us* a chance. I don't mind losing you as an employee, but I'll never stop kicking myself if I let you walk out of my life without telling you how I really feel about you. What you've come to mean to me these last few weeks.

"Because the truth is, I love you, Audrey Miller. It may have taken me way too long to realize it. And even when I did, I'll admit, I was trying to fight it—trying to give you time, trying to wait until you got over Mercer, trying to let you choose whether you wanted to stick around Halften or not, but now my time's up. I can't let you walk out the door without knowing the truth. I'm sorry I didn't let you know sooner. Honestly, I think I was scared. But I love you and I want you in my life, whatever way you'll have me. Although"—he dropped his voice in a conspiratorial whisper—"I really hope you'll want me to be more than your boss man"—he quirked his brows—"or I should say, comanager."

I stared at him, at his earnest eyes and hopeful smile, and my heart beat wildly. A million thoughts raced through my brain, but the first thing that tumbled out was "Jackson Crowe, you are the most confusing man I've ever met, do you know that?"

"I'm counting on it." Jackson's grin widened. "Because after meeting your ex the other night, it's clear you need more than just a pretty face."

I shook my head, then looked up at him, hoping he would hear the same sincerity in my words that I'd heard in his. "I was never in love with Mercer. I wanted to be, but it was never quite right. And I think now I know why . . . Because all along, it was you." I shook my head. "You have no idea how much it broke my heart to know I would soon be leaving this place—that I'd soon be leaving you."

"So does that mean you accept my offer to be my comanager and girlfriend?"

I nodded. "It does."

Jackson swooped one arm around my back and pulled me close. With his other, he reached behind him and grabbed a paper off his desk, then handed it to me. It was my two weeks' notice. "Care to do the honors?"

"Would I ever." I ripped the sheet in two, four, eight, then sixteen pieces, and with a laugh, threw them above our heads like confetti.

Jackson looked up as the little pieces rained down on us. "Why am I not surprised that your first official act as comanager is to trash our office?"

I quirked my brows and draped my arms across his shoulders. "And I'm surprised you're not welcoming your new comanager with a kiss."

He grinned. "Whatever you say, Boss Lady. I hope you know I take my job *very* seriously."

"I'm counting on it." I hopped up on the desk behind me, taking Jackson's arms with me.

Eyes full of heat, he leaned forward and his lips met mine. Sweet. Sincere. Insistent. He kissed me with the same fire as he had on the Fourth of July, and I responded just as intensely. But this time, our kisses weren't firecrackers, sizzling one moment and fading out the next.

No, they were the sparks stoking a flame that would be burning for a very long time.

Chapter 36

AUDREY

Two Months Later

"I'm so excited we're going to be roommates again," Penny said, leaning forward excitedly from the backseat of Jackson's truck.

"Me too," I said as we pulled up to the tree-lined drive where Penny's and my rental cottage was nestled. The leaves were just starting to change for the season.

From the driver's seat, Jackson laughed. "You realize you guys weren't roommates for only one summer, right? Codependent much?"

From the backseat next to Penny, Mr. Darcy let out a sharp bark, as if agreeing with Jackson.

"Hush, you." Penny rubbed her knuckles against his fur. "It's a good thing I'm back. You've been hanging out with Jackson for too long. You've completely lost your manners." She turned to her brother. "Although, I guess I should thank you for convincing Audrey to stay in Halften, or we wouldn't be renting this beautiful writing haven."

"Are you sure having me around isn't going to distract you too much from getting your next book written?" I asked Penny. I had been stoked when Penny told me she had found the perfect little cottage to rent in Halften for the year while she finished her next book. She had begged me to be her roommate again, and the timing couldn't have been better. Since I was planning on staying in Halften indefinitely—with a full-time job and a boyfriend that I adored—I had already begun looking to move out of my parents' house.

Even though my mother had eventually gotten over my and Mercer's breakup like my father predicted, I was definitely ready to have my own space. The turning point of her anger had been about a week after my confession, when my father had brought home a flyer from the local community theater stating that they were searching for costume designers. Turned out, it was the perfect project for my mother to throw herself into to relive the glamour of her former glory days. She had even landed a part in their next show, which she seemed really excited about. I was happy for her, but mainly, I was happy it was her and not me.

"You know you're invaluable to me when I need to talk out plot points," Penny said. "It's more *him* I'm going to have to get used to having around." She jerked her thumb Jackson's way. "I know you two lovebirds are practically inseparable now, but I still need girl time with my bestie."

"Don't worry." Jackson lifted one hand from the steering wheel. "I wouldn't dream of infringing on girl time." He wove that hand through mine. "Just promise you won't monopolize all of Audrey's time making her help you create fictional men. I don't want her forgetting about the real man in her life."

"Don't you get tired of him after seeing him all day long at work?" Penny asked me, ignoring her brother.

"No way." I squeezed Jackson's hand. "We're so busy at work these days, we definitely still need our alone time after."

"Plus we can't do this at work." Jackson threw his truck into park and leaned over and placed a heart-fluttering kiss to my lips.

"Unless we're in the office," I said with a laugh when we broke apart.

"I feel like I'm living in the twilight zone." Penny groaned as she opened the back passenger door. "I love you two, but I don't know if I'm ever going to get used to this." She held the door open for Mr. Darcy, who jumped out, then together they started up the stone-laden path.

I was about to follow after her, when Jackson put his arm around me and pulled me close. "Work seemed extra long today."

I grinned, then placed a kiss to his lips. "Did that have anything to do with it being my day off?"

"It might have." Another kiss. "Honestly, I don't know how I ever pulled twelve-hour shifts before you. Now eight hours seems like an eternity."

I laughed, but really, I was glowing. "I guess it's safe to say I mended your workaholic ways."

"You know it, Boss Lady, and not a moment too soon. The restaurant's running smoother than ever."

It was true, and the event venue was booked solid for the next four months.

"Don't forget our next endeavor," I said once we both exited the truck to join Penny in the yard.

"The fall festival? How could I forget?"

This year, the Stonewall Inn wasn't just manning a booth, we were also sponsoring the haunted house at the fall festival. I was thrilled. Penny was not.

"Oh good, you two finally came up for air," Penny quipped when we joined her and Mr. Darcy on the front lawn.

"We were actually just discussing our plans for the fall festival. You know, very important business stuff."

"Yeah-huh, sure." She rolled her eyes. "Are you sure you guys aren't sponsoring a kissing booth instead?"

"Speaking of." Jackson let out a hearty laugh. "I heard your favorite person is hosting a win-a-date-with-the-mayor raffle fundraiser. Better watch out or I'll put your name in."

"You wouldn't dare." Penny's tone turned caustic, and I couldn't help but cringe.

Halften's young and handsome mayor was also the town's most eligible bachelor, Camden Clarke. Aka, Penny's and my former classmate whom she had once tutored until that ended horribly. I could hardly believe I had once worried she was falling for him, since now he was the most hated man in Halften—in her eyes at least. The rest of the town obviously loved him enough to elect him mayor.

I wasn't quite sure whose bright idea win-a-date-with-the-mayor was, since it seemed kind of weird, but I had a feeling it would rake in a lot of money from the females of Halften, young and old alike.

"I hope Gwyneth wins it," Penny said. "They'd make a perfect pair."

I shook my head. "Gwyneth's long gone. And currently attached." I tried not to laugh, but it was as hard now as when Jackson had broken the news to me.

After he had deleted his social media app, he had confronted Gwyneth about the message, and sure enough, she admitted to being the culprit. But of course, in true Gwyneth-style, she had deflected all blame, saying she had only done it to "protect Jackson from crazy Audrey."

Turned out, she and Mercer had connected in Chicago—whether it was on purpose or by chance she wouldn't say. Although I strongly suspected Gwyneth had done some digging into my social media profiles and tracked him down. However, once she learned about our broken engagement, she saw it as the perfect opportunity to mess with both me and Jackson, all while pursuing her latest prospect. I guess that was her way of showing us up after karaoke night.

So Gwyneth had pursued Mercer and won him—they were dating now—and I was sure his fancy career and country-club lifestyle were right up her alley. But the good news for us was that we didn't have to deal with her popping up around Halften anymore.

I wondered if Mercer would ever realize he had traded in a semi-crazy ex-girlfriend for the real deal, but I figured he was smart enough to figure that out on his own.

But then again, I wasn't sure if he would care so long

as Gwyneth continued to look good on his arm and schmooze in his social circles.

Penny's jaw dropped after we filled her in on the latest with Gwyneth and Mercer, then she turned to Jackson. "I hope you know you traded waaaayyy up."

"Trust me, I do." Jackson grabbed my hand as we headed up the cobblestone pathway.

Mr. Darcy barked twice as if agreeing, and we all laughed.

"Well, let's hope our mayor gets stuck on a date with old Mrs. Gilford instead," Penny said.

We all laughed again, and I pictured the town gossip fawning over Camden Clarke while hounding him with requests.

"She'll probably ask to have a statue erected in her honor at the town park," Jackson said.

"Yeah, with a built-in recording device so she can get the latest scoop as everyone walks by." Penny fanned her arms out dramatically, standing in front of the porch. "So, whaddya think?"

"It's even more adorable in person," I said, taking in the cute porch, cedar shake roof, and buttercream-yellow door.

"You saw the pictures, right?" Penny asked excitedly. "The bedrooms are fully furnished. It's like something out of a fairy tale. Oh, and the backyard? It's the perfect place for me to write my next book. I'm telling you, there will be no end to the inspiration here—"

"Whoever renovated this place did a good job," Jackson said with a low whistle, taking in not only the updated siding and porch, but also the pristine, yet full and natural, landscaping. "I remember when this place was a dump. Like seriously, the roof was caving in and there were weeds everywhere—"

"Welcome to Halften's own little slice of paradise." A deep voice from behind interrupted us and we all turned around.

"Speaking of weeds," Penny muttered under her breath.

"Welcome to Clark Cottage." None other than Camden Clarke stood leaning on the other side of the white picket fence that separated this lot from the next. "I hope you enjoy your stay."

"Camden Clarke . . ." Penny said the three syllables between her partially clenched jaw, and I had a natural instinct to step between her and her former tutee—although whom I would be protecting, I wasn't quite sure.

I glanced at Jackson, who was clearly trying not to laugh.

How long had Mayor Clarke been standing there on the other side of the fence? Had he overheard our conversation? Was he going to write us a ticket? Or issue a citation? Maybe demerits? I wasn't sure how mayordom worked. Either way, it was hard to treat a man seriously whom you'd once seen drunkenly jump into a swimming pool.

Mr. Darcy on the other hand seemed to take him very seriously—or at least as a very serious threat—he started growling and barking in Camden's direction. I didn't think I'd ever seen him act like that before. Had Penny trained him to turn aggressive at the sight of Camden Clarke? Jackson rushed over and took the lead from Penny, which was probably a good idea.

Penny tossed her long, shiny black hair over her shoulder and lifted her chin, her tone cold, but formal—clearly her attempt at taking the high road. "Can we help you?"

"I think the question is, can *I* help *you*?" Camden unlatched the side wooden gate separating the cottage from the neighboring lot and crossed over into hostile territory—although the grin on his face said he wasn't bothered. "Considering I'm your landlord here to welcome you."

"What?" Penny's jaw dropped, and with it, her cool facade. "You mean you *own* this place?"

"Yup." Camden leaned back against the fence, seeming to enjoy Penny's shock. "I'm the property manager. Hello, Penny, it's good to see you back in town. It's been a while."

Penny didn't return his greeting. "But I thought you were the *mayor*."

"As the mayor of Halften, you can understand why I would want to invest in some of our real estate. This was one of my finer projects, I must admit. Surely you remember what a dump this place used to be?"

Jackson nodded. "You really made this into something."

Penny shot him a look that said, *How dare you consort with the enemy?*

He just gave a shrug. To be fair, even she was singing this place's praises a moment ago.

"I didn't see your name listed as the property manager when I signed the lease," Penny said, placing an indignant hand on her hip.

"Sure you did." Camden smiled easily. "Clark C.,

Property Manager of Halften Homes LLC. I just flipped my names around. Makes things a little easier when you're the mayor and want to maintain a little privacy. Surely you can understand that, being a national best-selling author and all." He glanced down at the phone in his hand. "And that must make you Edith Crowe?" His grin widened. "Gotta say, I pictured someone a little more elderly with that name. But"—he held up a finger—"every bit as stern."

"It's my middle name." Penny crossed her arms, not looking amused.

"Ah, I see. Well, I completely understand the need to protect your privacy due to your illustrious background. You're practically Halften royalty, after all." He slipped his phone in his pocket. "And rest assured, Halften Homes LLC protects our customer information very thoroughly, so you can feel confident that you have my discretion in this matter." He pushed off from the fence. "I'm sure you want to get settled, so I won't keep you. I just wanted to let you know where you can find me if you need anything." He pointed over the fence.

A look of pure horror washed over Penny's face. "You mean you live next door?"

"Great, isn't it? I find it makes managing this place much easier." He sauntered through the gate, then called back with a wave, "See you around, neighbor."

Once he disappeared through the trees, Penny turned on Jackson with accusing eyes. "Did you know he owns this place? And that he lives *there*?"

Jackson held up his hands, all while still looking like he was trying not to laugh. "I swear, I had no idea. Believe it or not, I'm not buddy-buddy with the mayor."

"What about you?" Penny turned to me, although she looked far less suspicious.

I shook my head. "Nope. I'm practically still a tourist here myself, remember?"

"Didn't the 'Clark' In 'Clark's Cottage' tip you off when you rented this place?" Jackson asked, heading to the truck to grab our luggage.

"No." Penny followed after him. "The little sneak took the 'e' off the end, so I thought it was a first name! You know, like Clark Kent."

Jackson chuckled. "So you thought you were renting from Superman?"

"And instead, got Mr. Hyde," Penny grumbled as she hoisted her suitcase and hauled it to the porch.

"What's the big deal?" Jackson asked, following after with my suitcase and another bag. "I mean, it's not like you're living with the guy." He waved a hand. "The property's huge and you can't even see his house."

"What's the big deal? He's a total snake! He'll probably sneak in here and steal from me." She dropped her suitcase on the porch with a thud. "Again."

"Wait—what? He stole from you? When?" Jackson's brow furrowed, legitimate concern crossing his face. "I mean, I knew you hated the guy, but I never really knew why."

I shot him a look that said I'd explain it all to him later, then turned to Penny, trying to make my voice soothing. "Stealing your senior paper and passing it off as his own is one thing. I very much doubt that he'd get away with stealing one of your manuscripts."

"I wouldn't put anything past him," Penny said.

"He stole your senior paper?" Jackson asked

incredulously. "No wonder you're mad. Why didn't you turn him in? And how'd he even get away with that? Didn't your teacher realize he'd copied you?"

"It wasn't *my* senior paper," Penny said. "It was the one I wrote in eighth grade when I went to that summer writing camp."

"You mean Nerd Heaven?" Jackson snickered. "I almost forgot about that. But wait—so let me get this straight, Camden Clarke stole your eighth-grade paper and turned it in as his senior paper because it was better than anything he could write himself? He better hope that doesn't get out because that's just embarrassing." Jackson glanced over the fence in the direction that Camden had disappeared. "And it really makes me doubt the abilities of our fearless town leader. I'm kind of regretting that I voted for him."

"You *voted* for him?" Penny practically shrieked.

I shot Jackson a look that said he wasn't helping.

He got the hint. He put his hand to his ear and tilted his head down toward Mr. Darcy. "What's that, Darcy, you need to take a dump? Oh, and you want to do it in Camden Clarke's yard? Lead the way." With that he hightailed it down the driveway with Mr. Darcy in tow.

"Yeah, you better run," Penny muttered at his retreating back.

I tried not to laugh. "Look, Camden Clarke is a jerk," I said to her. "But he probably has better things to do now, being the mayor and all."

Penny shook her head as she punched in the door code—quite viciously. "I can't believe he got elected—that the people of Halften actually trust him. He's such a schmoozing liar."

"Well, he is a politician."

Penny heaved a sigh as she flung open the front door. "So much for my beautiful writing haven."

Epilogue

AUDREY

Fourth of July

"I hope it's okay that I offered to stand in for Penny for your Fourth of July Ferris wheel tradition this year," Jackson said as we climbed into a familiar old rickety Ferris wheel car.

"I'll try to get over my disappointment." I grinned as Jackson lowered the bar across our laps.

"So do you have this year's wish all picked out?"

"You know, I actually don't. Isn't that crazy?" I snuggled against him as our cart started its slow climb, only to stop a few feet up to load more passengers. "But this past year has been so wonderful, I honestly can't even think about what to wish for that would make it better."

"In that case," Jackson said, "I think *I* should get the

honor of making the first wish."

"Oh, really?" I smirked. "I thought you didn't believe in the magic of the Wishing Ferris Wheel."

"I'll admit, I was a healthy skeptic—"

"You mean a scrooge."

"That's Christmas, not Fourth of July."

"Whatever."

"But I said I would believe if my wish came true. And it did."

"Really? What did you wish for?" I poked him in the ribs. "You promised you'd tell me if it came true. And it better not have been something boring like wishing that shrink in the restaurant would decrease by five percent."

"That's a good one." Jackson scratched his stubbly chin, looking thoughtful. "I should've thought of that . . . But no, I wished that you'd stay here"—he grabbed my hand, lacing our fingers together—"with me. And you did."

"You did?" My mouth dropped open. "Really?"

He nodded. "I'm not sure if you noticed, but I was falling pretty hard for you that day. All I wanted to do was kiss you." He placed a soft kiss to my lips, as if reveling in the fact that he could now do just that.

"I had no idea," I said softly. "But I have to admit that was a great wish. Because it made my wish come true too."

"And quite a few of your high school wishes, if what Penny tells me is true." He squared his shoulders, a cocky grin spreading across his face.

"I can't believe she told you that." I smacked his chest lightly. "I'm going to have to get back at her for that."

"Easy—vote Camden Clarke for reelection," he said

in a fake politician voice and we both laughed.

"I don't think that would be effective anymore." Penny's long-standing hatred for Camden had taken an interesting turn last fall.

"Oh, we're almost at the top," I said, glancing upward. "Get ready. And you have to wish out loud this year."

"Right. Don't worry, I'm a pro now." He cleared his throat as our cart crested the top, while I gazed out across the landscape, taking in the fantastic view for the first time this year.

"I wish that Audrey Miller was my wife."

No longer interested in the scenery, I whipped my gaze to Jackson's just as our cart jerked to a stop.

"Audrey Miller, I couldn't agree with you more that this year has been the best year of my life. You brought joy to my life that I had stopped searching for. And now that I've had it, I don't ever want it to end. I love you, Audrey." Jackson pulled a black velvet box out of his pocket and opened it, revealing a sparkling ring. "Will you marry me?"

As dazzling as the ring was—and much more brilliant than the fake one he had given me out of the Stonewall Inn machine—I only glanced at it, my eyes drawn to the serious, sweet, and vulnerable blue eyes of the man across from me. I'd said yes to a proposal once before—for all the wrong reasons. But today, I knew I was saying yes for the right ones.

"Yes, Jackson, I'd love to marry you—I love you. And I love the life we're building together. I never want it to end either."

His nervous smile turned broad and he slipped the

ring on my finger, then pulled me in for a deep, slow kiss. Just like our first kiss in the hayloft last Fourth of July, I got the feeling he—like me—was in no rush for this moment to end, cherishing every second. After all, we'd waited a long time for it.

When we finally broke apart, Jackson waved an arm at the attendant on the ground—no doubt in on his plan and paid off to stop us at the right point—and the cart started moving again.

"Well, that had to be a record for shortest amount of time it took for a Ferris wheel wish to come true," Jackson said as we started our descent back down to earth.

"I'm not your wife yet, just your fiancée." I playfully poked his chest. "But your prospects for wish fulfillment are looking quite good."

"I'll take it." He wrapped both arms around me and held me close as the cart started climbing upward again. "You know, if you had told me a year ago I'd find complete happiness in this rickety old Ferris wheel, I never would have believed it."

I laughed. "That's Ferris wheel magic for you."

No sooner had the words left my mouth than a lone firework burst across the sky in perfect view, still completely dazzling even though it wasn't dark yet.

I gasped, then laughed. "Did you plan that too?"

"No"—Jackson laughed too—"maybe they're testing one out before the show. Or maybe it's a sign."

"A sign of what?"

He pressed a soft kiss to my lips, then pulled back, grinning. "That all our wishes are going to come true."

Coming Soon!

Don't miss Penny & Camden's story, *Falling After All*, an enemies-to-lovers, second-chance sweet fall romance.

Never trust a politician – especially with your heart.

Also by Cece Louise

THE HAPPILY EVER AFTER ALL SERIES

Christmas After All (Book 1):
As if ruining my life wasn't enough, now he's back to ruin my Christmas. (Melissa & Tucker's story.)

Perfect After All (Book 2):
I would do anything for my best friend's sister – except tell her how I really feel. (Rob & Kelsey's story.)

Faking After All (Book 3):
Pretend to be in love with the most obnoxious man alive? I'm up for the challenge. (Victoria & Caleb's story.)

THE FOREST TALES SERIES

Desperate Forest (Book 1):
A princess on the run. An outlaw plagued by secrets. Will they lose everything to the dark forest?

Mazarine (Book 3):
A cursed mermaid. A disgraced prince. Can they find redemption, or will they be lost to an unforgiving sea?

In a Dark, Dark Wood (Book 3):
An imposter posing as a princess. A brooding prince hiding within his castle. An arranged marriage that could ruin them both.

Saving Vengeance (A Prequel):
He wants to save her life, but she wants revenge at any cost. E-book available for free at CeceLouise.com!

The Jabberwocky Princess (A Forest Tales Series Bonus Book 1):
He thinks she's peculiar. She thinks he's a joke. They're about to discover that nothing is what it seems.

To Escape a Wonderland (A Forest Tales Series Bonus Book 2):
A thieving maid with a secret. A tarnished knight with no purpose. Together, can they find a way out of Wonderland?

About the Author

Photo by Keri Ann Photography

Cece Louise writes clean novels filled with adventure, romance, and spirit for teens and adults.

Cece is an avid reader who has been making up stories in her head as long as she can remember. Despite all that daydreaming, she graduated with a BBA and highest honors from the University of Wisconsin, Milwaukee in 2012.

When she's not working on her latest story, Cece spends her time having adventures with her husband and two kids, hiking and biking in her home state of WI, and unfortunately, cleaning her house (which she is convinced is secretly inhabited by mischievous, mess-multiplying pixies).

Cece is currently working on more sweet rom-coms and fairytale romance books. Visit her online to stay up-to-date on her next releases:

Cece's website: CeceLouise.com
Goodreads: Goodreads.com/CeceLouise
Instagram: Instagram.com/CeceLouise_Author
Facebook: Facebook.com/CeceLouiseAuthor

Made in the USA
Monee, IL
19 August 2024

64097581R00184